Haunted

Sasha turned her head to glance at her and Paul's bodies reflected in the uncurtained window. She stared wide-eyed and disbelieving at what she saw. Her body was rising and falling, not under the familiar figure of Paul, but under that of a man she'd seen only once before, as a painted presence in the background of a portrait.

She stared with passionate intensity into the eyes of the dark-haired man as his big powerful body seemed to be driving ever deeper and harder inside her. And when Sasha opened her mouth in a silent scream of the fiercest pleasure she had ever known, it wasn't Paul's body which was the source of the rapture she was experiencing, but John Blakeley's – the man in the window.

By the same author:

THE NAME OF AN ANGEL

Haunted

LAURA THORNTON

Black Lace novels are sexual fantasies.
In real life, make sure you practise safe sex.

First published in 1999 by
Black Lace
20 Vauxhall Bridge Road
London SW1V 2SA

Typeset by SetSystems Ltd, Saffron Walden, Essex
Printed and bound by Clays Ltd, St Ives plc

ISBN 9780753541906

Chapter One

*S*asha twisted restlessly in her seat, her toes tapping out an impatient rhythm against the inside of her shoe, while she wondered in irritation how much longer the meeting would go on. The terms were very nearly agreed upon to everyone's satisfaction: the directors, lawyers, accountants and sales reps seemed eager to complete the deal, and the British marketing campaign for Gripp, ALM's new cologne for men, was about ready to be launched. Sasha had spent nearly twenty-eight hours out of the last seventy-two closeted in this hotel conference room with six of the best from the British advertising agency Rollit, and she was beginning to feel claustrophobic. She had made the trip to London with her boss Valerie and two other representatives, Robert and Ross, to strike a deal which would allow Rollit to represent the newest product line in the American men's cosmetics firm for which she worked. By now, though, she was utterly fed up with spreadsheets, demographics, sales figures and scent samples.

Sasha shifted yet again in her seat, and glanced at

the managing director of Rollit, who was elaborately ignoring her while staring at the multicoloured, transparent charts projected on the overhead screen. She watched while Paul absently flexed his strong, square wrist holding the black Mont Blanc pen, before jotting down yet more indecipherable notes on his impressive leather-bound legal pad. Sasha knew his writing was illegible because she'd tried to peek at it earlier that morning, while he was preparing to sneak out of her hotel room before any of her or his co-workers spotted him. Not being particularly good at industrial espionage, Sasha had merely smiled at the tiny, cramped scribble, the wayward dotting of i's and dashed-off crossing of t's betraying the writer's concentration and speed. She'd really glanced at his writing more as a way of analysing his character than in order to spy on his company's secrets about their sales pitch, but all his writing told her was that the man had been in a hurry to get it all down.

She glanced again at Paul now, his immaculately cut fringe sloping across his finely chiselled face, and she smiled to herself in dreamily remembered pleasure at the memory of their early-morning encounter. Despite the fact that they were brand-new lovers, Sasha had already experienced a great deal of ecstasy amid the flounced pillows and sheets of her king-size four-poster bed three flights upstairs.

'I think we can live with that, don't you, Sasha?' Sasha jumped and then looked guiltily at her boss. Valerie's question startled her, which must have been obvious, for Paul was watching his nearly confirmed new client with barely concealed amusement.

'Mmm?' Sasha hastily rearranged herself into a more professional position, her long, curved legs crossed sedately at the ankle, and her hands clasped tightly over the pile of files before her. 'Yes, I would think so,' she said firmly, fervently hoping that this signalled the end of the negotiations.

Valerie stared at her for a moment, her pale blue eyes unreadable behind the light-framed glasses she wore to appear more imposing, then smiled wearily at the exhausted group of businesspeople around the oval mahogany table.

'Well, then, I think we should bring this meeting to a close,' she announced. 'I just need to run the final details over with ALM's CEO, but I think we can all agree on the main points of the contract.'

As the relieved women and men rose from their comfortably padded chairs, shook hands, and called for champagne, Paul managed to sneak up unobtrusively behind Sasha and murmur discreetly into her ear, 'We'll have to slip away later and celebrate the new deal a little more privately in your room.'

Sasha felt her inner muscles pull tightly with anticipation at the feel of Paul's warm breath on her neck, but then she straightened up and gave a little cough at the approach of the senior managing director of Rollit. Paul edged away as Sasha shook hands with Roger Wickham and smiled modestly as he praised her company's product and remarked, 'I am most impressed with your success and professionalism, Ms Hayward, especially since you were so recently appointed to the position of marketing manager!'

Hah! thought Sasha, smirking as she remembered her highly unprofessional behaviour in her room upstairs that morning. That had been a different kind of consummation entirely from the delicate negotiations just completed here, but of course, no one must ever find out about that, even now that the deal was done. So instead Sasha smiled politely and replied, 'I think we qualify for a first-name basis now, don't you, Roger? And yes, I was promoted to the

New York office less than a year ago, but I'm working my hardest to make a successful contribution to the team.'

Sasha smiled again and excused herself to find another glass of champagne, moving randomly among the 'Get a Gripp' crowd, as the new campaign was tentatively entitled. As the champagne bottles were emptied and the toasts became increasingly hyperbolic, people began to drift towards the door, talking longingly of food. It had been four hours since the tea and biscuits had been served, and Valerie had booked a table in the hotel restaurant for eight o'clock in the expectation that negotiations would be completed and the reps from both companies could dine together (at Rollit's expense, of course).

'Sit next to me at dinner,' Paul whispered in Sasha's ear as the party headed for the dining room, and Sasha found herself all atremble at the thought of finally being alone with him later on that night. She paused at the ladies' room door near the entrance to the restaurant, caught Valerie's eye, and said, 'I think I'd like to freshen up before we go in to eat, if you don't mind.'

Valerie joined her in the large, luxurious bathroom, and together they emptied out their make-up bags and began to reapply lipstick, powder and scent in the scalloped, gilt-edged mirror.

'That Paul is amazingly handsome, don't you think?' asked Valerie casually, adjusting her cleavage, which could just be glimpsed at the top of her linen blouse beneath her lemon-yellow business suit.

Sasha looked carefully away as she reapplied her eyeliner, hoping she sounded coolly non-committal as she replied, 'Yes, it's nice to finally meet him in person after speaking to him so often on the phone.'

'Well, now that the negotiations are over,' Valerie

confessed, brushing out her long, thick black hair, 'I can finally admit what a crush I've had on him these past three days. Not that I'd do anything about it,' she added hastily, as Sasha raised an eyebrow at her boss. 'Of course, as you and I are their clients, it would be most unethical for us to date anyone from Rollit's team,' Valerie concluded stiffly.

Hmmm, thought Sasha, glancing at Valerie out of the corner of her eye. Once inside the restaurant, she made a dive for the seat waiting for her next to Paul, but then felt a little guilty when she saw that Valerie was forced to sit next to the slimy head of Rollit's creative team, who smiled greasily at her as she sat down, his eyes resting on her hinted-at cleavage.

'Glad to see you finally made it,' commented Paul, officiously filling Sasha's glass from the newly opened bottle of champagne. 'I was beginning to get desperately horny – er, worried,' he chuckled under his breath while his hand surreptitiously began a slow seductive climb up Sasha's stockinged thigh.

'Menu?' the Rollit secretary asked brightly, apparently unaware that across the table from her Paul had now slipped his warm, narrow hand under the lace-edged band of Sasha's stocking. He then began to caress her thigh, slightly tickling the sensitive skin as Sasha's muscles tensed under his wickedly sensual touch.

'Yes, please,' gulped Sasha, trying not to squirm as those long, lean fingers continued to stroke her leg.

'So, is this your first trip to England?' enquired Jean politely, still seemingly oblivious to the havoc Paul was wreaking underneath the table.

'Er – yes,' replied Sasha, pulling more of the table-cloth over her lap. 'It certainly is beautiful here: not that I've been able to see much of the country,' she managed to add.

'Are you going back to the States tomorrow?' continued the woman, sliding the slim vase of flowers away so she could see Sasha's face more clearly. Irritably, Sasha wished that Jean would shut up so that she could concentrate more fully on the delicious feel of Paul's fingers moving upward towards her now-liquid sex.

'I'm afraid so,' she croaked, as Paul's long index finger gently stroked the dew-moistened lips of her sex, while he miraculously carried on an easy and comfortable chat with his colleagues across the table. As the food orders were placed and the waiters brought in bread and more wine, Sasha shifted about uncomfortably in her seat, while Paul's fingers continued their devilish torment inside her underwear. Soberly discussing the newest exhibit at the Tate gallery with his boss across the table, he held on to Sasha's sex, pressing lightly against her outer lips and circling slowly round her clitoris, always nearly but never actually quite straying inside her desperate cavern. Sasha could only grip the table and hold her breath while she urged her pelvis forward, willing Paul to thrust his fingers inside her and bring her off right there, in full view: she didn't give a damn who might see her come.

'Sasha? Are you quite well?' enquired her boss loudly, apparently taking note of Sasha's flushed face and lustfully sparkling eyes. 'You look a little feverish.'

'Actually, I would like to splash some water on my face, I think,' Sasha gasped out, grateful for an excuse to release herself from Paul's naughty torment so she could dash off to the bathroom to finish the job herself. With unobtrusive grace, Paul gently slid his slick fingers away from Sasha's liquid vulva and casually folded them under his nose as though deep in thought. Sasha could see, though, that he was inhaling

6

her womanly scent, and he smiled secretly at her and touched the tip of his tongue to his top lip as she moved away.

Sasha nearly ran from the table, hoping no one was watching her awkward exit from the room, though she thought she could feel Valerie's eyes boring questioningly into her back.

Once she was safely locked inside the luxuriously clean and delicately scented stall, Sasha hastily ripped up her navy suit skirt, pushed down her damp blue satin panties and quickly worked herself into a quietly satisfying climax. One – two – three rapid strokes inside while her finger pressed against her clitoris, and she was done. Her orgasm may have been a little brief and businesslike, but it was, after all, only an appetiser before the main course which was to follow with Paul in her bed very shortly.

Getting to that bed would be a bit of a problem, however, Sasha realised as dinner progressed. The past two nights had been relatively easy to manage, for Paul had simply crept into the men's bathroom when the meeting had adjourned, before sneaking up into Sasha's room after the others had gone. Tonight, though, things would be a little more difficult, since now that the meal was over, the Rollit and ALM people were planning to congregate in the hotel bar for the rest of the night.

Having apparently worked out a strategy beforehand, however, Paul simply dropped a note into Sasha's lap as he brushed by her chair on his way out of the dining room. Sasha remained seated, sipping her wine, while watching the others disperse. She giggled to herself now as she surreptitiously unfolded Paul's note beneath the table. Such subterfuge! she thought, and laughed inwardly. Such stratagems were involved in flouting office convention!

The note merely said, 'Your room. Midnight.' How romantic, Sasha thought to herself dreamily, as she finally rose and pushed back her seat. A secret midnight rendezvous: a last blast of passion before she had to fly back home tomorrow. In her mind she had already constructed the pair of them as ill-fated lovers, forced apart, not by ancient family feuds, but by the more modern pressures of conflicting business loyalties and the pitfalls of international commerce. She was American, he was English; she was the client, his firm provided the service – and Sasha couldn't wait to have Paul start servicing her properly pretty damn quickly!

She hastily downed her obligatory drink at the bar with her co-workers, before graciously excusing herself, pleading last-minute packing. No one seemed to notice or care as Sasha, with the slightest nod of her head to Paul, strode swiftly towards the lift which would whisk her away so she could begin her amorous preparations.

Well, not exactly whisk, Sasha thought in amusement as she leant against the book-lined walls of the lift: more of a groan and a whirr, really. The lift seemed nearly as ancient as the hotel claimed to be: the Asher Hotel bore a proud plaque in the lobby which dated its foundations to the late seventeenth century, when it had been the stately home of the Asher family, a long lineage of lower-level nobility. Viscounts, earls and barons glared down their stately noses from portraits ostentatiously displayed throughout the hotel: too few of them were women, Sasha had noticed with disapproval. Looking around the lift now as it slowly ground its way to the third floor, she studied the leather-bound volumes that were crammed in haphazardly on the shelves. They were probably there to keep the passengers entertained in case the elevator broke down, as, she thought sardonically, it certainly sounded in danger of doing. Idly, Sasha trailed her fingers along the cracked vellum bindings, noting that many of them seemed to be first editions of Behn, Smollett, Burney and Defoe, as well as lesser-known seventeenth- and eighteenth-century writers. Sasha had studied English literature at university and had written her senior thesis on radical writings of the 1790s, so she thought now she might have a quick glance through the second volume of Mary Wollstonecraft's *Vindication of the Rights of Woman*. When she tried to ease out the book, however, it wouldn't budge, and Sasha realised that the books were all actually fixed in place, undoubtedly to prevent theft. She was surprised by the depth of her disappointment, and she wondered irritably how the volumes could be attached to the shelves without permanent damage, for they were probably extremely valuable. She was just about to try to wriggle two books apart when the lift suddenly ground to a halt with an abrupt jolt, and the doors slowly opened to allow Sasha to disembark.

Startled, she glanced at herself in the mirror above the bookshelves in the lift: her cheeks were flushed, her eyes shone darkly, and her glossy chestnut hair was unravelling from its topknot. She looked remarkably dreamy and seductive, she noted, and attributed it to her growing excitement at her impending encounter with Paul. Or was that all it was? She paused before leaving the lift, casting a final glance around its deep crimson-and-mahogany interior. It was the first time she'd been inside it: before this she'd always taken the stairs, as a poor substitute for the sessions at the gym she'd been missing while in England. Now, however, reluctantly leaving the elevator while the doors slowly closed behind her, Sasha thought to herself that there was certainly something eerie about that antiquated piece of machinery, something she felt compelled to investigate further. It was almost as though she felt a kind of presence in that lift, she thought: it seemed as though something inside was calling to her, urging her to re-enter and examine the interior more closely.

The feeling of compulsion was so strong that Sasha actually turned around and reached out her hand to call the lift back, but then she mentally shook herself, her mind calling out sharply, Don't be ridiculous! Paul will be coming up in a little while and you need to get ready! So with a wrench, Sasha turned away from the lift, scurried down the corridor to her room, and hastily fitted her card-key into the computerised lock on her door. The lift might be out of date, but everything else at the Asher Hotel was state of the art and designed for maximum comfort and pleasure. The towels were thick and plentiful, the mini-bar was well stocked, the bed was firm, the shower strong, and there were even fresh flowers, chocolates and fruit in a charming little basket on the dressing-table. True, the room didn't have a TV and telephone in the bathroom as the more prestigious American hotels did, but then they were so much more impersonal, Sasha thought, as she stripped off her suit. The calculated modernisation of this sumptuous old hotel couldn't detract from the beauty and grandeur of the Ashers' former estate.

Nonetheless, Sasha silently blessed modern technology as the power shower rained down on her body, unlocking the tension which sat deep within her muscles, and washing away all of the dull, stuffy atmosphere of the negotiating table. Although Sasha loved her job, and was genuinely excited about getting in on the ground floor of the Get a Gripp campaign, she was eager now to forget all about sales pitches and company contracts and get down to an entirely different kind of business.

She lavishly stroked her expensive scented lotion into the strong muscles of her calves and thighs and over her firm biceps, smooth belly and gently rounded buttocks. Sasha worked hard on her body, continually plagued by her tendency to plump out at the slightest provocation: a pint of beer here, a slice of cake there, skip a couple of workouts, and her hips suddenly gained five pounds. She knew she would never be model-thin, and at five foot five she veered between sizes twelve and fourteen, depending on the designer, but she was proud of her body and revelled in her strong, womanly curves. OK, so her breasts could be a little larger and her hips could certainly be smaller, but Sasha refused to give in to the body-image paranoia so common among other thirty-year-old women she knew, for which, she privately admitted to herself, the advertising and cosmetics companies were partly to blame. If only chocolates weren't so tempting! With a sigh she reached for one now, luxuriating in the feel of the creamy smoothness sliding down her throat as she slithered into a matched set of black satin panties and bra. She paused to admire her new tattoo, only recently acquired and without quite as much pain as she'd expected: the rounded ball of her upper arm was now enhanced by a small black swan, its long graceful neck following the curve of her shoulder. Fondly, Sasha stroked the pretty design, then turned to her suitcase to consider her wardrobe. As usual, she had overpacked for this trip, uncertain about the English weather, which she had been pretty sure would be both wetter and chillier than the muggy New York midsummer air – and she had been right. But the room was warm and her mood enticing, so Sasha knew with certainty the outfit she should choose, which she'd packed for just such an emergency. She certainly wasn't going to put on the clichéd silk negligee Paul would probably be expecting, the soap-opera costume of the stereotyped feminine woman passively awaiting her man. Instead Sasha drew on a pair of wide black crêpe trousers, nearly transparent enough to reveal a glimpse of her underwear, but not quite. Over this she floated a matching chiffon tunic which settled gracefully around her throat in a mandarin collar, with sheer black sleeves through which her swan could clearly be seen, and only the flimsiest of fabrics to cover her breasts, stomach and hips. Not quite pyjamas, certainly not to be worn outside the most intimate gatherings, Sasha's outfit was part of the new 'At-Home' collection being marketed by one of her company's subsidiary firms. A quick stroke of blusher, the merest dab of lipcolour, and a single coat of mascara, and she was ready.

By now fully primed and in the mood, she poured herself a glass of wine – from the Asher vineyards in France, she noticed from the bottle – settled herself on the bed, and flicked on a music video channel. Oh good, she thought: it was the hard rock and heavy metal hour, a welcome antidote to the anaemic Britpop and pretty-boy dance bands. In fact, Sasha was so entranced by the sight of Steven Tyler's generous lips widening in a sneer on the TV screen that she very nearly didn't hear the faint knock at her door.

Certain it was Paul, Sasha hastily snatched the remote, aimed it at the TV and switched it off, then checked to make sure she'd left an open packet of condoms by the bed before walking purposefully towards the door. Arranging a smile of shy seduction on her face, Sasha took a deep breath to quiet her rapidly beating heart, and opened the door.

But there was no one there. Curiously, Sasha stepped out into the hallway, and glanced up and down the long corridor, straining to hear a sound, but there was nothing. Shrugging, she pulled the door shut and reached for her glass of wine, figuring that whoever had knocked must have passed on to the room next door. She was just about to turn Aerosmith back on when she caught her breath, as she felt something brush right by her. Now this was getting weird, Sasha thought crossly. She certainly didn't believe in ghosts, she wasn't at all superstitious, and she had no time for New Age spiritualism or even traditional religion, for that matter: but there was no doubt about it, she had certainly felt something ruffle the air by her face. She was just starting to become seriously worried about this, when a firm, hard rap at the door told her this really was Paul now, and she could forget this whole silly business.

'Sorry I'm late, darling,' Paul called out airily as he came towards her for a kiss, 'but the boss persuaded the barkeeper to open a vintage bottle of Benedictine from the cellar.'

Whew! Sasha could certainly smell the fumes on Paul as he enveloped her in an embrace, fitting his lips to hers and stroking the back of her neck under her hair in a long, satisfying kiss. 'You're lovely,' he breathed against her skin, as he began to undo the top button of her blouse. 'Let me get a better look.'

Sasha stopped his hands. 'Just wait,' she whispered as she kissed him again. 'I want to make this moment last.' She grinned up at him wickedly. 'And besides, you deserve to pay for your naughty behaviour at the dinner-table tonight.'

She drew him to the bed and lay down, watching while Paul stood to slip off his jacket and loosen his tie. He then eased off his shoes and tidily arranged his discarded clothes, while Sasha smiled to herself at his obsessive neatness. The man certainly was gorgeous, though, she thought, with his fair English colouring, his slanted blonde fringe and his sea-green eyes. She sighed as she gazed at his fingers, remembering the thrilling delight they'd so secretly bestowed at dinner, and she couldn't stop herself from reaching for his hand now and placing it on her breast. Paul watched Sasha's face flame as he gently stroked her nipple through the satin fabric of her bra, smiling a little at her obvious pleasure.

'Do you know,' he whispered, moving closer to her on the bed, 'I knew I had to lay my hands on you the moment I saw you at the first meeting.'

'Oh, yes,' Sasha sighed: whether in agreement with Paul's words or to encourage his fingers to do more, she didn't know.

'I was already intrigued by our telephone conversations,' Paul continued, his other hand now sliding up Sasha's thigh as it twined itself around him. 'But meeting you in the flesh was even better than I'd hoped for. You're so talented, sensitive, warm, and – ' his mouth lingered at her throat ' – wonderfully, wonderfully sexy.'

Sorry now that she'd stopped him from unfastening her blouse earlier, Sasha reached for her buttons herself as Paul's lips travelled down from her throat to her cleavage, enhanced by the uplift of her bra, while she revealed more and more of her creamy flesh to Paul's warm and wet mouth. She clasped her breasts in her own hands for a moment, her fingers slipping in between Paul's lips as his tongue played over her skin, and he briefly sucked on her fingers while continuing to kiss her breasts. With an impatient grunt, Sasha pushed down the shoulders of her blouse along with her bra straps, her breasts now gloriously naked and pressed upward by the underwired cups. As Paul's mouth closed over a nipple, Sasha wrenched at the buttons of his crisp cotton shirt, and, his mouth never leaving her breasts, Paul struggled to help her pull the shirt off him. Frantically, she ripped apart the buttons left on her tunic, and, with one sure twist, unhooked her bra and flung it to the floor.

Their bare stomachs now rubbing deliciously together, and their bodies arcing intuitively towards each other, Sasha and Paul worked their way to the centre of the bed, upending pillows and shoving aside covers and sheets in their haste. She then nudged him over on to his back and ran her mouth up and down his neck, while he grasped her buttocks and cupped his hands around them, pressing her against him. Wriggling his hands between their bodies, Paul deftly undid the top button of Sasha's trousers and helped her slide out of them, slipping off her underwear until she was completely naked and lying on top of him. Sasha sighed and inhaled deeply into the muscles of Paul's chest, his silky golden chest hair tickling her nose as she bit gently at the curve of his breast. She then turned her attention to one tiny pink nipple and ran her tongue around its puckered edges, feeling Paul's stomach muscles tighten and the hard bulge of his cock press urgently against her thigh. Slowly, teasingly, she moved lower and touched just the tip of her tongue to Paul's navel, dipping it ever so slightly into the enticing indentation in his stomach before giving it one full lick of her tongue. Sliding further downward, she grasped his cock tightly with one hand before nipping at the waistband of his button-fly trousers, smiling up at him saucily, and then using her teeth to slip the top button out of its tight enclosure. She pressed her lips briefly to the throbbing pole helplessly imprisoned behind the row of buttons, before swiftly undoing the remaining three; then she drew back to help Paul rip off his trousers and striped boxer shorts in one quick move.

Looking up into Sasha's face, Paul gently positioned her over his ready cock, helping her to straddle his hips while she carefully lowered herself towards his rampantly erect penis. She looked down to watch as her sex moved to meet his, and she was one millimetre from clasping Paul's cock in her hot, fluid flesh when she heard it, and froze, her body suspended a fraction of an inch over Paul's.

Sasha's head jerked up, her eyes focusing on nothing, her ears straining to hear it again, and her brow knotted in concentration.

'Darling? What's the matter? What is it?' Paul asked, clearly not daring to move in case he never got her back in this position.

Dazedly, Sasha looked at him, her eyes glazed and unblinking. 'Didn't you hear it? Didn't you hear *her*?' she asked in a trembling voice. 'Hush! There she is again. What is it? What's the matter? Why is she crying? Or is she laughing?'

For indeed, what Sasha could hear – and what Paul, apparently, could not – was the sound of a woman – what? Crying? Sobbing? Laughing? For although the sound appeared to be coming from somewhere behind Sasha's shoulder, it was too chaotic to be clearly deciphered. It was wordless, as a baby's noises are wordless, though the voice clearly came from an adult. The sound seemed to be coming from deep within the woman's throat, rapid and high-pitched, at times almost gurgling, or perhaps almost choking. But then, just as Sasha began to think she had a hold on it, the sound started to move farther away, as though the woman was stepping backward, and then it became fainter and fainter, though no less urgent, until finally, try as she might, Sasha could hear the woman's voice no more.

Shaken, startled – and yet, oddly, not frightened – Sasha shook her head once, and then her eyes cleared and she turned her gaze once more towards Paul, her face calm and even smiling a little.

'Didn't you hear it?' she asked again. 'Didn't you hear her?'

But Paul just looked at her blankly, his face registering his utter incomprehension, and suddenly Sasha knew that she wasn't going to tell him, that she was going to keep this mystery to herself, at least for a while. So instead she decided to lie about what she had just experienced, and to hug this enigma to herself like a private treasure.

'Whoa! I must have had too much to drink!' With a great show of cheery indifference, Sasha manoeuvred herself off Paul and rolled on to her back, one arm dramatically thrown across her forehead. 'I thought I just heard a baby crying, can you believe that?' She laughed brightly at Paul, hoping it didn't sound too forced. 'And I'm not even thirty-two yet! I hope this doesn't mean I'm getting broody!' She glanced at him, hoping he wouldn't suddenly back away from her, frightened off by the prospect of her sudden interest in procreation, but he didn't even seem to notice. Instead, he looked back at her, clearly still puzzled.

'I didn't hear anything,' he said, baffled, then added curiously, 'And how did you know it was a she?'

'Must have been the TV next door!' Sasha responded, choosing to ignore his question. There was only one way to distract Paul from his line of enquiry, she realised, and reached for his now rather flaccid penis. 'Now, where were we?' Deciding to file away this mystery to the back of her brain for tomorrow, she returned her attention to the cock in her hand, though, to be frank, she wasn't as keen to reanimate it now. Still, this was their last night together before her plane left the next day, and who knew how long it would be before she saw another such tasty specimen? So she leant over Paul's stomach and delicately laid her tongue against the purple plum of his penis, then gently drew the whole thing into her mouth where, sure enough, it slowly began to thicken and grow. As she sucked, Sasha could feel Paul's cock starting to throb, so that soon she had to reluctantly release a little of it before she gagged. While Paul watched in approval, Sasha rose up on her haunches and licked up and down the length of his cock, wrapping her tongue around the indentation under the head and lapping off the drop of salty cream at the top.

With a groan, Paul suddenly reached down to pull her back up and rolled himself on top of her, scrabbling for the packet of condoms on Sasha's bedside table. He braced himself on his hands, while Sasha quickly unrolled the sheath down over his cock before guiding it inside her.

'It's been a great three nights with you, Sasha,' Paul murmured as he began to thrust with vigour, his hands curving up under her shoulders. 'Definitely worth the risk,' he added, before playfully nipping at her ear.

Well, Sasha wasn't so sure it was worth risking her job for, because if anyone at ALM had found out she'd been sleeping with one of the ad-men from Rollit she'd have certainly been in disgrace. But Paul's cock made her feel satisfyingly full as it delved deeper inside her, and she rocked her hips forward to take in as much as she possibly could. As the welcome spasms of orgasm began to ripple through her sex, she gripped Paul tightly to her, her cheek pressed against his as he, too, sought his climax. Even in the depths of her vaginal ecstasy, though, Sasha found herself listening into the silence, broken only by her and Paul's breathy cries and the rustling of the mattress beneath them. There was nothing else. The woman – whoever she was – had gone.

Chapter Two

*T*he next morning, after a succession of rapid but extremely pleasurable orgasms, Sasha bade Paul a fond farewell, knowing they would be communicating often via fax and e-mail during the whole of the Get a Gripp campaign. Moreover, Paul promised to clear his schedule for her the next time she flew over on business, so that they could repeat their amorous encounters. With a lingering last look and one final kiss, he reluctantly released her and left, scurrying frantically down the corridor lest anyone from ALM should spot him. Sasha watched him go, wondering if he'd take the mysterious elevator, and whether it would affect him as it had her, but no, he disappeared around the corner to dash down the stairs. Sasha had to admire a man who, like her, preferred to expend the energy to take the stairs rather than recline lazily in the lift, but perhaps Paul just thought he'd have a better chance of avoiding her boss that way. And besides, Sasha herself intended to inspect that lift a little more closely later that day.

With Paul gone, she could now climb back into bed

and indulge herself shamelessly in that staple of hotel luxury, room service. She ordered herself a full English breakfast, secure in the knowledge that she could eat the entire tray without feeling obliged to put on any ladylike pretence of a delicate feminine appetite in front of a man: not that she usually did. Instead, she ate with gusto, working her way through mushrooms, eggs, bacon, sausage, toast, and fruit, ignoring the tomatoes and beans. Afterwards she lay back against her pillows, wonderfully replete, and sipped her coffee, planning what to do with the few hours she had left before she and the rest of the team had to board the mini-cab that would escort them back to the airport.

As if on cue, the phone rang, and Sasha reached over with one hand to pick it up, while scrabbling for the last strawberry under her plate with the other.

'Hello?' she said, hoping she sounded crisp and alert.

'Sasha?' It was Valerie. 'The boys and I are going into the centre of London this morning: we're hoping we have enough time to take a quick walk through the exhibition at the Tate. Would you like to come along?'

Casting about frantically for an excuse, Sasha's eyes fell on her handbag and she replied firmly, 'Oh, that's kind, Val, but I was really hoping to get in some shopping before we leave: I'd promised my – my niece that I'd buy her some English toys, and I was also hoping to pick up something for myself.'

Desperately hoping that Valerie didn't know that she had no nieces, Sasha breathed out a little and relaxed when Valerie responded, sounding not in the least bit disappointed, 'Oh, dear, what a disappointment. OK, well, I just thought I'd ask. We'll meet you back here at one o'clock then, all right?'

She's probably delighted I'm not coming, Sasha thought: there's nothing that woman likes more than to have a man or several all to herself. In the nine months or so that Sasha had been working in the New York office, she had come to realise quite a few things about her boss, one of them being Valerie's continual lustful interest in males. Sasha figured that was probably why Valerie had specialised in the marketing of cosmetics for men: there were plenty of opportunities to pull in the still male-dominated fields of market research and advertising, not to mention the plethora of gorgeous male models. Valerie insisted upon being personally involved in interviewing and hand-picking the handsome young blades that ALM featured in its ads; no doubt many of their customers were gay men who were drawn to the products by the enticing male spreads in the glossy magazines. And, of course, those great-looking men helped to persuade women to buy moisturiser, shaving gel, toner, and face-wash for their husbands, fathers, lovers and sons (or so the research implied) in the hope that their men would become almost as attractive as those photogenic beauties.

Well, Sasha had other things to consider this morning, as she showered in the spacious stall and dressed quickly in the most comfortable clothes she had brought, stretchy black leggings and an oversized cotton sweatshirt. She could never see the point of wearing restrictive clothing and loads of make-up on a transatlantic flight, and so she dispensed with her usual routine of hair gel, base and powder, as well as eye, lip, and cheek colour, opting instead for moisturiser and a pony-tail. As she wound her shoulder-length chestnut hair into her velvet scrunchie, she glanced at herself approvingly in the mirror, noting the pleasing length of her legs, flattered by the Lycra in her leggings, her shapely hips not quite hidden by her sweatshirt, the creaminess of her skin, the gloss of her hair, her round brown eyes, and the well-cut shape of her slightly full mouth. She stepped closer to the mirror and admired the slight glow in her cheeks and the sparkle in her eyes, due, she supposed, to the great sex she'd shared with Paul. Or perhaps, she mused to herself, the glow was inspired by the compelling mystery of the ghostly laugh she'd heard last night. She was sure that that laugh was somehow connected to the eerie feeling she'd had in the lift, and she was determined to investigate both matters now. Tying on her high-topped sneakers with a quick jerk of the laces and pulling up her chunky white socks, Sasha felt more than ready for some amateur sleuthing, beginning with the good-looking bartender she'd spotted in the lounge last night. She hoped he was on duty again this morning.

Sure enough, there he was, polishing glasses and pouring coffee behind the high oak bar. He glanced at Sasha as she bounded in, feeling optimistic and full of energy, and hoping for some local gossip.

'May I have a cup of coffee please?' she asked politely, noting that there were few patrons in the hotel bar that morning. She watched, a little nervous now, as the man poured her a steaming cup of Java, and as he handed it to her she wondered how to begin.

'This really is a lovely hotel, Simon,' she said, indicating the name on the tag pinned to his black waistcoat. 'Have you been working here long?'

He glanced at her from under his heavy black brows and nodded. 'About two years,' he replied, handing her a plate of biscuits.

'Two years.' She bit reflectively into her bourbon cream, trying to decide how to continue. 'I see this hotel is over three hundred years old,' she said chattily, and sipped at her coffee. 'There must be a lot of history in this old building, hmm?'

The man nodded. 'A fair bit,' he said shortly.

'A place like this must even have a few ghost stories about it,' Sasha went on, innocently widening her eyes and hoping she looked guileless.

'Yep.' He continued to polish glasses, looking a little away from her.

Sasha realised she would have to be more forthright. 'I don't suppose any guests have ever complained about hearing noises or anything, have they?' she asked lightly, trying to sound as though even she wouldn't believe such stories.

The bartender, however, was not fooled. He put down the glass he was working on, and, looking Sasha directly in the face, he said heavily, 'You want to know about her, don't you?'

Stunned, Sasha looked up at him. He was staring at her, unsmiling but not particularly unfriendly, but all she could say was, 'Her? Do you know something about that?'

'You're staying in room 323, aren't you?' he asked, and watched her flush in response. When she nodded, he continued, 'This happens every couple of months or so. A guest – a woman – will come into the bar, usually in the morning, alone and a little nervous, and either pretend to be casual and offhand, like you – ' he nodded at her '– or else a little more hesitant and shy, but they always want to know the same thing.' He paused – for dramatic effect, Sasha thought irritably – then explained. 'They always want to know if I've heard any good ghost stories about this place.' He almost sneered at Sasha now, a little bitterly, she thought with a jolt, and wondered why he was being so unpleasant. She didn't think he was at all good-looking any more.

24

'Ghost stories?' she could only echo dumbly, staring at the man. When he merely nodded but said nothing, she leant across the bar and said, a little impatiently, 'Well? Are there any?'

The bartender looked back at her unkindly. 'Look, all I can do is tell you what I tell the other guests who ask me about her. All I know is that there is a rumour that this hotel is – well – haunted by a lady who cries or laughs or something.' He shrugged, looking a little less mean. 'We call her The Weeper. But apparently only other women can hear her: for some reason men never know what the ladies are talking about, me included.' He looked a little defiant now, and backed away slightly from Sasha as she demanded, 'But who is she?'

Simon hesitated, then said, almost respectfully, 'They say she is Amelia Asher.'

Amelia Asher. It was the first time Sasha had heard the name, yet her skin seemed to prickle in some kind of recognition, as though she somehow knew something about this mysterious ghost. At the same time she felt an entirely irrational surge of jealousy at the thought that Amelia had appeared to other women, that she hadn't been waiting for Sasha alone: that there were others who had, if not seen, at least heard her.

'Has anyone ever actually seen this ghost?' she asked eagerly, leaning further forward.

Simon looked at her and shook his head. 'No. All I know is that they hear her, but only in room 323, and only at night.'

'So who was Amelia Asher?' Sasha asked, annoyed that the man seemed so reluctant to talk.

In fact, he seemed positively anxious to end the conversation. 'All I know is that she is supposed to be the daughter of the people who lived here in the late eighteenth century; she had some kind of broken love-affair and died suddenly. That's all I know, and that's all I can tell you,' he said firmly, and actually stepped away from her.

Sasha was now seriously perturbed. Without another word or glance, she rose from her seat and moved towards the door, barely noticing the young woman busily clearing glasses behind her. But as Sasha stepped out of the lounge, the girl came up to her and whispered shyly, 'I heard you ask about Amelia.'

Startled, Sasha turned and looked at the girl. 'Do you know something about her?'

The young woman glanced around the empty lounge and whispered, 'Shhh. We're not supposed to say anything about her. That's why he – ' she jerked her head in the direction of the bartender '– was being so grumpy with you. He's never seen her, and I think he thinks the stories about her are all made up, and the manager doesn't want to scare away guests with the rumour that a ghost lives here.' The girl, whose name-tag identified her as Claire, steered Sasha into a corner and looked at her excitedly. 'But I'm just going on my break now, and I can take you to her, Miss, if you like.'

Mystified, intrigued, and a tiny bit scared – as well as a bit put off by being addressed as 'Miss' – Sasha followed the girl out of the lounge bar and along the entrance corridor, past the reception desk and hotel lobby, and around to an empty back passage. She felt a slight chill as she scurried silently behind the girl, who seemed a little nervous herself, and repeatedly looked left and right as though ensuring that they weren't being followed. Sasha wasn't at all sure what part of the hotel they were now in, and she'd had no idea the building was so large: they seemed to have turned several corners past rows of shut doors. At one point she thought she spotted a pile of hotel laundry, and it seemed by the sudden smell that they were passing a rubbish tip, but they now seemed to be leaving behind all signs of habitation.

As though guessing her thoughts, Sasha's young guide stopped for a moment and turned to smile at her bewildered fellow conspirator, as Sasha felt she had become.

'Guests aren't supposed to see this part of the hotel,' she explained. 'We've just passed the manager's office and staff rooms. We're now entering the back part of the house where the servants used to live: it's been closed off for as long as anyone can remember.'

Sasha stared curiously at the girl, wondering how she came to find her way around this maze when it was so clearly forbidden. Claire simply smiled and shrugged at Sasha, then gestured that she should follow her up a wide, dusty staircase, which had clearly been unused for some time: probably decades, Sasha figured, given the decaying state of the carpet and the grimy, dark, wooden walls which seemed to muffle all sound and absorb all light. It was quite dim up this staircase: the windows were curtained off by heavy velvet drapes and the illumination from below was becoming fainter and fainter. There was a musty smell of age and neglect in the air, and the ceiling and the walls as they climbed the stairs were thick with cobwebs and dust. Just when Sasha decided she'd had enough, and was getting tired of following her guide up an ancient set of stairs that seemed to lead nowhere, the girl suddenly stopped. Sasha looked around: they were standing on a landing, though the staircase clearly continued on up, apparently for ever. Sasha then looked back at Claire. She was leaning back against the banister, gazing in wide-eyed adoration at the portrait on the wall that was miraculously clean and grime-free.

'Here she is,' breathed Claire, in what was nearly a sigh of worship. 'This is Amelia.'

Sasha looked. She studied the portrait before her, trying to emblazon its image on her memory. The background of the painting was in dull hues of grey and green, as though to make the central spotlit figure all the more startling for the contrast. Sasha gazed at the painting of a young woman – probably about eighteen or so, she guessed – wearing a magnificent dress rich in hue and texture. The painter had paid minute attention to detail, so that Sasha could clearly make out the layers of lace ruching at the throat, the heaviness of the fabric, and the way the deep pink shaded into crimson where the material creased and folded at the bosom and waist. The lady in the picture wore no jewels, except for a ruby-studded ribbon threaded through the intricate golden curls that were piled up so artfully, and apparently quite precariously, on her head. But it was the woman's face that held Sasha's gaze: she made careful mental note of the delicate pink ears, the porcelain-and-peach complexion, the long, aristocratic nose, the full rosebud mouth, and the huge green eyes, thickly lashed and stunningly framed by arched brows. She gazed at this woman in fascination, dazzled not so much by her beauty as by the shock of recognition, almost an erotic thrill, as though she somehow knew her, as though young Lady Amelia were a flesh-and-blood woman, not merely some aesthetic image. As Sasha continued to stare at her, it seemed as though Amelia breathed an almost imperceptible sigh, as though her lips actually trembled for a moment and her eyes grew moist as Sasha looked into them.

This is crazy! Sasha told herself, jolted out of her

reverie by the realisation that her own eyes actually had tears in them, and her own mouth was beginning to tremble. It's just an old painting! she chided herself, anxious to break the spell. She glanced at Claire, who was now looking at her rather than at the portrait, and smiling a little at Sasha's obvious stupefaction.

'She's lovely, isn't she?' Claire sighed. 'It almost seems as though she's alive, doesn't it? That's why she was moved back here to hang in this dusty old part of the house: the guests complained that they were disturbed by her when she was hanging in the residential part of the hotel. In fact,' Claire went on meaningly, watching Sasha while she spoke, 'several women said that Lady Amelia's eyes seemed to follow them.' She looked closer at Sasha. 'You feel it too, don't you, Miss?'

It was true: it did seem as though the painted eyes flickered whenever Sasha looked away. However, she said nothing, but turned to walk away, determined to forget all about this silly investigative nonsense. She started down the stairs, when, out of the corner of her eye, she saw him, and stopped.

Claire saw Sasha's eyes widen. 'Yes,' she whispered, as if afraid of being overheard. 'Oh yes, he's here too.'

Ignoring her, Sasha stepped closer to the portrait, peering at the periphery of the painting where the background dissolved into the wooden frame. No, she was too close: she had to step back a bit in order to get a better perspective on the shape that had only barely come into view.

'Who is that?' she breathed.

'That's Johnny,' replied Claire, in a tone of hushed awe.

Johnny. Sasha adjusted her position on the staircase until she could get as clear an image as possible of the shadowy figure who lurked in the margins of Amelia

Asher's portrait. Whereas the lady had been lovingly painted, with intensive attention to detail and almost photographic accuracy, the man in the background was only sketched in, his small figure and indistinct features dwarfed by the luminescent presence of Amelia. Still, Sasha could discern enough of his face to retain a clear impression of curved black brows, burning dark eyes, unruly dark hair, and a firmly chiselled mouth. Unlike Amelia, whose rich dress and aristocratic mien revealed her powerful class status, this man was dressed in simple workman's clothes: boots, breeches, rough cotton blouse and leather waistcoat. Like Amelia, the man was gazing at something outside the portrait, and, for an unnerving moment, Sasha actually thought he was looking directly at her, even smiling a little. Inexplicably, she felt an erotic pull as she looked at this man: a kind of electric charge that buzzed in her head, pounded in her heart, beat in her breast and throbbed between her legs. She felt herself grow warm and moist, and her lips actually parted a little as though in expectation of a kiss. Sasha stared until she could look no more, the painted images blurring before her eyes until she felt dizzy and faint. Stumbling a little, she backed away down the stairs, her eyes still held by the portrait, until Claire came down behind her and gently turned her around so that she was facing in the right direction again.

'Come on,' she said tenderly, taking Sasha by the arm. 'I'll take you back down.'

Carefully, Claire guided the still-dazed Sasha all the way down the stairs, back through the dimly lit passages, past the rubbish dump and laundry piles, until they were once again back in the main part of the hotel, blinking a little in the sudden sunlight pouring through the windows that was such a contrast to the gloom of the staircase hidden somewhere in the back.

'Wow.' Sasha shook her head, still a little disoriented, then focused clearly on Claire. 'Thank you. Thank you for taking me to her.'

'Would you like a cup of tea?' Claire asked gently. 'I still have some time left on my break; if you like, I could tell you what I know about her.'

'Oh, yes, please,' Sasha agreed eagerly. 'I want to know everything!'

'Come with me.' Claire gestured for Sasha to follow her to a set of guest rooms on the ground floor, where, with a furtive look down the empty hall, she quickly shook out a key from the pocket of her skirt and opened one of the rooms, ushering Sasha inside.

Sasha looked around the empty room, its bed stripped of sheets, a hint of bathroom freshener in the air.

'This is one of the rooms that's left unoccupied in case there's a sudden rush of emergency guests,' Claire explained, then gestured to the bed. 'Sit down.'

Sasha sat, her hands clasped between her knees like a schoolgirl, and said, 'Tell me. Tell me everything.'

Claire smiled. 'Well, I don't know very much, but I do know more than that prat behind the bar: or, at least, I know more than he's telling. My mother told me the story about Amelia when I first started working here; you might say it's kind of a local legend.'

Sasha nodded impatiently. 'Tell me. I want to know.'

'Well, the Ashers were one of the most famous families around this part of the country in the seventeenth and eighteenth centuries,' Claire began, seating herself across from Sasha. 'I guess they were the local nobility; they were certainly rich, because they owned most of the village right outside the town, including the chapel and churchyard. Apparently they were also pretty unpleasant people, especially Amelia's grandparents on her father's side, whose lineage was supposed to reach back to Norman times.' Sasha could hear the note of bitter scorn in the girl's voice, but then Claire brightened and continued, 'But Lady Asher, Amelia's mother, was different. She didn't come from royalty: her father had been in some kind of trade, and they say Lord Asher married her out of true love, even though his parents disapproved.' The girl sighed romantically, then continued, 'But his parents died soon after the Lord and Lady married, so the Ashers moved into this house and had Amelia soon after. My mother says that Lady Asher was very charitable and good, and believed in education for all women and fair wages for servants; everyone was supposed to have loved her. But she died in childbirth when Amelia was twelve years old, and after that they say that everything changed.'

Claire paused, and Sasha said nothing, but waited for her to continue.

'Lord Asher, Amelia's father, is said to have become cruel and mean after his wife died, and to turn out to be just as wicked as his parents. Apparently he couldn't bear to have his daughter around him, probably because she reminded him too much of his dead wife, and so he sent Amelia away to a so-called ladies' school to be educated. She hated it, though, and she wasn't allowed to come back home until she was seventeen, except for Christmas and the short summer holidays.' Claire waited until Sasha nodded, and then added dramatically, 'And that's when she fell in love with him.'

'Johnny?' Sasha felt she didn't even need to ask.

Claire nodded. 'John Blakeley. He was the gardener whose family had worked on the estate for generations; in fact, he and Amelia used to play together when they were children, because Lady Asher didn't

32

believe in segregating the children of different classes. Well, when Amelia returned from Mrs Sinclair's School for Ladies, Johnny was all grown up, and they began to see each other secretly: Mama says they used to meet in the rose garden.' Claire's voice grew wistful, and then she glanced at Sasha and continued, 'But eventually they were found out. And you can just imagine how happy that made Lord Asher. He had planned on Amelia marrying some titled gentleman, and had willed the property to her on that condition: or, rather,' Claire corrected herself bitterly, 'the title and property would go to the man Amelia would have to marry. Her father seemed to have forgotten that his own lovely wife didn't come from nobility, because he ordered Amelia to stop seeing John, and he actually locked her in her room when she refused.'

Sasha held her breath for a moment, then asked, 'Room 323 in this hotel?'

Claire nodded. 'They say Amelia went quite mad for a little while, and that finally her father actually had Johnny banished: nobody knows to where.'

Sasha felt she knew what was coming next. 'What happened?'

Claire turned sorrowful eyes towards her. 'This is the really sad part,' she said. 'The story is that as Johnny's carriage was rolling away, Amelia broke out of her room and ran outside after it, calling his name and crying. I guess he didn't hear her, though, because the carriage never stopped. Amelia fell down in the mud in the drive, screaming and sobbing, until her father found her the next day, still weeping. He brought her inside and called the doctor, but it was too late. They say she had caught influenza that night in the rain and died, but I think she died of a broken heart.' Claire paused, then finished her tale by saying, 'After that, Lord Asher moved away – to South Africa,

I think – and the house was closed until it was turned into a hotel in the 1920s.'

The story was melodramatic, absurdly so, and so ludicrously simplistic that ordinarily Sasha would have dismissed it as a ridiculous fairy tale. However, the memory of the woman's voice from last night was still strong, and the kinship she felt with the figures in the portrait too powerful to deny. So, instead of ridiculing the story and Claire's childishly sentimental belief in it, Sasha asked instead, in all seriousness, 'And so it's Amelia Asher who's said to haunt room 323? And only women can hear her?'

Claire nodded. 'I've never heard her myself,' she said sadly, 'but I often sit there when it's empty and call to her.' She shrugged regretfully. 'I guess she just doesn't hear me.' She looked at Sasha. 'But you – you're the lucky one. She came to you.'

Sasha remembered her own envy when the bartender had told her that other women had heard Amelia's voice, and she said nothing, but smiled sympathetically. Then, with a small shriek, Claire pulled out her watch and hastily stood up.

'I've got to go,' she said breathlessly, urging Sasha towards the door. 'I'm sorry I didn't give you any tea.'

Impulsively, Sasha hugged her. 'Thank you for telling me Amelia's story, and for bringing me to see her,' she said as she released the girl. 'I hope she comes to you someday soon.'

Claire let them both out of the room, after first ensuring that no one was lurking nearby, and then whisked away down the hall without a backward glance. Sasha stood there a moment, then turned, lost in thought, for the lift. She knew it must almost be time to meet Valerie and the others, but she wanted one last moment alone in the elevator, if only to absorb the atmosphere.

Sasha pressed the call button, expecting it to take several minutes for the lift to respond, but to her surprise, the doors immediately opened for her, as though welcoming her in. Hesitantly, she stepped inside, not sure of what it was she expected to find, and watched as the doors slowly closed and the lift began its ascent. Lingeringly, almost seductively, she trailed her fingers over the backs of the books on the shelves, fingering their leather bindings and stroking their textured spines. She closed her eyes and breathed in the faint musty smell, then opened them as she ran her fingers up and down the back of the fourth volume of Ann Radcliffe's *The Mysteries of Udolpho* which stood at the end of the bookcase on the bottom shelf. It was clearly the original edition of the novel, first printed in 1794, and as Sasha fruitlessly attempted to ease the book out, the thought occurred to her that no one had probably touched it in nearly two centuries: no doubt people were put off by its length and cumbersome, unfamiliar title. Too bad, Sasha thought, shrugging to herself as she tried, again unsuccessfully, to extract the volume: it really is a great read. She finally gave up on trying to work the book loose when, with a sudden thump of her heart, she realised that the creaking, grinding noise of the elevator had stopped, and so, apparently, had the lift. Puzzled, surprised, but not really frightened, she looked at the row of buttons that numbered the floors, but saw that none were lit. We must have stopped between floors for some reason, she thought, unsure why she was thinking in the plural. She pressed the button to open the doors, but nothing happened. Instead, she seemed suspended in space and time, and for a moment she did nothing. Then, thinking to herself how silly this all was, she turned her back on the books and aimed her index finger firmly at the red alarm button. Just before her finger made contact, however, a peculiar dry, fluttering sound broke the eerie silence. Sasha froze for a moment, refusing to believe what she was hearing. There it was again: a persistent crackling, crinkling noise that suddenly stopped as abruptly as it had begun. Slowly, almost afraid to turn around but daring herself to do so, Sasha pivoted to gaze again at the bookcase below the mirror on the wall of the lift. She glanced down at the copy of Radcliffe's *Udolpho* that stood at the end of the shelf, and now she noticed that there was a thin sheaf of papers wedged between the book and the bookcase. As the lift suddenly whirred noisily back into life, Sasha slowly reached out her hand and gently slid out the rustling object.

It was a faded, yellowed manuscript tied up with a decaying length of red ribbon, and clearly written on the outer page was the date: 8 April, 1795.

Chapter Three

Sasha sat uncomfortably in her aeroplane seat, deliberating whether she should ask for another whisky before landing at Kennedy Airport. The trip had been intolerably long, with Valerie flirting shamelessly with her two male employees, the three of them cheerily ignoring Sasha. Actually, that was fine with her, as she preferred having the time to herself to contemplate the mysterious goings-on she'd experienced during the last twenty-four hours. First the strangely compelling lift, then Amelia's ghostly visitation, she mused, staring moodily out of the window. A darkly seductive portrait, a tragic tale of a woman confined, driven mad, and then dying for love, and now a hidden manuscript! It was just too ridiculous, Sasha reflected: it was almost as though she were living in a Gothic novel like *The Mysteries of Udolpho* herself!

Yet the thought of that manuscript and the secrets it might contain set Sasha's heart thumping; she'd tucked it hastily away in her suitcase just as Valerie had tapped on her door to call her to lunch, and of course she'd had no time to read it since. She'd carefully wrapped it in tissue-paper before repacking it tenderly in her carry-on bag, where it was now safely stored away underneath the seat in front of her.

Since boarding the plane she'd done little else than sip whisky and stroke her hold-all protectively with her foot, heedless of the marks she might be leaving on the expensive leather bought at last year's post-Christmas sale at Bloomingdale's. Now, as the cabin steward passed enquiringly by, Sasha signalled to him for yet another drink to fortify herself before touchdown.

It seemed ages before the plane finally jolted to a halt, the doors opened and the Business Class passengers began to disembark. Sasha grunted tipsily to herself as she trailed down the exit corridor behind the ALM team, through passport control, and down to collect her luggage at the carousel with all the other Virgin passengers. Finally she paused at the arrivals lounge to say goodbye to Valerie, Robert and Ross, and to graciously decline their offer to share a cab back to midtown Manhattan. Instead, she watched them depart with relief, promising to see them at 8.30 sharp Monday morning to report on the Rollit contract with the rest of the ALM staff. She then went out into the grimy New York air to hail herself a cab to take her back home.

Once inside her spacious twelfth-floor apartment, Sasha dumped her bags on the floor, hastily stripped off her clothes, and headed for the bathroom without even glancing at her breathtaking view of Central Park. Although it was only 9.00 p.m. New York time, she was exhausted after the seven-hour flight, as well as by the events of that morning – had it really been only that morning? – and all she wanted was to brush her teeth, take a shower, and climb into bed with her mysterious eighteenth-century document. But first, messages.

Sasha rewound the tape on her answering machine to see who had missed her while she'd been away. She shuddered when she heard the nasal voice of Newt, her latest ghastly blind date, who had called to ask when he could take her out again. As if! Sasha grimaced, vowing never to put herself at another's match-making mercy again. Her dry-cleaner had called to remind her to pick up her winter coat that she'd left nearly three weeks ago, and there was also a call from Xenia, asking if she was back yet. With a smile at the sound of her best friend's voice, Sasha switched off the machine and went to turn on the shower. Only three calls – two, if you didn't count Mr Kwik Clean – but then, she'd only been gone since Tuesday. Well, she'd call Xenia back tomorrow.

Freshly showered, unpacked, tucked up in bed wearing her favourite L.L. Bean men's pyjamas, and sipping a cup of Lemon Zinger tea to wash away her whisky hangover, Sasha at last held the exciting roll of manuscript in her hands, almost unable to believe what she was looking at. England now seemed very far away, surrounded as she was by the elegance of her New York apartment, the noise of the traffic floating up faintly to her window as the air conditioner hummed. Sasha was almost beginning to wonder whether the lift, the portrait and the story of Amelia Asher were just a murky dream; but no, she held the evidence of them in her hand, for there had never been any doubt in her mind that this roll of paper was the property of the mysterious, ghostly woman. She stared again at the inked date on the outer page, gently stroking the decaying red ribbon that tied the papers together. Again she felt a puzzling but unmistakable erotic thrill down her spine just from touching the pages in her lap, as though she was actually in the presence of some powerfully enticing man – or woman, she shrugged to herself. Sasha was nothing if not pragmatic, and she was broad-minded enough to accept the reality of her senses; although she'd never believed in ghost stories before, she was willing now to suspend some of her disbelief.

With that thought in mind, she slowly slipped the ribbon off the rolled-up sheaf of papers and carefully smoothed them down with her hand. Dry, thin, yellowed and crackling, the pages were made from a cloth base, the texture quite different from modern paper. Sasha briefly caressed the watermark on the back of each page, and stared at the handwritten words, the graceful curves, and the strange shape of the 's' which looked like an 'f' to the twentieth-century eye. The style of script was so different from the cursive of modern-day writers that Sasha had at first a little trouble in deciphering the characters. There were surprisingly few blots, considering the implements the writer had to work with: although, as Sasha leafed through the sheets, she saw that the writing became progressively more chaotic and indecipherable, and that several of the pages were mere fragments, as though parts had been ripped away. Chiding herself for skipping to the end first, which she would never have done with a novel, Sasha turned back to page one. She reached up to reangle her lamp, poured herself another cup of tea from the pot, adjusted the pillows behind her back, and began to read.

17 June 1794
Can it be? Is this love? My head is in such a rush, my heart is pounding so, I can barely speak or write! Yet write I must: I must get this all down

on paper, while I see it all before me – while I see *him* still before me – and what a man he is! Those eyes so dark and tender, his complexion so brown and clear, that curling black hair and – dare I comment? – that shapely mouth! Such a fine figure of a man, in his simple breeches and blouse, and what long, strong legs! Can this be the Johnny I played with as a child? True, I have been away five long years, only visiting at home at Christmas and a fortnight in the summer, but to have missed seeing him all that time? And now, to see him grown so tall and fine, a man at last – yet, is he not the same age as I? Are we not both seventeen? What a contrast he is to my toady, oily cousin Gareth, who I know is here only to try to wheedle a marriage settlement out of my father! I know that Gareth thinks he can persuade Father to coerce me into marrying him, just so he can appropriate the inheritance that will be mine when Father dies! They think that I should want to marry him just so I can retain my title as Lady Amelia Asher, but I refuse to be wed to someone I so loathe, and who only wants me for my property! I know how hopeful Gareth has become ever since he found out that he could claim ownership of both my title and property if only I would agree to marry him, as Father has no male heir – poor Mamma! Dying while trying to give birth to Father's so longed-for son!

But I digress. It is John who holds my thoughts. I will never forget that glimpse I had of him on my return home. We'd only glanced at each other, but I could see – could I not? – a warmth and light in his fine dark eyes as he gravely bowed along with the other staff who had lined up to welcome me home. 'Good to have you back,

Lady,' was all he said then, but such a fire that voice struck in my bosom! Since that day – but a week ago – I have strained to catch a glimpse of the handsome gardener, yet not daring to let anyone see, lest they report back to Father! Oh, he has been so hard and cruel since the death of Mamma, especially to me, his only child! He has let go of almost all of his civic responsibilities, except for acting as local magistrate, and even that business he conducts mainly in the public houses with that tiresome lot of solicitors and City agents! He never has any time for me, and I can't bear to be around Gareth; the staff don't dare approach me as a friend because I am Lady Amelia, and I have no real friends here, but suffer in loneliness.

At least, until now. Now I have handsome John to dream about, and just the thought of him starts such a fire in my blood and in my body, especially in that most secret of places which even now throbs so unaccountably!

Is this love? I must see him, I *must* – somehow I must contrive to meet with him, but where? And how? Perhaps sweet Rosie, the scullery-maid who used to play with us as children? Can I trust her? Perhaps she is hoping that one day she and Johnny might . . .? Oh, but I have no one else to ask, and she has always been especially kind to me! Perhaps Rosie will help me to find a way to meet with Johnny, for meet with him I absolutely must.

Here the first entry, or whatever it was, seemed to end, for Sasha noted that the bottom half of the page was empty, and the next page was dated 29 October. In need of some fortification after such an exhausting overflow of emotion, Sasha got out of bed to pour herself a brandy. Settling back in amongst her pillows, she took a long drink before picking up the manuscript to read the next entry. I hope Amelia has calmed down by now, Sasha muttered to herself as her eyes scanned the page. The first few lines, however, soon convinced her that she hadn't.

29 October
Can one woman contain such bliss in her body? Can one die of the rapture of love? It is now four months that Johnny and I have been seeing each other in secret, and I feel I will go mad if I do not confide in someone! I have even considered confiding in sweet Rosie, my dear maid, who has been so instrumental in helping to provide opportunities for Johnny and me to meet to express our love! But I dare not involve her too deeply in our affairs, lest harm should ever come to her from knowing too much. Oh, if only I had a woman friend to talk to! But since I have no one, I will write to an imaginary confidante: I will pretend that this is a letter going out to a beloved sister or friend. Anna, I shall call her, as Mr Richardson's Clarissa had her best friend Anna Howe to write to.

Sasha jumped a little at this. Her middle name was Anna. After a moment, she continued reading.

Well, my dearest Anna, last night I finally persuaded my beloved Johnny to fully initiate me into the ways of love. After long hours of passionate kisses and caresses, my body would frequently scream out – for what, I did not know. Some kind of relief was what I craved, but how

43

to achieve it was beyond me, and Johnny would often pull away as some crisis seemed to be mounting. We were both in despair that we could not consummate our love as woman and man, as Johnny put it, always afraid that somehow we would be discovered and Father would marry me off to Gareth after all. Ever since our first secret meeting at night in the ha-ha by the rose garden, where the wall of the ditch would hide us from view, we have both been tormented by the most delicious longings for fulfilment! And then, last night, I finally convinced him to make love to me the fullest way he knew how, so that I should discover all the delights of heaven! How did I do it? Well, my dearest Anna, I shall be but too happy to reveal all . . .

Whew! Sasha poured herself another drink, glad that at last Amelia and John were going to get it on and get it over with. She continued to read.

As we lay together in the grass under a bundle of warm blankets that Johnny had placed there earlier, I turned to him, and, laying my lips tenderly against his, I whispered, 'And now, tonight, we will do as we've both desired for so long.' I wrapped my tongue around his and urged him on top of my body, moulding my hips to his as we moved against each other in sweet sensuous harmony. Johnny withdrew himself from me for a moment, reared up on his powerful strong arms, and, looking down at me fondly, he teasingly asked, 'And what might that be, my dearest?'

Embarrassed, I looked up at him. 'I confess, I do not know,' I murmured shyly, for indeed, I was still unsure about the ways of a woman's – or a man's – body. I knew, though, that my lower body – what Johnny said was my 'fanny,' or, naughtier still, 'cunny' – was desperate for something other than the insistent rubbing against each other we'd been engaged in, and I guessed that my form of relief – and his – must be connected to that thick, hard rod that leapt and pulsed in the front of his breeches. And so, bold now with desire and daring, I placed my hand on that great strong thing and pressed against it, sliding my fingers up and down in some kind of natural rhythm. John shut his eyes briefly and let out a low moan, indicating silently that my hand was engaged in exactly the motion he craved. Although it is now late in the autumn and the air is chill outside, neither Johnny nor I felt the wind or the cold as we lay in our blanketed cocoon, our limbs wrapped securely around each other, our lips pressed feverishly together as our tongues eagerly probed the sweet recesses of each other's mouths. Our hearts beat together as one, just as the throb of John's manhood pulsed so steadily beneath my hand, and my own seat of desire was grown moist and warm and full, and yet, somehow, achingly, tormentingly empty.

'Oh, stop a moment, my love!' John breathed against my ear. 'Or I swear I shall spend too soon and ruin both our pleasure! Indeed, I know we mustn't linger too long out here lest your father start searching for you inside, or your odious cousin Gareth stumble across us on some ill-fated midnight ramble. And besides, my dearest – ' and here he placed a wickedly thrilling kiss right at the valley between my breasts '– there are so many, many delights which await us both.'

All atremble with the fever of desire, I nevertheless could not stifle a gasp of shock when Johnny reached his hands deep within the bodice of my dress, unlaced my stays and drew out both my breasts, freeing them from the confines of my whaleboned corset and pressing down the fabric which covered my shoulders and arms. I had never felt so naked or exposed in all my life, and the wind was cold on my flesh, but the chill lasted only a moment, until John bent over and ran his warm tongue across the crests of my bosom now grown quite tight and hard. Oh, Anna, I cannot express the joy that I felt when my beloved parted his lips and drew first one puckered bud, then the other into his mouth, rubbing them with his tongue and sucking on them gently. I pushed my fingers through the glorious thickness of his hair and arched my back, thrusting my breasts yet further into the deep cavern of his mouth. We lay there for many minutes this way, with John raining sweet kisses on my naked and trembling bosom, until my senses were further inflamed by the feel of his hand inching its way up the length of my leg. His fingers were hard and callused from the long hours of manual labour he performed every day in the gardens, yet they felt devilishly soft as they crept under my skirts and petticoat until at last they reached that part of me that burnt and pulsed so desperately. The feel of his fingers against my bare flesh sent such a wave of fire sweeping through my veins that I unthinkingly shunned the last vestiges of my modesty and actually freed myself of my confining underclothes, tugging away the cumbersome garments right up to my waist so that my lower body was completely naked beneath my cloak and dress.

And then – oh! how to describe it! Those clever fingers gently stroked at the outer edges of the channel between my thighs, working their way inwards till they reached some secret spot I didn't even know I had. While the two fingers of John's hand stole shamelessly right up inside my woman's space, his thumb slowly circled round the little nub at the apex of my – dare I say? – cunny. (Such a pleasurable flush even writing the word brings to my cheeks!) John pressed against that funny little button with his thumb, while I bucked and writhed beneath him, hardly knowing where I was or what he was doing, until a sudden spark of the purest, fiercest delight I had ever known, a kind of paroxysm, went off inside my head and body, and I nearly screamed aloud with the rapture of it all.

When I came back to myself, I blinked to see my handsome John looking down at me tenderly, smiling at me with the greatest love as he said gently, 'You just spent, my dearest. And now I want to show you how to do this for yourself.'

I looked up at him, a little puzzled as to what he meant, but then rapidly understood as he took my hand and led it down the length of my body, along the curves of my waist and hips and underneath the heavy velvet of my dress, until my own fingers lay against the deep crevice between my legs.

I had never dared to touch myself there before, hardly even knowing what to do, but I was baffled now as to why I had so foolishly restrained myself. Impatiently, I released my hand from John's so that I might explore the mysteries of my own body myself. John then moved back a little, respectfully averting his eyes so as not to intrude on my private moment of bliss. Quickly my fingers discovered my pleasure button, still overly sensitive from its recent vibrations, so I left that alone for a moment while I explored the dewy softness of my complex set of petals. They felt rather like the lips of my mouth, I realised in surprise, and there seemed to be two distinct pairs of them, a fuller, velvety set, and smaller, more delicate twins. Delighted, I stroked and rubbed at them, tangling my fingers in the soft curls that partly shaded this curious nether mouth, until I dared to venture a hesitant, shy finger inside. And what a surprise! The interior was not only just as soft and plush as the outer crevice, but also ridged and intricately textured, full of interesting places to stroke and press. I had nearly forgotten about Johnny now in my own sphere of self-discovery, and I ventured a second, then a third finger into this most precious of places in my own body. At first I mimicked the rhythm I had applied to the hard pole in John's trousers, but found that motion a little too rough for my liking. It took but a moment for me to discover the rhythm that suited me best, and as I rubbed my fingers to and fro in this pulsing hot cavern, that stiff little bud at the top throbbed for attention. Gently I began to caress it with my thumb, marvelling at its pearl-like shape and feel, until again my body was racked by the sweetest of spasms, and I seemed to float away in a self-induced delirium of delight.

When at last I returned to my senses, I saw that John was gazing at me intently, and smiling with an expression of pure devotion. As his fingers gently caressed my cheek, I murmured up at him,

'Is this the way of love you had promised to show me?'

Johnny let forth a low chuckle, and shook his handsome head. 'Oh no, my dearest,' he whispered into my neck. 'There are many, many more joys to share with you, but I fear that time is running out and your father will soon be searching for you. I would not cause you any trouble, so I will help you to dress and head back to the house.'

'Oh, John, no!' I cried, my senses newly inflamed at the prospect of yet more pleasures to come. 'Not yet! Do show me just a little of the wonders still left unexplored!'

He looked at me meditatively for a moment, then with a joyous laugh he flung himself back upon me. 'Oh, Amelia,' he ground out in a low whisper, 'I cannot resist you! My body is crying out for you, even as my head bids me stay! Look,' he proclaimed, placing my hand back on to the curious staff in his loins, 'look at the response you unknowingly call forth!'

Wickedly, I smiled up at him while saucily pressing my hand against the bulge in his breeches, then, daringly, I began to unbutton the sturdy fabric to finally discover what lay beneath. Imagine my astonishment when out popped such a massive stalk of flesh as I had never imagined possible! It was firm and erect like a finger, but ever so much thicker and warmer! The steel-hard core was enwrapped in a lovely soft sponge-like cowl which I could slide up and down, and it was capped by a deliciously smooth and round head with a tiny little hole, from which crept a shining drop of sweet-smelling cream. Tentatively, I wiped the drop off with my finger and lifted it to my mouth, testing with my tongue the richness of this curious stuff. I could feel the hot blood pumping through his wondrous staff, and discovered to my surprise two other little treasures tucked in a curious sac that nestled in the thick crisp curls at the base of this rod. This precious pouch seemed much more fragile and sensitive than the pole that throbbed in my hand, and instinctively I stroked it more gently, marvelling at its delicate weight and incredible moleskin softness.

I must have been doing something right, for John gasped and moaned above me until, with a little cry of desperation, he urged away my hand and positioned himself between my willingly spread thighs. I could feel the hard knob at the top of his staff pressing urgently against the entrance to my cunny, and I could hardly breathe with the excitement of wondering what it would feel like once it was finally inside my secret space.

'And now, Amelia,' he breathed against my ear, 'let me share with you the most heavenly pleasure that I know.' He paused for a moment and gazed with loving concern into my eyes. 'There may be a moment of pain, dearest,' he murmured, then added, 'but be not afraid. It will not last long, I promise.'

Well, but I wasn't in the least bit afraid, only tremblingly eager to experience yet more thrilling delights. But oh! What a strange sensation it was at first! Johnny moved slowly and with the greatest of care, giving me time to become accustomed to the feel of this hot, pulsing shaft as it gently eased itself inside me. There was no pain, only the slightest edge of discomfort as he pressed himself deeper and deeper inside, pausing every now and then to allow me to accommodate myself to his strength and size. At last it seemed he could go no further, for he lay still inside me for so long that I wondered whether this was all there was. And so, a bit disappointed, but not meaning any insult, I hesitantly whispered, 'My love? Is . . . is this it?'

Apparently unable to answer, John merely sighed between his gritted teeth, moved back a little to allow himself the tiniest bit of withdrawal, then moved forward again, this subtle movement mysteriously activating sensations from deep within my cunny. I didn't think of it at the time, but now, writing to you, my dearest Anna, I realise what fearsome control and determination my lover must have been exercising so as not to force himself upon me too quickly. Indeed, his next movement imparted a greater feeling of urgency, for this time he pulled back a little farther and pushed back in a little harder, eliciting a tiny cry of pleasure from my lips.

Immediately he stopped. 'My lady, are you well?' he asked with real concern.

Insistently I nodded my head, then arched up my hips to drive him back inside at greater depth. 'Move,' I whispered into the dark night, desperate for real fulfilment. 'Please, move,' I entreated again.

He needed no further encouragement, and so we began the motions of love, he and I, our bodies working together in the sweetest of harmonies, hips rocking together as one. I have no words to describe the emotions, the passions, the ecstasy of it all, other than to say that Johnny and I are as one now, our hearts and minds wedded together in the sensual bliss of physical union, and no one and nothing can sunder this bond of love. I no longer fear discovery: nay, I welcome it. I would rush to Father tonight and boldly proclaim our love, but John bids me wait. He says the time is not right, that Father would never allow his daughter Lady Amelia, his only child, to marry a lowly gardener. Indeed, it may prove dangerous to us both if we are discovered. When John said this it gave me pause, and reluctantly I must agree with him – at least, for now. I am willing to carry on our meetings in secret, for the present, though how am I to keep silent when inside I am bursting to tell all, so great is my happiness? And so I confide in you, my dearest Anna, though you are but an imaginary friend of the pen; and yet, I almost fancy I see you now, your eyes glowing with joy for me, your generous heart so happy for my good fortune. Good night, sweetest friend! May you also find happiness so true!

Sasha finished the page she was reading, grunted, then poured herself another drink. She had about had it with Lady Amelia's bloated and self-satisfied paroxysms of rapture, refusing to admit to her envy of this perfect relationship Amelia had found for herself. Men in the real world on the edge of the millennium aren't nearly this tender or compassionate, Sasha growled to herself: it seemed that these days high-pressure jobs, low-fat diets, all-terrain vehicles and football scores took precedence over issues such as dating, relationships, commitment and sex – for men, that is. As for Sasha, she certainly didn't believe in the kind of eternal love and soul-mate mush that Amelia was mooning on about: that sort of thing belonged strictly either in the past or in fiction. She was just about to roll over and turn out the light, a little disgusted with herself for becoming so readily absorbed in the love life of some long-dead woman, when her eyes scanned the next page of the manuscript, half of which was missing, apparently having been torn off. When she'd first opened the manuscript she'd noticed that the latter half appeared to be far sloppier and more illegible than the first pages, and so she examined the remaining sheets in closer detail: in contrast to the elegant, mannered lettering of the pages she'd read so far, these were full of blots, scribbles, crossings-out and chaos. Intrigued, mystified, and beginning to feel increasingly uneasy, Sasha carefully smoothed out the remaining sheets and read on.

17 March, 1795
Oh, God, it is just as I'd feared! We are discovered! My debauched, cruel, lecherous cousin came upon Johnny and me as we lay in the rose garden, our lips pressed together and our arms round each other as we thought no one was near. We'd grown so indiscreet of late, our heady passion leading us to take more and more risks, foolishly trusting to love that we'd be safe – and now it is too late! Gareth has sworn to go to my father unless I – I – oh, God, I cannot write it! No, never, I swear I will never let him touch me, despite what he may threaten! But to save Johnny? To protect the man I love from the hideous schemes of my cousin, who will delight in bearing tales to my father, who is not only lord of the manor but also the local magistrate? What shall I do, what shall I do? I must write to John – I must let him know the danger! Rosie must help me find a way to write a note to Johnny to warn him . . .

Here, squint as she might, Sasha was unable to decipher the rest of the writing leading to the ragged, torn edge: presumably Amelia had used the rest of the sheet to send a note to John. With a heavy feeling of dread, remembering Claire's story, Sasha turned to the next page and tried to read her way through the blots and slurred handwriting on the torn and fragmented sheet. There was no date.

Oh, my head aches so, I can hardly write. Have I been drugged, perhaps? My vision is so blurred, my hand trembles so I can hardly hold the pen ... I must lie down ... but I cannot sleep for fear I will see *him*. There! Do you see him? Does he yet approach? Is nowhere safe?

Whose voices are those I hear? Who mocks me so? Let me out! Father! Father! Unlock this door! My Johnny needs me! I must –

Here the writing broke off into what looked like a private code of symbols, or maybe Amelia's ink had simply spilled over, or perhaps she had gone a little deranged from being shut up in her room. Certainly this fragment of a page Sasha held in her hands seemed to indicate some kind of violent struggle, even if that struggle was mostly in Amelia's head. And yet, when Sasha turned to the final sheets of the manuscript, she saw that the writing, though perhaps a little feeble and lacking the robust curves of the characters that had dominated in the beginning, was now far clearer and more legible, as though Amelia had come back to her senses. Sasha read Amelia's final words, feeling an uncanny surge of recognition come flooding through her.

8 April, 1795
And so it is done. I do not know how long I had been locked in my bedchamber, nor for how long

I must have raged in some kind of delirium, but judging from the state of this room, my hair, my eyes, and my clothes, I must have been beside myself in some kind of violent whirl. I must collect my thoughts and recount what I remember as clearly as possible, so that whoever finds and reads this story may somehow be able to put right the incalculable wrongs that have been committed in this household.

The last thing I remember before my strange period of unconsciousness was being discovered by cousin Gareth while John and I embraced in the rose garden. Gareth threatened to go to my father and tell all unless I ... unless I ... No. I must be strong and get it all down. Either I give my body to Gareth in a mockery of the holy communion of love, or he would go straight to the study in the hopes that his rich uncle, Lord Asher, would finally force me to marry, yes, marry Gareth! – and pass all of what should be my rightful property over to him.

I could hardly decide which was worse: to be touched and fondled by one so loathsome in order that my love remain undiscovered, or else resist, and take the chance that Gareth would reveal all to Father and somehow persuade him to coerce me to enter into a most unholy alliance. In the end it was John who convinced me to take the risk, once I managed to smuggle my note to him; he vowed he would kill Gareth before he let him lay a finger on me, and he persuaded me into believing that we could convince Father of the sanctity of our love. Indeed, John welcomed the opportunity to finally bring our love out into the open: so sure was he of the strength of our devotion that he believed that together we could withstand any onslaught!

I remember little of what followed. I have a dim recollection of standing hand-in-hand with my lover in Father's study as he bellowed and raged, of shouts ringing out, my own included, of threats made, duels warned, swords brandished ... I know little else other than that I was somehow transported here, to my bedchamber (how I know not), the key was turned in the outside lock, and I was incarcerated, a prisoner in my own home.

I have vague memories of horrid dreams, of demons with red eyes glaring, of strange voices whispering in my head, and of John being racked by the most hideous of tortures ...

And then, yesterday morning, I was able somehow to come to my senses and form a kind of plan. Last night, when Father's butler came to pass me my evening tray through the door, I managed, with a dexterity that surprised myself, to slip a folded piece of paper into the lock so that, although the key was turned when Browning closed the door, the bolt did not shoot all the way home but left a tiny wedge of space. Once Browning had gone, I carefully inserted a hairpin into the lock where the bolt pressed, and after some time of patient work, managed to push the bolt back.

With a fearful sense of foreboding I glided noiselessly across the corridor and down the stairs, intending to seek out my beloved by whatever subterfuge I could devise. But lo! – what treachery was this I saw as I darted out of the back door towards the labourers' cottages? A black carriage, a huddle of three men: one a

stranger, one my cousin, and the other so achingly, heart-rendingly familiar to me, who was
being hauled cruelly into the waiting carriage! I
could dimly discern voices, my cousin's clearest
of all, as he mockingly called out to Johnny, while
delivering a vicious blow to his head, 'And the
best part of all is that Amelia is now mine! You're
banished from this town, you're banished from
this county, and from all areas where Lord
Asher's power and influence extend! You're as
good as dead around here from now on, John
Blakeley!'

As the door slammed shut and the carriage
started to roll away, the two men disappeared,
laughing, inside the house. I flung myself madly
down the drive, desperately chasing the carriage,
hoping against all reason I could somehow make
it stop. But alas! – the horses soon outran me, and
as the heavens opened and rain poured down
from the unforgiving black sky, I realised my love
had gone, gone for ever – and I hadn't even heard
his voice one last time.

How long I lay out there in the drive, in the
mud and the rain, sobbing out Johnny's name, I
do not know, but I suppose it was all night. As
the early grey dawn began creeping in this morning, I found myself being tenderly lifted up from
the gravel by, of all people, my father. He looked
at me in that pale grey light, his face nearly as
ashen as mine must have been, but said nothing
other than to murmur, 'My child! How like your
mother!' Then, saying nothing else, he carried me
gently into the house and into my bed, where he
carefully laid me down and bade Clarice draw
me a warm bath and bring me some hot tea.

The doctor has been here, and they try to tell

me I will be well. Father says I mustn't worry, that I'll not marry Gareth; I must just rest and get well, for it appears I am very ill.

And so I will myself to die. It has taken nearly all my strength to write these few pages, and I must stop every so often to cough, trying to clear my chest of some blockage which makes it difficult to breathe. I will somehow manage to sneak down to the library tonight and tuck this manuscript away within the newest novel of Mrs. Radcliffe: she is such a favourite in this house that someone is bound to read her book and discover my sad tale. And so, to you, whoever reads this story, please, find my Johnny for me! Tell him I died loving him, that I died freely and of my own unfettered will, and that the last words on my lips shall be his name! I entreat you, kind Stranger who reads these words, find my John Blakeley for me, his desperate, dying Amelia!

Sasha woke with a start. She had no idea how long she had lain there in her bed, her nightlamp still shining, tears damp on her face, and Amelia Asher's manuscript clutched tightly in her hand. She looked at the clock: 3.30. With the greatest of care, Sasha laid the sheaf of yellowed papers on her night table, carefully smoothing them out before she reached up to turn off the light. She needed her sleep now: she had a lot to think about in the morning.

Chapter Four

'*I* feel as though I'm living in a Gothic novel.'

It was Monday morning, two days after Sasha's return from England, and she and Xenia were walking down 5th Avenue towards Rockefeller Plaza, squinting despite their dark glasses in the glare of the hot summer sun. Sasha had asked her best friend to meet her for lunch, as she was desperate to confide in her about the extraordinary events of the past few days. As head director of human resources for a major financial firm, Xenia had the counselling skills and experience to guide Sasha through any kind of professional or personal crisis, and she could always be counted on to provide a steady dose of compassion, common sense, and emotional support, as well as a continual supply of fine wines and decadent comfort food.

'You certainly look different,' Xenia commented now, much to Sasha's surprise. Funnily enough she thought she was looking a little different as well: she felt energised, vital, even glowing, though she hadn't thought anyone else would notice. Come to think of it, she mused to herself, she looked a little as women are generally said to look when they are in the first heady stages of a love affair. Indeed, this clearly must have been what Xenia was thinking, because she gently nudged Sasha in the side and knowingly asked, 'So, are you in the midst of some hot new English passion, or what?'

Sasha stopped and looked at her friend for a moment. The vibrant intensity that hummed throughout her body certainly seemed to be erotic in origin, but she didn't think it was due to Paul. Sasha couldn't really explain it very clearly to herself, nor did she think she could convince Xenia of this passionate new interest she was taking in some as yet ill-defined experience, but she was certainly going to try.

'Let's get some lunch first,' she suggested hastily, pointing to the hot-dog vendor who was standing by his cart on the sidewalk, expectantly awaiting new customers. 'I've been dying for one of those ever since I got back.'

It wasn't until after the two women had seated themselves on the steps leading down to the skating-rink and had carefully squirted the mustard and arranged the sauerkraut neatly on their hot dogs that Sasha began to talk. She told Xenia the whole story, beginning with when she first heard Amelia's ghostly voice, and sketching in her encounter with Paul as the necessary background to her narrative. She described her odd sense of recognition when she'd confronted Amelia's portrait, her leaping pulse as she'd deciphered John Blakeley's image, her feeling of an uncanny presence in the lift, her excited discovery of the manuscript, and her eerie fascination in reading Amelia's story.

'And now I feel ... well ... kind of involved or something with this dead woman and her boyfriend,'

Sasha confessed, half-embarrassed, to her friend. 'I don't know how to describe it, except as a crazy sort of identification or . . . or obsession, I guess, with these two people; whatever it is, I can't seem to get their images out of my mind.'

Xenia said nothing for a moment, merely patting Sasha absently on the thigh with one hand while daintily licking the mustard off the fingers of the other. She continued to say nothing, and merely sucked thoughtfully on the straw of her Diet Dr Pepper, while Sasha watched her with a mounting sense of frustration.

'Well?' she finally demanded as Xenia slurped up the last of her drink. 'Aren't you going to say something?'

'Sasha, my dear,' Xenia sagely opined, inclining her head towards her friend, 'what do you want me to say? It's a crush that you're having, that's all, like the fantasies you used to have about those absurdly pretty pop-star boys when you were fourteen, or the way you sigh over some of those gorgeous ALM models today. What are you getting so worked up about? You thought you heard some spooky voice, you stumbled across some mouldering old manuscript –'

'Not *thought* I heard,' Sasha interrupted, 'but heard for real. I know I wasn't imagining that sound! Amelia was in my room that night!'

Xenia turned wise eyes her way. 'Sasha, darling,' she said in a tone of aggravating reasonableness, 'didn't you say that not even Paul heard that voice?'

'But that's part of the – the haunting!' Sasha burst out in exasperation. 'Amelia only ever comes to women! Don't you get it? I think that I was – oh, I don't know – somehow destined to find that manuscript! It's as if someone – or something – had deliberately inserted those pages into that space on the

61

bookshelf when I wasn't looking, then rustled them around a bit so that I was sure to turn around and find them! Don't you see?' she went on, quite red in the face now, and oblivious to the passers-by who were staring at her. 'The lift stopped mid-floor on purpose, it was waiting for me to discover Amelia's story! Maybe I'm the "stranger" Amelia is beseeching at the end of her journal, or letter, or whatever it is! I know that other women have heard Amelia crying in room 323 at night, but maybe I'm the one meant to somehow find this Johnny and pass on her message!'

Sasha was suddenly embarrassingly aware of the astonished silence that seemed to surround the two women. She realised that she had half-risen off her step and was bending over Xenia, heedless of the way her brief skirt had inched further up her legs, practically up to her bottom. She quickly took a mental step backward and surveyed the scene she must be presenting to the nosy New York lunchtime crowd. She rapidly sat back down again and tried to pull her skirt down to her ankles.

Xenia merely cocked a cool brow towards her friend. 'John Blakeley is dead,' she said gently, with real concern in her voice, but not without a trace of her usual good humour. 'You do realise that, don't you?'

Sasha took a shaky sip of her not-diet Dr Pepper and nodded her head quickly. 'I know that,' she muttered, half-ashamed, to her friend. 'You must think I've gone quite crackers.'

'Well, I can see that you really believe that you've experienced some kind of, um, otherworldly occurrence,' Xenia conceded comfortingly. Sasha shot her a grateful look.

'Let me just ask you one favour,' she said pleadingly, but trying to sound rational. 'Will you please just take a look at the manuscript itself? Will you do that much for me, if only to reassure me that I'm not going crazy?'

Xenia leant over and gave Sasha an affectionate squeeze. 'Sure I will,' she said fondly, flicking Sasha's shining chestnut hair behind her ears. 'I'm a little curious about this thing myself.'

Sasha hugged her back, flicking her hair back the way it was. 'And could I ask another favour? I'm all out of one-dollar bills; do you think you could buy me one of those zucchini muffins from that vendor over there?'

When Sasha hurried back into her office after lunch, having practically run all the way up 5th Avenue, she nearly hurtled straight into Valerie, who was loitering around the reception area looking positively dewy with delight.

'He's coming back,' she sighed dreamily, gently cradling the files she was holding in her arms. 'He's coming over next week.'

'Who?' asked Sasha indifferently, not caring in the least, but only anxious to get back to work. 'Who's coming over?'

'Paul,' breathed Valerie, finally focusing on Sasha. 'The handsome ad-man from Rollit is flying over on Monday to talk us through their redrafted mock-ups after I briefed him on this morning's meeting.'

Paul! Sasha blinked rapidly as she absorbed this information, then cast another bemused look at her boss. Valerie was practically swooning with pleasure, and smiling hazily at Sarah, her unimpressed administrative assistant, who was waiting patiently for her boss in a corner.

'He sounded awfully impatient to get here,' Valerie went on rapturously, tossing out her luxuriant black hair as she spoke. 'Do you think he might possibly have been coming on to me?'

Sasha nearly choked with laughter as Valerie, oblivious, turned to her and added unconvincingly, 'Of course, as I've always said, it would be most unethical to become involved in a personal relationship with any of our co-workers or colleagues: I was merely speaking hypothetically. Oh, and by the way, Sasha,' Valerie called over her shoulder as she turned to walk down the hall, 'Paul left a message for you with Heather: something about places to stay uptown, I think. I guess you're the designated accommodations officer.' Her tinkle of laughter drifted down the corridor as her assistant trailed doggedly behind her, struggling under the weight of her files.

Sasha's own administrative assistant, Heather, shared a sympathetic smile with her as Sasha cautiously reached out for the yellow Post-It she was fluttering Sasha's way. 'It's a little more personal than that,' Heather whispered conspiratorially; Heather was the only co-worker at ALM who was privy to the most serious breaches of professional ethics Sasha had committed since she'd been with the company. Heather knew what no one else at work did, including the time that Sasha had lost a vitally important demographic spreadsheet and blamed it on her predecessor; she was also the only witness to the time that Sasha, wildly drunk at the staff Christmas party and faced with a locked ladies' toilet, had, in desperation, urinated in the potted parlour palm Valerie kept to adorn the corner by the bookshelf in her office. Heather also knew that at that same party Sasha spent forty-five minutes in a parked car madly kissing one of the account executives who, thankfully, no longer worked there. Sasha never did find out whose car it was they had climbed into.

As a consequence, Sasha felt distinctly uncomfortable treating Heather as a secretary and an underling; she disliked delegating minor tasks to her assistant, and so she often performed her own menial tasks in secret, guiltily typing away at her own memos and completing her own filing, with the end result that Heather often complained she had too little to do.

Now, as Sasha took the proffered memo held out between Heather's fingers, she wondered how much her assistant had guessed about her relationship with Paul. She glanced at the nearly coy note in her hand: 'Will be flying in Sunday night. Needs a place to stay. Any suggestions?'

Ghosts and haunted hotels seemed absurdly out of place in modern-day Manhattan as Sasha returned to her office, leant back in her plush revolving chair, kicked off her shoes and spun around in her seat, feeling a renewed surge of interest in Paul kindling in her belly. Maybe Paul is just what I need to reground me in reality, she mused, as she sifted through the charts and figures piled haphazardly on her desk. Maybe Xenia's right: this whole ghost story thing is crazy, and I should just put it out of my mind and concentrate on the life I have here. After all, she reminded herself crossly, I'm so fortunate to be instrumental in shaping the campaign for a brand-new product: most marketing women I know are still waiting for an opportunity like this to prove themselves at work. A sexy English boyfriend is a great perk of the job, she thought, grinning to herself as she dug her muffin out of her bag; surely I have enough to occupy myself with in the here and now, rather than obsessing about some long-dead ill-fated love-affair between two people I'd never heard of! And so, with that thought, munching happily on her muffin, Sasha

65

dusted off her mouse and began to craft an e-mail reply to Paul's request.

Sasha's good intentions regarding the shelving of her fascination with the story of Amelia Asher didn't hold for very long, however. Other forces seemed to be conspiring against her.

Although she had to work late in the office during the week in preparation for Paul's arrival from England with the new mock-ups, she made time on Saturday night to go to a new comedy club in Greenwich Village with Xenia, after which Xenia came back to her apartment to take a look at Amelia Asher's manuscript. By this point both women were giggling and out of breath, partly as a result of the new stand-up talent at the club, and partly due to the Zombies and Long Island Iced Teas they'd been drinking with such enthusiasm. However, as Sasha went to retrieve the precious document she'd so carefully wrapped up and stowed away on top of her closet, she knew that her giddiness had little to do with either New York humour or a combination of white spirits, and it was with a kind of hushed reverence that she tenderly laid the yellowed papers in Xenia's outstretched hands.

'Wow,' Xenia breathed as she respectfully stroked the dry, crackling papers and caressed the decayed red ribbon. 'This is really it, isn't it?'

Sasha said nothing, merely nodded and seated herself opposite her friend on her expensive cocoa-coloured leather couch. She sipped nervously at a cup of peach blossom tea and, stretching out her legs, crossed her ankles on the glass table while she watched Xenia read raptly through the ancient sheets of paper. 'Well?' she asked tentatively when her friend finally looked up from her reading, her expression inscrutable. 'Now do you see why I find this whole experience so fascinating?'

'It certainly is a remarkable document,' Xenia said reflectively, rolling up the pages and tapping them lightly against her knee. As Sasha breathed a sigh of relief, however, thankfully assuming that Xenia now shared her sense of uncanniness, her friend cast a sharp eye her way and tartly remarked, 'But I think that's all it is: although it's obviously of great historical interest, it's just a crumbling old document you had the good fortune to stumble across while you were in some creaky old lift. It must be worth a fortune. Why don't you consider selling it to a museum or a university library?' she suggested. 'I bet Barnard or Columbia would pay a bundle for it.'

'You don't understand!' Sasha snapped irritably, snatching the pages out of Xenia's hands and laying them carefully on the table. 'Why do you so stubbornly refuse to admit what you see? I couldn't possibly sell Amelia's story! I feel as if I know her now, as if I've been fated to carry her message further – yes, I know they're both dead,' she interrupted herself peevishly, glaring at her friend. 'I haven't gone completely round the bend; I just don't think this story can be laid to rest until I – oh, I don't know – I just have to do something about it, though I don't know what yet.'

There ensued a long silence; Sasha poured more tea for them both while the women jointly contemplated the pages lying quietly on the table, as though they somehow expected them to perform some magical act. Finally Xenia shrugged her shoulders and came to sit beside Sasha on the sofa opposite the table.

'Listen, girl, I'm your best friend, and you know I support you in just about anything you decide to do,' she said gently. 'It's true, I don't feel the kind of phenomenal pull that you do: in fact,' she added, shuddering briefly, 'I think the whole thing is kind of creepy. And I do think that in a little while you'll be able to put this in perspective. In the meantime – ' she gave Sasha a brief hug '– you do what you feel you have to do. And who knows?' Xenia smiled encouragingly at Sasha. 'You might even convert me into some kind of supernatural groupie.'

'You're right,' Sasha said resignedly as she carefully wrapped the pages back up in tissue-paper. 'I guess I have been reacting a little crazily. I can't really afford to get caught up in this any more, what with the Gripp campaign getting underway and Paul coming over tomorrow night.' She grinned mischievously at Xenia and slyly whispered, 'Valerie thinks he isn't coming in until Monday morning, and I'm not about to tell her he's spending tomorrow night here with me!' She took another sip of tea and giggled naughtily. 'Monday and Tuesday nights he'll have to stay in a hotel, of course – he's leaving Wednesday afternoon – but I'm really beginning to enjoy this clandestine, cloak-and-dagger kind of relationship!' She stood up and pushed away the teapot, gathered Amelia's manuscript in her hands and said cheerily, 'Enough of this herbal nonsense: why don't I get us a real drink to enjoy with the late-night cable-TV sex shows? You might as well spend the night; I'll make popcorn and lend you that Victoria's Secret nightie you always borrow. Do you want a banana daiquiri or a strawberry margarita?'

As Sasha went to check there were fresh towels in her guest bedroom, she decided that she wouldn't look at the manuscript again for – for at least a week, she bravely resolved. With that thought in mind, she fetched her small step-stool and tucked the document securely away on the uppermost shelf of her linen closet, under the stack of frothy Laura Ashley sheets she'd vowed she'd never use, and shut the closet door firmly. 'Good night, Amelia,' she muttered under her breath, and went into the kitchen to dig out her blender.

It was therefore with a great deal of shock – but an oddly comforting sense of welcome as well – that when Sasha awoke the next morning, the first thing she saw was Amelia Asher's manuscript, the pages neatly unrolled and lying silently on the night table next to her bed.

Chapter Five

'*P*aul! Over here!'

Frantically waving, her face flushed with excitement, Sasha pushed her way through the hot, sweaty mass of people crammed by the velvet ropes demarcating the arrivals' corridor at Kennedy Airport. It was a sweltering August night in New York, and Sasha could feel her make-up practically sliding off her face as she leapt about by the continually opening and shutting doors, feeling the muggy blasts of hot air envelop her body as she strained to attract Paul's attention.

Paul, however, was looking remarkably cool and crisp as he finally spotted Sasha and strode purposefully her way; despite the internationally-recognised logos of his Levi's jeans and pale-blue Gap T-shirt, he seemed to exude English elegance with his asymmetric blonde fringe and his classically cut features. For a dreadful moment Sasha had feared he might be wearing shorts. She couldn't bear the thought of Paul in shorts, not even denim cut-offs, as she always thought men looked silly in them, with their great hairy legs sticking out, neither sandals nor sneakers looking quite right. But no, Paul was looking enormously sexy as he came towards Sasha, sweeping her up in his firm, strong embrace, smelling not at all of sweat and only faintly of cologne.

'Come on,' Sasha said after a moment, releasing herself from his grip and taking one hand while Paul slung his luggage casually over his shoulder with the other. 'I've got a driver waiting.'

Sasha had indulged herself by ordering a sleek grey limousine from the company she normally used for business and claimed as an expense; although she was paying for the luxury herself tonight, she knew that the cool, dark privacy of the interior was well worth the seventy-five-dollar fare, and far preferable to jostling about with the other airport arrivals, all competing for the dirty yellow cabs that were also incredibly noisy and hot.

'This is nice.' Paul smiled appreciatively as he slid smoothly into the car, after first making sure that Sasha was comfortably seated. 'Thanks for coming to pick me up.'

'It's just nice to see you again so soon,' she replied, a little nervously, for she felt suddenly shy with him, as though they were on a first date.

Paul, however, seemed eager to re-establish their intimacy. 'I've brought you something,' he whispered seductively into her ear before pausing to bury his mouth in her neck. 'To show you how much I've missed you.' He then withdrew himself from her to reach into the outside pocket of his impressive leather bag, and drew out a rustling, silver-wrapped package. 'Actually,' he said as he placed the package in Sasha's lap, 'it's for both of us.'

With tremulous fingers Sasha untied the pretty gold ribbon that held the paper together and then slowly

71

drew out a shimmering length of delicate ivory silk, which was actually a calf-length lace-edged nightslip bearing a South Moulton Street designer label.

'Oh, Paul,' she breathed, quite overwhelmed by the extravagance of his gesture. 'I don't know what to say.'

'Don't say anything, then,' he advised, trailing his fingers along the back of her neck and stroking lightly along her coiled-up bun of heavy chestnut hair. 'I hope you like it: I wanted to bring you something pretty.'

She turned to him, her eyes shining in the dark of the spacious interior of the car. 'It's lovely,' she sighed happily, holding the slip up against herself. 'It's absolutely divine.'

'I can't wait to see it on you,' Paul growled throatily in her ear, causing Sasha to shiver in delightful anticipation.

'I can't believe it's only been a little over a week since I last saw you,' she murmured against the smoothness of his shaven cheek. 'It seems like it's been so much longer; I've missed you.'

She cast a quick, apprehensive glance at the silent driver in front, but he didn't seem to be paying any attention to the couple in the back, concentrating instead on negotiating a difficult path through the warring taxis that were fighting it out in the crowded lanes of the road that led to the Queens-Midtown Tunnel. As if to confirm Sasha's thoughts, the driver turned up the volume of the slushy female vocalist he was listening to in the front, her voice drifting out through the glass that separated him from his passengers.

Having assured herself that the driver's attention was otherwise engaged, and secure in the knowledge that no one could see through the darkened windows

72

that shielded them from intrusive eyes, Sasha leant over and placed her mouth gently against Paul's, her tongue slipping out to stroke lightly along his lower lip. He responded by opening her mouth with his, allowing their tongues full access while easing her on to his lap so that her legs were wrapped around his waist and her crotch was pressed tightly against his, separated only by the bulk of his jeans and the thin satin panel of her pale grey tap pants. As they kissed with passion, Sasha reflected that it was a good thing she'd dressed so sensibly in the heat, wearing only her panties underneath a lemon-yellow sun-dress that criss-crossed at the back, leaving most of her shoulders bare. The feel of Paul's hands on her exposed skin made her purr low in her throat with pleasure, and she worked her tongue against his, thrilling in the urgency building in her belly as she felt the unmistakable ridge of his cock surging beneath her. Heedless now of the driver in front, Sasha ground her hips against Paul's, feeling him respond with an answering arc of his hips, and she rocked her body against his in time with the movements of their searching mouths. Arms clasped tightly around each other's shoulders, their mouths slanted across one another's, they simulated the motions of sex through the constrictions of their clothes while the wheels beneath them picked up pace and the car drove smoothly through the tunnel. As Sasha continued to grind herself against Paul's cock, the pressure on her clitoris mounted, and she thought to herself with a delicious panic that she might actually orgasm on the spot. Feeling that this might be a little undignified, she attempted to ease herself off Paul's lap, but he only gripped her to him tighter. Then, with an admirable show of dexterity, he effortlessly flipped her around so that Sasha was leaning against the car seat, her back pressed into the

73

rich-smelling leather while Paul knelt on the floor of the car before her. Fruitlessly, Sasha tried to draw him back up on to the seat beside her, indicating the driver with her eyes, but Paul only pressed himself against her more firmly, his body feeling irresistibly hard and strong between her thighs.

'Sssh.' His voice was deep and warm against the curve of her throat, his hands on her shoulders holding her in place. 'Just let yourself go.'

'I . . . I don't know if I can,' Sasha whispered, even as she was closing her eyes and lifting up her hips as though inviting him to venture further between her spreading thighs. She felt the strength of Paul's hands as he reached underneath her buttocks and held her tightly to him, his mouth moving downward from her throat to her heaving bosom. He then released his grip on her bottom to deftly unbutton the straps of her dress at the back and slowly draw them down her shoulders and across her front, brushing the ends of the straps against her breasts and flicking them lightly at her stiffening nipples. By now Sasha's sex was warm and moist, poutingly open and desperate for more direct stimulation. She was only dimly aware of the wheels rolling beneath her, as the hum of the car seemed to be emanating from within her own body, and it was with the greatest of efforts that she restrained herself from reaching her own fingers down and into the throbbing ache at her core. Instead she held back, digging her nails into Paul's shoulders as he continued to tease the pink crests of her breasts with the ends of her straps, using the fabric like feathers that delicately stimulated her flesh. Finally, when Sasha thought she could hardly stand any more, Paul bent his head and gently captured one engorged nipple between his lips, kissing it lightly before drawing more of it into his mouth, sucking on the hard, pointed nub and rubbing against it with his tongue. Sasha heaved a great sigh of relief when she felt Paul's hand creep down between her thighs and press against the hot wetness that was seeping through her panties, as though he was testing for himself the level of her arousal. She wound her fingers in his shiny, soft hair and arched her back, trying to push more of herself into his mouth, while she cupped her own hand around her other naked breast, pressing against her own nipple with her fingers and urging herself on to a higher state of pleasure.

Paul then released Sasha's breast from his lips and leant forward to whisper deep in her ear, 'I want to taste all of you now.' With a gasp she felt him lift up her bottom so he could slip his fingers under the top of her French knickers; sneakily, stealthily, ever so smoothly, he slid them down her bare legs and over her strappy sandals to presumably discard them on the floor of the car.

Sasha now lay against the slick leather of the seat, the billowing skirt of her dress hitched up around her waist, her breasts bare above and her sex naked below. She opened her eyes briefly to check that the driver was still facing stonily ahead at the road, then shut them in bliss as she felt Paul settle himself down between her feet and gently nudge her thighs apart so that he was directly facing the moist richness of her flowing sex. Sasha held her breath and squeezed her eyes shut, waiting in suspended silence for that first sweep of Paul's tongue as he gave her what she so craved: but there was nothing. She could feel her inner tension grow as Paul simply sat there, his fingers pressed against her lower lips, holding her sex open but stubbornly refusing to do more.

Sasha couldn't stand it another moment. 'Please,'

she breathed, hardly daring to say more. 'Please,' she said again, the urgency evident in her voice.

'Please what, Sasha?' Paul's low voice could hardly be heard above the hum of the car, and through the haze of her desire Sasha was hoping whole-heartedly that the driver couldn't see Paul kneeling between her spread thighs in his rear-view mirror. 'What do you want me to do?' Paul asked quietly, his breath warm against her thigh.

'Please . . . kiss me . . . there,' she whispered, feeling her arousal heighten yet another notch, the driver be damned. 'I want . . . your kiss.'

She didn't have to say any more. With a wild surge of joy, Sasha felt the heat and strength of Paul's tongue as he swept it long and slow up the glossy length of her sex, his hands gripping her buttocks and bringing her closer to his mouth. She strained her legs even further apart, replacing Paul's fingers with her own as she shamelessly spread herself for him, feeling the smooth stroke of his tongue against her thumbs and forefingers as he licked along the intricacies of her sex. When he pointed his tongue and reached it inside her, she arched her hips as if trying to suck it deeper within. Again and again Paul drove his tongue into the satiny recesses of Sasha's vagina before finally withdrawing it to seek out the shining nub of her eagerly expectant clitoris. As he gently drew the slick little pearl into his mouth, Sasha's climax erupted in a series of shattering sparks along her body, and she twisted herself away from Paul as her exquisitely sensitive clitoris continued to vibrate all on its own, her thighs squeezing together as if to wring out the last traces of pleasure still pulsating along her thrumming bud.

'Whew,' was all Sasha could say when it was finally over, her hair dishevelled, her dress askew, and Paul looking mightily pleased with himself. A quick glance around, however, and she realised with a start that they were practically at her Central Park West address. Flaming with embarrassment, she cast a wild look at the driver who continued to silently steer the car, looking steadily ahead, the histrionic notes of the lady vocalist still playing obscurely through the glass.

It wasn't until the limo had pulled up in front of Sasha's building and she was about to pay the driver an overly generous thirty per cent tip, that she realised she'd left her panties on the floor of the car behind the front passenger's seat. As she handed the money to the driver, Sasha's eye caught the discarded satin scrap tossed so carelessly aside, and she gasped out in horror, then looked helplessly at the man behind the wheel who was smiling at her kindly.

'Happens all the time, Miss,' was all he said, and then he drove off while Sasha and Paul nearly collapsed with laughter on the sidewalk.

'Do you think he really knew what we were doing while we were doing it?' Sasha asked for the twelfth time that night, as she anxiously hitched up the strap of her sexy new nightslip.

'Sasha, please!' Paul laughed in exasperation, rolling over to curl his body up against hers. They were now lying on top of her bed, she in her new satin slip and Paul in his boxer shorts because of the heat, despite the low hum of the air conditioner in the background. After a delightful shower à deux, they had set up a picnic in Sasha's bedroom, giggling as they fed each other like children on chilled asparagus, rolls of smoked salmon filled with cream cheese and dill, peeled shrimp, stuffed olives, marinated mushrooms, and a bed-full of other treasures Sasha had picked up from Balducci's delicatessen earlier that afternoon. The lights were low, the music was soft, the atmosphere romantic, and Sasha continued to obsess about what the limo driver had or hadn't seen on the way back from the airport.

In an effort to distract her, Paul reached across the bed and into his Loewe wallet he had placed earlier on Sasha's night table.

'Still hungry?' he asked suggestively, while extracting a shiny foil-wrapped disc from his billfold.

'What are you up to now, you shamelessly indecent man?' Sasha asked happily, reaching for the packet. 'What's this? A chocolate-flavoured condom?' She hooted with laughter. 'Paul, please – how tacky is this? I've got something much, much better.' She looked at him teasingly for a moment, then ordered, 'Stay there: I'll be right back.' She jumped lightly off the bed, rummaged briefly through the top drawer of her dresser, then walked back to the bed, swinging her hips exaggeratedly and dangling a black silk scarf seductively from her finger. Paul's eyes met hers with the merest flicker of consternation.

'Sasha . . .' he began, but she cut him off.

'Now be a good boy and just lie quietly for a moment,' she instructed him, then gently placed the scarf over his eyes before tying it just tightly enough at the back of his head. 'Wait there.' She left Paul on the bed for a moment, while she disappeared into the kitchen, returning almost immediately with a silver bucket of ice. 'Let's see how much you like this idea, lover,' she murmured quietly, and before Paul had a chance to respond, she pulled out an ice-cube and brushed it lightly across his lips, watching his tongue sneak out in a vain attempt at a lick.

'No, no,' Sasha breathed warningly, withdrawing the ice. 'You just lie still and let me do all the work.'

Blindfolded and apparently pliant, Paul seemed

content to merely lie back and await Sasha's next move. She ran the ice-cube one more time around his lips, then trailed it down his throat, watching his neck arch and the nipples on his naked chest prickle, while cool droplets ran down his skin. She glanced down the length of Paul's body, noting the tented rise of his cock beneath his cotton boxer shorts which indicated his excitement at the game they were playing. She bent over to briefly kiss his lips, then twirled the ice-cube around his left nipple, noting the tense flexing in the flat muscles of his stomach as she did so. She then reached over and licked at the erect little bud, chilly and firm in her mouth. The ice-cube she was holding was beginning to melt, so she reached into the silver bucket for another one, but this time she put the ice between her lips. Paul stayed silent, merely breathing a little more rapidly than usual, while he waited for Sasha to touch him, and she hoped that he hadn't guessed at what she was doing. She tried to suck quietly on the ice while she eased off his underwear, and when she was sure that her mouth was quite cold, she took a firm grasp on Paul's penis, spat out the cube and guided his fully erect cock into her icy-cold mouth.

Paul's hips arched with the shock, and his cock seemed to grow even larger in the wet confines of Sasha's mouth. He muttered something incomprehensible under his breath and wrapped his fingers in her hair, while he guided Sasha's mouth further down his throbbing shaft. She resisted, however, and, withdrawing her mouth, reached for another piece of ice; even though blindfolded, Paul seemed to know what was coming, for it looked as though his body was tensing even more as Sasha, with a purr of delight, bent low again and took his prick back in her mouth, where it jostled for room with the ice-cube.

The contrast of the cold ice and the warmth of Sasha's tongue seemed to be almost too much for Paul: already Sasha could taste the drop of salty-sweet cream that lingered at the tip of his cock, indicating a rush of more to come. Again she withdrew, but this time she ducked her head lower and sucked the delicate pouch of Paul's balls into her mouth, where their heat quickly melted the remains of the ice still left. While Paul squirmed in pleasure above her, Sasha sucked gently on the sac of his scrotum, running her tongue over its peach-like softness and kissing her way all over its contours. As she did so, she thrust her finger in the ice bucket on the floor by her feet, ensuring that her finger was thoroughly cold and wet before sliding it slyly up the secret stretch of skin between Paul's balls and his clenching back passage. She then plunged her finger into the tight enclosure of Paul's puckered anal opening, feeling the ridged walls contracting around it.

As Paul moaned with bliss, Sasha twisted her finger further up inside his rear orifice, congratulating herself on her recent manicure which had filed all of her nails out of harm's way. She removed her mouth from his balls and placed it back over his penis, slipping her tongue inside the foreskin and swirling it around the sensitive ridge beneath the rich plum of the head. She strove to match the rhythm of her mouth with the beat of her driving finger as it stroked in and out of Paul's most private space: as her mouth came down, her finger drew out, and as she slid it back in again, she sucked back up the length of Paul's cock. Finally, when she judged by the increase in tempo in the frantic movement of Paul's hips that he was close to climax, she withdrew her finger and grasped the base of his cock in her hand, urging as much of it into her mouth as she could, while she concentrated on matching her rhythm to his. She sucked on his penis with pleasure, tracing intricate patterns with her tongue, her cheeks hollowing with the effort. Just when Sasha was beginning to think that her jaw might collapse with the strain, Paul grasped her head and held on tightly as his motion slowed to a pause before that final ecstatic burst of fluid pumped out of his cock into Sasha's expectant mouth. She held perfectly still and calmly allowed his semen to fill her full before drawing away to swallow it down completely.

'Well,' she breathed with a little laugh as she struggled to sit back up and help Paul to slip off the blindfold. 'You don't seem to be suffering from any jet lag.'

Paul smiled at her fondly and ran a hand through his hair, straightening it out from the scarf before gathering Sasha to lie on his chest. 'Oh, I'm not nearly finished for the night yet,' he promised into her ear, one hand straying between her thighs. 'It's not even nine o'clock here yet.'

'No, but it's nearly two o'clock in the morning in London,' Sasha advised him, trying in vain to move his hand away from her crotch and on to his chest. 'And don't forget you're due at the ALM offices early tomorrow morning.'

'Yes, supposedly after a tiring overnight flight,' Paul reminded her, referring to the elaborate ruse they had constructed with their respective assistants about the rejigging of Paul's schedule. 'My people know I'm coming in tonight, but yours think I am currently still airborne, so I need to look suitably worn-out in order for our story to be truly convincing. Let's just hope,' Paul added with a wry grin, 'that no one at Rollit feels the urge to confirm my arrival with anyone at ALM before I've officially landed.'

'Doubtful,' Sasha said thoughtfully, as she chewed

on a piece of asparagus. 'They're hardly about to call just to check up on you: after all, Rollit's your employer, not your babysitter.' Still, she couldn't ignore the uncomfortable niggle of unease that what they were doing was a compromise of both their professional ethics. She was a little nervous about how she was going to pull off the charade in the office tomorrow: she and Paul arriving separately and both pretending that they were meeting on work-related grounds only, a situation made more complicated by the thought of Valerie prowling predatorially around Paul, waiting for an opportunity to compromise some professional ethics of her own. Sasha briefly debated with herself the efficacy of confiding in Paul her boss's personal interest in him, then decided against it: he was sure to discover that little fact for himself tomorrow, she thought.

'Let's not talk about work now,' Paul murmured, stroking the swan tattooed on Sasha's shoulder and kissing her behind her ear in a way that made her shiver. 'We've got far more interesting things to concentrate on right now.' He moved away from her a little and smiled, reaching across her body towards the drawer in her night-table. 'Since you sneered at the novelty value of my Sweet Shoppe condom, have you any spares of the more unpalatable variety lurking around in here?'

Paul opened the left-hand drawer in the night-stand and reached in, but then held still for a moment, a puzzled expression on his face. 'What's this?' he asked curiously, and drew out Amelia Asher's manuscript.

Sasha held her breath and said nothing, avoiding Paul's eyes as he held the document up for inspection. She had carefully placed the manuscript back in her night table drawer that morning after deciding not to say anything to Xenia about its mysterious reappearance. She had thought that it might be better to keep this uncanny experience to herself for a while, though she decided to keep the sheaf of papers by her bed, since it seemed to be what Amelia wanted. Sasha couldn't even believe she was thinking in these terms, worrying about what would please an eighteenth-century ghost, but she felt very protective towards the little bundle of pages as well as towards the woman whose sad story they told. Indeed, there now seemed to her to be something crude, vulgar, almost obscene about the way Paul was handling the manuscript, and she virtually snatched it out of his hands, cradling the pages securely against her bosom and away from Paul's intrusive, though innocent, interest.

'Sasha? What is that?' he asked again, attempting to unclasp her arms and retrieve the sheaf of papers from her safeguarding grasp. She pushed him away and stood up to place them carefully in the top drawer of her dresser, tucking them safely beneath her pile of frothy underwear.

'It's just something I found,' she said shortly. Paul, however, seemed undeterred.

'Come on, darling, let me have a look at it,' he coaxed her, adding, as Xenia had, 'It looks quite old, and must be valuable. What is it?'

'It's nothing,' Sasha nearly snapped, then, a little ashamed of her rudeness, she said more gently, 'It's just an old bundle of letters or a journal or something that I discovered a little while ago, and I'm holding on to it while I decide what to do with it.'

'Why are you being so secretive?' Paul asked, sounding a little annoyed as he sat up and leant against the pillows. 'Why won't you let me take a look at it?'

'Because it's private,' Sasha responded crossly, not bothering to ask herself why she so resented his justifiable curiosity. 'It's just not something I want to share with anybody right now.'

With an exaggerated shrug of dismissal, as though to show he wasn't really interested anyway, Paul rolled on to his side, leant over the bed and dug out a fat textbook on management practices for the millennium from his overnight bag. 'Forget it, then,' he said indifferently, opening his book at the place he'd marked. 'Forget that I even saw the damned thing.'

Feeling even more ashamed of herself now, Sasha came over to sit on the bed and stroked back Paul's fine blonde hair. 'I'm sorry I sounded so irritable,' she apologised lamely. 'It's just that I'm feeling a little bit possessive about this very old document that I found, and I feel kind of awkward about showing it to anyone just now. I promise I'll tell you all about it sometime very soon,' she added with as much conviction as she could muster. 'I'm sure you'll find it all a bit boring anyway.'

Mollified, and apparently willing to concede like a gentleman, Paul slid over a little and made room for Sasha on the side of the bed. 'Get in,' he said, patting the space beside him invitingly. He smiled and threw her a saucy wink. 'I think I'm over my . . . jet lag by now.' He laid aside his book and slid Sasha's slip up her thighs and over her belly and breasts so that he could draw it off her entirely, leaving her as naked as he.

'Now, where did that condom go?' he muttered abstractedly as he fumbled around on the floor until he located the chocolate-flavoured sheath.

Sasha was surprised by the level of arousal she seemed to be suddenly experiencing. She gazed eagerly at Paul's nearly erect cock as he expertly slid the saccharine-smelling condom down over himself, and she wondered where her excitement originated from: it almost seemed as though simply handling the manuscript had begun to turn her on. Suddenly craving the feel of another's flesh against her own, she reached out for Paul to pull him over her body, when with a jolt she realised that she had actually placed Amelia's manuscript in the right-hand drawer of her night table, the one furthest from her bed, but Paul had found it in the left-hand side: how, then, had it moved from one drawer to the other? As she urged Paul to manoeuvre himself into position between her parted thighs, it suddenly seemed to Sasha that she could sense another's presence in the room, almost as if someone was watching her body beginning to join with Paul's.

'Amelia?' Sasha mouthed silently, even as she was guiding Paul's cock towards her sex. Eyes wide over Paul's shoulder, she looked anxiously about the room, before shutting them in bliss at the feel of Paul's long, thick staff starting to ease slowly and smoothly inside her satin-slick channel. No, the presence didn't really feel female, Sasha decided as her hips began to move, her legs drawing Paul closer while she arched up and down to meet the rising tempo of his thrusts. Indeed, as Paul's cock began to drive steadily faster and harder within her, his head lowered against her shoulder and his breath warm against her neck, Sasha now knew that if there was a ghostly presence in the room, it wasn't Amelia Asher who hovered invisibly by the bed, an otherworldly witness to their passionate coupling.

'Johnny?' Even as she whispered his name, Sasha turned her head to glance at her and Paul's bodies reflected in the uncurtained window that faced Central Park, the light of the moon illuminating the room within. But whereas Sasha expected to see a mirror image of herself and Paul in the pane of glass, their bodies thrusting and heaving towards each other, what she saw instead seemed to trigger her orgasm almost instantly.

Sasha stared, wide-eyed and disbelieving, at the backlit, reflected image of her own body which was rising and falling, not under the familiar body of Paul, but under that of a man she'd seen only once before, as a painted presence in the background of a woman's portrait. Instead of Paul's long, lean body gyrating vigorously between her thighs, Sasha saw herself arcing in syncopated time with a strong, dark-haired man, his tangle of wild curls tumbling over his shoulders and back, his cheek pressed against hers. And this was perhaps the most startling thing about the whole experience: when Sasha looked up at the man whose body was above hers on the bed, she saw Paul facing away in pre-orgasmic bliss, his eyes shut in concentration, his head turned towards the wall. When Sasha looked back towards the reflected image in the window, however, the man whose body was pumping away forcefully into hers had his head turned her way, his eyes meeting hers in the glass panes of the window. As Sasha's liquid sex began to grip and convulse around Paul's cock, she stared with passionate intensity into the eyes of the dark man reflected in the window whose big, powerful body seemed to be driving ever deeper and harder inside her unstable reflection in the glass. And when Sasha opened her mouth in a silent scream of the fiercest, most unbearable pleasure she had ever known, it wasn't Paul's body which was the source of the rapture she was experiencing, but John Blakeley's.

Chapter Six

'*A*re you sure there's nothing going on with you?'
This must have been the third time that day that
Valerie was asking, and her blue eyes were slitted in
what Sasha hoped was friendly suspicion. 'You're looking awfully dreamy, you know, sitting over there with
your head on your hand and your eyes half-closed.'

Not for the first time, Sasha had to clamp her mouth
tightly shut to stop herself from telling her boss what
she really thought of her. As a manager and a businesswoman, Valerie was challenging but fair, capable
of praising her team when she needed to, but demanding and precise about the level of achievement she
sought to wring out of her workers. As a woman,
however, she seemed to lack the kind of supportive,
empathetic qualities Sasha expected from her friends
such as Xenia, qualities which she tried hard to culti-
vate within herself. Sasha couldn't stand assertiveness
or toughmindedness either in women or men, and she
often wished privately that Valerie would translate the
support she could demonstrate within the office to
circumstances that weren't strictly work-related.

'Do you have the latest reports on the UK regional sales figures yet?' Sasha asked politely, in an attempt to steer Valerie away from the much speculated-over subject of her relationship with Paul. It had been over three weeks since Paul had been in the New York office, and although he and Sasha had both acted with cool professionalism, not giving potential gossips any material they could digest and regurgitate over coffee, Heather had discreetly informed Sasha that rumours did seem to be circulating about the newest romantic indiscretion in the office.

Sasha had tried hard to discourage such speculations, even though she and Paul had been together practically every minute of the two days he had spent at ALM-New York, since she was the second-in-command on the UK marketing and distribution project. Although neither Paul nor Sasha had allowed themselves the slightest indecency, or even familiarity, while in the presence of others, Sasha could almost smell everyone else's salacious interest in the two of them, the atmosphere was so palpable. The odd thing was, however, that once she and Paul were back in the office, she really felt surprisingly little for him. The episode in her bedroom seemed to have quelled any sexual interest she had in Paul, and even had an opportunity arisen for them to sneak off for another sexual encounter, Sasha seriously doubted whether she would have bothered to risk it. Indeed, Paul seemed to sense her withdrawal from him, with the result that they parted cordially, and had exchanged a few pleasant but impersonal computer messages since, which was probably a good thing, Sasha figured, since Valerie was probably monitoring her e-mail.

So Sasha couldn't quite figure out where all the subterranean gossip was coming from (though she suspected it originated in Valerie's simmering sexual interest in the English ad-man from Rollit) and she trusted Heather's quiet tact and good judgement to lay such idle rumours to rest. In the meantime she politely side-stepped her boss's pointed comments and intrusive stares, choosing instead to concentrate on focus groups and market shares, and to hell with what her colleagues thought.

And a good thing too that she had so much work to keep her busy, she thought now as she scrolled through the regional breakdowns on her screen: it kept her from dwelling on the sudden emptiness she'd been experiencing lately in her private life. There had been no more ghostly visitations in her bedroom, no more intuitions of any otherwordly presence, and Amelia Asher's manuscript insisted on staying disappointingly, stubbornly, in one place. Each morning Sasha would leap eagerly out of bed, hoping for some indication that she really was experiencing events of Gothic proportions in her contemporary Manhattan life, but each day there was nothing. Occasionally, as she pushed her way through the crowds on the street, feeling dwarfed by the towering architectural wonders of the city, she thought she could almost catch a flash of curly dark hair, a hint of a billowing workshirt, a seductive, dark-eyed glance, always teasingly ahead of her grasp. Such visions were always quickly demystified, however, and revealed to be nothing more than ordinary, dull New Yorkers, and Sasha continued to search in vain for a glimpse of the man of whom she dreamt, wetly, at night.

Baffled and frustrated, she obstinately refused to believe that it had all been the result of her own overheated imagination, that she was like some modern-day Catherine Morland, Jane Austen's ludicrously hypersensitive character, who insisted on seeing herself as some kind of Gothic heroine, when in fact she was a rather ordinary young woman. It seemed as if the spirit manifestations – if that was what they were – of the long-dead John Blakeley and Amelia Asher were playing a capricious game of paranormal hide-and-seek, and Sasha was beginning to get mightily tired of it.

'Do you have a moment to look over these test shots?' Valerie asked Sasha later that day, not bothering to conceal the creamy undertones in her voice. 'I have a rather interesting project for you, if you've got the time.'

Sasha looked up from the mountain of market research freshly dumped on her desk by Heather, and blinked. 'Sure,' she said unenthusiastically, not at all inclined to take on more work. 'What is it?'

Valerie took a moment to preen. 'Well, as you know,' she began importantly, 'preliminary figures seem to indicate that our product is doing extremely well in Great Britain, well enough now to justify the launch of the rest of the range. Since the US division downstairs are in the midst of conducting the first round of interviews in their search for the American Face of Gripp, I thought we might jump on their bandwagon and do a little research ourselves on some of the models they're thinking of using to promote the line.' She indicated the bulk of photos in her arms. 'These are the test shots of the hopefuls they'll be interviewing today, and I thought you might like to take a run downstairs and sit in on the interviews in case any of the models turn out to be more suitable for the UK campaign than the US one.'

Sasha groaned inwardly. When she'd first started out in advertising, she would have leapt at the opportunity to mingle with the glamorous women and men whose bodies were being so openly utilised to sell the American Dream in the form of everything from deodorant to toilet cleaner. At that time it had been a continual thrill for Sasha to be involved, however peripherally, with the behind-the-scenes detail that made up the sexy, glossy images, and she used to view the models with an adolescent sense of wonder. Now, however, the whole advertising project had begun to bore her, and she vacillated between viewing it as, at best, the most mundane aspect of her job, and at worst, as a downright pernicious influence on society. The fact that her company was objectifying the image of the male body, rather than the female form, did little to appease her social conscience, and whereas others in her company spoke in reverential tones about the creative geniuses who dreamt up the innovative and inspirational tags that identified the ALM line, Sasha would often snort in derisive amusement to herself. The cartoonishly macho implication of names such as Slick Blades (gel-based aftershave) and Smooth Grooves (moisturiser) had been patently designed to offset the regrettably effeminate sound of the eau de toilette for men, though the products were remarkably similar to many products aimed at women. The models Valerie had approved to represent the cologne were also appropriately testosterone-charged, all tensed six-pack stomachs and suggestively bulging biceps. The idea of spending a valuable hour or two listening to would-be Hollywood actors drone on about their modelling 'art' made Sasha shrink in distaste, but it was, after all, part of her job. So, with as much good grace as she could summon, which frankly wasn't a lot, she said, 'Sure, Val. Love to.'

Valerie looked disgruntled. 'Actually,' she sniffed, 'this was supposed to be my job: I had already spoken to Charlotte and Mitch about sitting in on their interviews, but there's been a sudden computer crash in demographics, and I have to run upstairs to help disentangle the mess. Anyway – ' she tossed the stack of photos on to Sasha's desk ' – let me know what you think about these before you head downstairs; the meeting's at three o'clock. I'll check in with you later.' And without bothering to stop and say 'thank you', she turned and stalked out of the door.

Great, Sasha thought glumly, as she contemplated the stack on her desk before reaching for another cup of extra-strong coffee. She glanced at the clock. If she was to complete her report on projected costs so it would reach the finance department in the morning, she'd probably be up all night, thanks to this last-minute assignment. And how much would this new marketing project cost, and would it fit into their budget? Sasha wondered sourly, as she started to thumb with great uninterest through the pile of pictures.

As she continued to flick through the stack, however, she quickly forgot about financial spreadsheets and billing breakdowns, concentrating instead on the stark black-and-white photographs in front of her. The ads that had started the American campaign had been relatively predictable and of a certain genre: handsome male stud shot from the waist up, dressed in either a leather jacket or a polo-neck and blazer, and gazing thoughtfully into the distance or smiling slightly off-camera. These test shots, however, were far more provocative and daring, so much so that Sasha seriously doubted they'd ever find space on the pages of any glossy magazine in the States – though perhaps Britain and the Continent might be a little more receptive, she mused, intrigued in spite of herself by the marketing possibilities of the mock-ups. There was no doubt about it: these pictures were witty, sexy, edgy, and anything but dull. She crossed and recrossed her legs, checked that the door to her office was shut, settled herself deeper into her chair and meticulously examined the photos again, beginning with the one on the top of the stack.

All of the black-and-white prints contained just the images of the models, a discreet shot of the product, and the caption reading 'Get a Gripp' in bold black letters on the white border at the bottom of the page. The male models were all young, probably aged between twenty and thirty years old, Sasha figured: some wore sleeveless white T-shirts, some were bare-chested, some were wearing jeans, some wore white briefs, and some, apparently, were wearing nothing at all.

The first shot featured a particularly stunning young man, his straight chestnut-brown hair parted on the side and flipped boyishly over his forehead, the honed muscles of his chest rising suggestively above the deeply scooped neck of his T-shirt. The viewer was invited to follow the model's line of vision down to the white long-leg briefs he wore, the camera having caught every enticing curve and swell of the quiescent jewel that lay sleeping within. Indeed, the man's hands and arms seemed to be braced on something behind him, so that his pelvis was thrust a little outward, as if he were deliberately calling the viewer's attention to the bulges of his cock and balls. The combination of his apparent vulnerability, indicated by his lowered eyelids, which seemed to suggest a kind of retiring bashfulness, and the arrogance of his out-thrust genitals caused a flutter in Sasha's sex and a pounding in her veins. With a sigh she set the photo aside and paused to take a good look at the next.

The second photographic image was of the same man, the pose similar to the first, except that in this case the expression in his eyes was not one of shyness or vulnerability, but a winning kind of coyness – a sexy, wicked grin, because he knew that what he was doing was naughty, and he knew the viewer was watching. This time, instead of bracing both arms behind him, he had one hand slyly cupping the unmistakable outline of his penis which seemed to be semierect, as though he had been interrupted in the act of stroking himself through the white cotton of his underpants. Indeed, though the man's head was bent downward, his eyes were looking up at the camera, his mouth caught in a knowing grin as he met the gaze of his viewer, confirming his spectator's suspicion that the young man was in fact enjoying a private moment of masturbation.

Whew! Sasha fanned her flaming cheeks for a moment with Valerie's obnoxious memo reminding all employees of their responsibility to refill the coffee and cookie tins as prescribed in the weekly rota. She looked again at the mock-up on her desk, the monochromatic image mounted on heavy black cardboard, and was tempted herself to engage in the same kind of physical expression of self-love as the man in the ad, but decided neither the time nor the place was particularly appropriate. Instead, she tried to ignore the developing ache in her sex, and reached for the next picture in the pile.

This photograph was even more intriguing than the last: it featured a stunning black man, his ebony beauty highlighted by the starkness of the photograph, his apparently nude body cut off an inch or so below his navel, with the barest suggestion of a line of dark hair leading downward, beyond where the camera refused to go. The model was being embraced from behind by a tall white woman who was also significantly older than the man, a pale blonde beauty whose arms were wrapped around the man's waist, her hands out of sight, presumably wrapped around the model's invisible cock. Both the woman and the man were staring defiantly into the camera, meeting the gaze of the viewer, and although the images were truncated right below the waist, it was inevitable that the spectator would conjure up in her mind exactly how the lower parts of their bodies were posed. Sasha could practically see right in front of her how the woman's legs were intertwined with the man's, their two bodies braced against each other, his hands lightly covering hers as she enfolded his cock in her fingers. The vision was so real, in fact, that Sasha had to look away for a moment and readjust her position in her seat before turning back to the remainder of the pictures in the stack.

The rest of the prints followed a similar theme: lone shots of men cradling the contents of their underpants, several pictures of a woman poised behind a foregrounded man, her hands curving up under his arms to press against the muscled wall of his chest, or dipping below the bottom of the photograph out of sight, and there was even one photo that nearly made Sasha's eyes pop out: one lucky man was surrounded by three women, none of whom were looking at the camera but instead were engrossed in each other, breasts and thighs being caressed by a confusion of hands, while the man in the photo smirked impudently at his unseen audience.

Becoming increasingly uncomfortable with the rising state of her own arousal, Sasha decided she needed a brief break to cool herself down before the interviews started, when out of the corner of her eye she noticed one last print, practically hidden under the pile of pages and printouts that littered the top of her desk. That's funny, she thought, as she unearthed the photo from the rubbish that had nearly concealed it: I thought I had already reached the bottom of the pile. But as she moved the print into the glow of the lamp on her desk, taking a full, long look at the image it revealed, she knew without a doubt that she had certainly not seen this shot before, for if she had, she would have ignored the other pictures on her desk and focused all her attention on this one.

How could she possibly have missed this photo on her first time through the stack? Staring moodily up at her on the page that bore her company's logo were not one, but two, yes, two flesh-and-blood images of the man she thought of as John Blakeley.

The men in this picture resembled each other so strongly they might have been twins: dark curling hair tumbling over their foreheads, sharply-cut cheek-bones, full, sensual mouths, and deep-set, nearly black eyes which gazed directly out at Sasha. On closer inspection she noticed that there were enough facial differences to decide that no, they weren't twins, but their similarities, both to each other and to the painted image of John Blakeley, were so immediately striking that Sasha had a momentary fear that she wasn't in full possession of all her mental faculties.

Unlike the other photos, this shot pictured the men at full-length, the camera having caught their bodies from the tops of their curly heads to the toes of their shiny black boots; both dressed identically in leather trousers, but both bare-chested, they seemed to be of the same height, but the man in front was seated on a tall wooden stool, his long legs stretched indolently out on the floor, and his sculpted upper body leaning back into the man who was embracing him from behind. The man at the back had one arm carelessly slung across the impressive chest of the man on the stool, his other arm reaching around his partner's stomach and disappearing beneath the man's waistband to cup the handful of promise hidden by the leather jeans. Two semi-naked men, one slyly gripping the cock of the other: the message implicit in the caption underneath the picture was sure to strike home.

Sasha gazed in heated silence at these two exquisite young men, photographic replicas of the ghostly lover who had been haunting her visions at night for so many weeks. She stared and stared, her breath coming in gasps, her hair beginning to loosen from its elaborate French plait, her nipples tightening, her belly shimmying, her thighs beginning to tremble and her underwear starting to liquefy. How could the two young models look so like him? she wondered dazedly to herself. Was the resemblance to that indistinctly painted image as strong as it seemed, or was she slowly beginning to go out of her mind? Sasha stared down at the picture of the two eerily familiar men on her desk until she felt she was growing dizzy and faint, the photographic images starting to blur and swim before her.

'Sasha? How are you getting on with those test shots? Have you discovered any favourites yet?'

Sasha's head snapped to attention, her eyes taking a moment to focus until she recognised the figure of her boss standing in the doorway. Without waiting for an answer, having apparently let herself into the room, Valerie strode purposefully over to Sasha's desk and gazed down at the photo that had so enthralled her colleague. With a proprietorial finger, she stroked the cheek of the model on the stool, and then lingeringly caressed the black-and-white contours of his finely chiselled chest and the striated planes of his stomach with such an evident display of lust that Sasha began to feel a little queasy, not to mention jealous. It almost seemed as though her boss was actually handling the real-life bodies of these two Johnny-wannabes, whereas Sasha had somewhat irrationally begun to feel as though they belonged to her.

'This one's a honey, isn't he?' Valerie sighed dreamily, her long tapered nail scratching lightly at the chest of the man in front. 'Actually,' she mused, 'they're both pretty gorgeous. Is this the only shot of the two of them?' Before Sasha had a chance to respond, Valerie took a closer look, a puzzled expression clouding her eyes. 'In fact, I don't remember seeing this particular print before. Who are these guys? These aren't any of the models the US division normally uses.' Curiously, she flipped the board over to inspect the back. 'Now this is weird,' she said quietly to herself. Catching sight of Sasha's single arched brow, she explained, 'The agency that sent the shots is supposed to supply all the relevant details on the back of the mock-up, aren't they?' At Sasha's mute nod, Valerie asked impatiently, 'Well? Why is this blank?' And she turned the back of the print so her co-worker could see for herself.

Valerie then carelessly scattered the rest of the shots over the piles of printout that cluttered Sasha's desk, nearly knocking Sasha's half-empty coffee cup on to the floor as she did so. She carefully inspected the backs of all the other prints to confirm that they contained all the usual data. 'Well,' she said indifferently, indicating the boards, 'the rest of these seem to be in order. We can always call the agency if there's a real interest in these two great-looking lads.'

Anxious to protect her precious picture from any more of Valerie's lascivious fondlings, Sasha restacked the photos carefully, placing her favourite at the bottom, and said thoughtfully, 'These are all much too racy for magazine publication, don't you think? Surely not even our big-name competitors who are so keen on edgy ads would touch these.'

'You're probably right,' Valerie commented as she picked up the pile of prints. 'That's why these are only mock-ups: the company just wanted to get a feel for what the models are capable of, and I guess the creative team got a little carried away in their quest for the New Face of Gripp.' She glanced over at Sasha's face. 'So did any of them strike you in particular? Do you think any of them might be suitable for our UK campaign?'

'Well, yes, actually.' Sasha strove to appear terribly casual as she flicked through the stack in Valerie's arms until she withdrew the enthralling photo of the two mystery men. 'Do you think I might hold on to this one until the interviews are over, just to be sure?'

She averted her eyes from her boss's smug expression as Valerie handed over the requested shot. 'I thought you seemed awfully interested in this one,' Valerie said in a nerve-jangling tone of self-satisfaction. 'But they are a bit different from blonde men such as Paul, don't you think?'

Sasha allowed herself a moment of childish mimicry as her boss turned and left the room. 'Bit different from Paul, aren't they?' she sneered quietly to herself, then gazed again at the picture of the two dark-haired men, the monochromatic images seeming to stare right back at her. She checked her watch. She had an hour and a half to wait before it was time to go downstairs, and the thought of actually meeting these two men who so reminded her of her ghostly lover was causing her palms to dampen and her heart to pound. She needed the upcoming ninety minutes to get herself under control.

* * *

It was ten minutes to three when Sasha slipped inside the heavy glass door that led to the US division of the ALM marketing team on the eleventh floor of her building. She nodded a quick, nervous hello to Wendy, the receptionist, then turned the corner and followed the corridor to Charlotte Campbell's office, where the scarily efficient department head was seated in conference with Mitch Clarke, her second-in-command.

'Hello, Sasha: thanks for coming down,' Charlotte said brightly, indicating for her to take a seat. 'We're just about to get started next door. I know that you're thinking of launching a similar campaign upstairs, and we'd be happy to exchange information with you.' She gestured towards the photo Sasha was clutching to her breasts. 'You particularly like that one?'

Still clinging tightly to the photo, as though reluctant to relinquish it to Charlotte's outstretched hand, Sasha nodded and tried to act cool. 'I think both of these models show some promise,' she said, trying to sound businesslike rather than enthralled. 'But, of course, I'd need more to go on than just one shot,' she added slowly, as if deliberating the matter over.

Charlotte looked at the picture Sasha held out, looking as puzzled as Valerie had. 'I don't remember seeing this picture before, do you, Mitch?' she asked, turning to her colleague. He gave an equally puzzled shake of the head, then both briefly consulted the printed information on their laps before looking at the picture again in bewilderment. Also like Valerie, Charlotte examined the blank back of the board before saying, with a shrug, 'Well, we'll soon find out if any of the names on our list match up to these guys.' She tucked the test shot in among the stack of photos in her arms and rose from her seat. 'Come on, let's go.'

The interviews were being held in the large conference room further on down the hall, and when Sasha walked in she took a seat at the far end of the table, wedging herself in between two other managers from the US division. She smiled nervously at the – to her eyes – shockingly young men, then bent her head over her legal pad and tried desperately to look as casually indifferent as they.

Nearly two hours later, Sasha was fighting off the yawns for real. All her dissatisfaction and weariness with the tedious details of the advertising world were rising to the fore of her otherwise-engaged mind. Although her obligatory attendance at the interviews today was spiced by her decidedly unprofessional interest in the two models still due to appear, the continual parade of young men who streamed in, some fashionably sullen, some annoyingly outdoorsy and wholesome, had her doodling offhandedly in bored frustration. Nearly five o'clock, and still no sign of the hauntingly evocative men she'd come here to see, Sasha grumbled to herself, then she jerked down her skirt and reached for her third cup of coffee.

'Well, I think that's about it,' Charlotte said gratefully after the last model had strutted out of the room, and she shut her briefcase with an authoritative snap. 'That was the last one on our list.'

Sasha looked up in confusion. Where were the two young men she had wasted all afternoon waiting to see? Why was Charlotte barking out orders about the need to debrief and regroup, and why was everyone leaving the conference room before the last two candidates had arrived?

Mystified, uneasy, but already beginning to suspect some supernatural intervention, Sasha was about to follow the others back into Charlotte's office when out of the corner of her eye she caught a flicker of movement by the elevator. Impelled by some inner sense of urgency, she hurried to catch the lift before the doors shut. Barely mindful of her actions, Sasha called out, 'Hold the lift!', dashed inside the elevator, and found herself face to face with the very men she had been seeking.

As the elevator doors closed behind her, Sasha stared in heated fascination at the two men before her. Both clad in black leather jackets, jeans and boots, with virtually identical dark hair, deep-set eyes, sculpted cheekbones and chiselled mouths, the men in the lift merely gazed intently back at Sasha, the corners of their mouths lifting in the merest hint of a smile.

'Why . . . why weren't you at the interviews?' Sasha stammered breathlessly, feeling her heart pound with agonising pressure. 'I've been waiting for you all day.'

The two men merely smiled a little more broadly, both of them leaning back casually against the far wall of the elevator, their hips arched out towards Sasha, their thumbs in their pockets and their shoulders braced against the wall. They continued to say nothing, but simply stood smiling and motionless until, with a jolt, the elevator came to an abrupt stop at Sasha's floor. As if in a daze, she left the lift first, then walked dreamily down the corridor to her office, knowing by instinct that the two men were following wordlessly behind. As she closed and locked the door of her office after them, only dimly aware that everyone else on her floor seemed to have left, Sasha switched on the lamp on her desk, then stood nervously by her filing cabinet, watching anxiously as the two strangers seated themselves in the leather armchairs across from her desk with the easy familiarity of two people comfortably at home.

'Don't be afraid, Sasha,' said the one on the right, in a voice so husky and low it took her a moment to realise with a start that he was English. 'We know you've been expecting us.' Sasha stared at him for a moment, then decided he must have been the man in the photo who had been sitting on the stool while the other one reached for his cock. She would have liked to check the print again to be sure, but it wouldn't exactly have been appropriate, and besides, she had left the picture with Charlotte.

As if enjoying Sasha's scrutiny, the man in the chair leant far back and crossed one long, lean leg over the other, almost striking a pose. As he flicked back the dark curls that rested over one brow, he gestured to his companion and himself. 'We've been waiting a long time for this.'

Sasha wasn't exactly certain what it was they had been waiting for, but the effect of the man's warm, lilting voice, the accent so much richer and more distinctive than Paul's stuffily precise Queen's English, was like a kind of opiate on her senses, filtering out the irrelevancies of their situation and causing her to focus only on the rush of desire that was pounding through her veins.

'What shall I call you?' was the only thing she could think of to say, her voice coming out in little more than a whisper, even as she knew what it was they would answer.

'Why don't you call me John?' the one on the right offered easily, while the other said, 'And I'll be Jack.'

Sasha stared at the two of them, the thunder of the pulse in her ears nearly deafening – and what was that rushing sound, like the rustling of wings?

'You look so familiar,' she breathed to the two of them, coming forward a little to examine their faces in the lamplight, which was the only light in the room. 'I feel as if I know you.'

Hesitantly, she reached out one finger to trail it

wonderingly over the features of John, the man closest to her in the chair on the right. He said nothing, merely sat quite still as Sasha stood over him and brushed her fingers lightly over the bristling arch of his brow, the strong, straight line of his nose, the high curve of his cheekbone, before allowing herself to experience the yielding firmness of his finely cut, beautifully shaped mouth. The man leant back a little in his chair and closed his eyes while parting his lips just enough to let his tongue flicker out and gently lick the tips of Sasha's exploring fingers. She gazed at him as he sat with his head pressed against the back of the chair, and she ran her fingers down the exposed arch of his neck, marvelling at the texture of his skin and the feel of the pulse that beat, warm and alive, in his throat. She leant further over him to run her fingers through the silky black ringlets that curled over his forehead and tumbled down the collar of his jacket to rest a mere fraction above his shoulders. She was so wrapped up in the feel of her fingertips against this man's skin and hair that she had nearly forgotten about his companion, deep as she was in the intimacy she was pursuing with this stranger.

Sasha inched a little closer to John, positioning herself between his long thighs as he parted his legs to let her in then closed them around her knees, pressing her closer to himself. He opened his eyes briefly to look at her, as if to reassure her that she could go ahead and touch him, then shut them again and sighed quietly as, with trembling fingers, Sasha slowly slid off his heavy leather jacket to reveal the plain white T-shirt he wore underneath.

It was then that she finally remembered the silent other man, and, still leaning over John, she turned her head to stare at his companion, who had swivelled his chair around to watch in tacit encouragement as Sasha bent over the body of his friend. Jack's jacket had somehow also been removed, and his posture in the chair mimicked his friend's, his head tipped back and his legs outstretched. She turned back to the man whose thighs were enclosing hers, and, with great delicacy and hesitation, hardly able to believe her own daring, she eased his T-shirt up over the rounded curves of his shoulders and gently tugged it completely off, leaving him blissfully naked from the waist up. Sasha caught her breath and bit her lip at the sight of the expanse of male beauty before her, the flesh-and-blood reality of the man far surpassing his one-dimensional photographic image. She pressed both hands against the smooth brown hardness of his chest, noticing with a kind of detached interest the curious glow that seemed to illuminate his skin. Sasha leant slightly into the strength and density of this stranger's breast, pressing her palms tightly against the sharply defined pectoral swell, and feeling his small, tight nipples that were puckered and ridged against her hands. Her fingers curved over the rounded muscles of his shoulders and chest, and she half-closed her eyes and breathed out quietly, a barely formed 'oh' of delight rising in her throat. She then drew back a little to trace her finger enquiringly down the fine arrow of silken hair leading to the mysteries that lay below his belt, and she lingered for a moment at his shiny silver buckle, smilingly catching his eyes with hers. He smiled back at her gently, still sitting passively in the chair, but the thrilling bulge of hardness that strained against the leather of his jeans belied his quiescent stillness.

Sasha firmly gripped that impressive length in her palm for a moment, pressing lightly against it, and rubbing her hand up and down with a smile of promise before cradling it one final time, then releasing it in order to turn her attention to his partner. She was not surprised to discover that Jack now sat similarly bared to the waist, the strangely luminescent beauty of his body an obvious mirror of his friend's. Sasha moved to stand over him now, observing how naturally his legs opened up to allow her to stand between them, and she gazed fully into his face, noting with almost clinical observation how his features differed ever so slightly from the other man's. She suddenly hoped that the men weren't brothers, the very thought of any incestuous interconnection being altogether too perverse for her. No, she decided to herself as she reached out to touch Jack's cheek, these two men aren't brothers – at least, not biologically. She was so engrossed in marking the distinctions between Jack and his companion that she only half-heard the creak of the leather chair as John rose from its depths to come to stand behind her, and then she felt the warm, strong length of his bare arms encircle her from the back. She felt no jolt of surprise, only the welcoming rush of pleasure as she leant back slightly against John's naked chest, her thighs still gripped by his friend Jack who sat before her in the chair. For the briefest of moments Sasha hesitated: what exactly was she doing here in her office at this late hour with not one, but two strange young men? She felt no anxiety or fear, however, only a confident feeling of rightness, that she and these two men who were so reminiscent of John Blakeley somehow belonged together, here, at this moment, in this place.

And so Sasha leant forward to lay her lips along the convex column of Jack's throat, her tensed body extending over his prone one, her groin pressed to his, her breasts along his chest as her buttocks pushed outward to find an answering pressure against the bulge of John's leather-clad cock. She arched even further into Jack's inviting embrace, feeling his hands slide up and down the lengths of her arms as her mouth pressed tightly to his throat and her crotch pressed hard against his erection, still constrained beneath his clothes.

As Sasha moved her mouth to the strong curves of Jack's chest, she felt John shift slightly behind her so that he could assist his friend, who was, Sasha realised, starting to edge the powder-blue jacket of her suit down her shoulders and on to the floor. With a whimper of desire, Sasha slid slowly to her knees, her mouth sliding urgently against the ridged planes of Jack's stomach, her arms held momentarily above her head as the two men eased up her cream silk shell blouse and lifted it up and completely off. And then, as Sasha reached for the tightly clasped buckle of Jack's belt, she felt John's fingers behind her unclasp her lacy cream bra and slip the straps from her shoulders so that, as she deftly unbuttoned Jack's trousers, the tips of her now-naked breasts rubbed deliciously against the rich, smooth leather of his jeans.

With eager fingers she reached inside to clasp her hand around Jack's thick, heavy shaft, and as she palmed his ready cock, still crouched on the floor between his legs, she saw John reach for Jack's right foot and tug firmly at his boot, releasing it from his foot with one smooth pull. He repeated the operation with the other boot, then paused, waiting expectantly as Jack arched up his hips, allowing Sasha to ease down his trousers and pull them off entirely, so that the man in the chair was now wholly, gloriously naked. Sasha shuffled back a moment, still on her knees, and gazed up at the man seated before her in silent admiration. There was a quick rustling behind her, and she knew without looking that John had similarly stripped off his clothes so that he too sat splendidly nude on the floor behind her, the two men now arranged in a decadently erotic circle, the positions of their bodies mirroring each other's, with Sasha kneeling on the precipice of tingling suspense between them. She wasn't at all afraid, only tense with the heat of a shimmering arousal.

She inched a little forward now, so that she was firmly wedged between Jack's naked and spread thighs, her eyes focusing on the thick, soft cowl of foreskin which had rippled back on itself so that the glossy purple head of his cock could clearly be seen. She gripped the iron-hard length in her hand and aimed it straight into her mouth, hearing a barely audible sigh of pleasure, which seemed, curiously, to come from both of the men. As the soft, wet recesses of Sasha's mouth enfolded Jack's hot, hard cock, she started to settle herself more comfortably on the floor, but then gave a muffled sound of surprise, her mouth so completely filled with Jack's throbbing shaft, as she felt John's warm, strong hands on the sides of her hips, coaxing her up on to her knees and guiding her arms on to the seat of the chair, Jack's cock still embraced by her mouth. Sasha's upper body was now braced securely on the chair, while she knelt on the floor, her buttocks thrust outward, her sex close to John's face. In this position John was able to expertly unfasten Sasha's skirt, unclip her stockings, unclasp her suspender-belt, and roll down her panties so that she was effortlessly, gracefully, oh-so-slowly released from the confines of her clothing. As Sasha slid her mouth downward and took even more of Jack's penis deeper inside, she felt a surge of excitement as John urged her thighs further apart, and then she felt his long, slim fingers on the flushed lips of her sex. Sasha sucked desperately on Jack's length, waiting with a desperate urgency for the feel of John's mouth on the aching wetness between her legs.

When it came, the heat and strength of John's tongue along the plush groove of her channel, Sasha nearly choked with the pleasure, and she had to pull her mouth sharply away from Jack's cock so she could concentrate fully on the movements of John's mouth against her spread and rosy sex. She glanced up at the man in the chair even as she pushed backward on to John's tongue, and felt a warmth swell within her as she saw Jack smile gently at her, one hand stroking the wildly disarranged strands of her topknot, the other trailing softly over her hot and flaming cheeks. As Sasha opened her mouth in a soundless 'oh' of rapture, her hips swivelling back and forth as John sucked on her clenching, straining sex from behind, Jack slid one long finger between her lips and stroked her grasping tongue as she closed her mouth around the substitute penis. As Jack's finger pushed gently in and out of her mouth, its reduced heft and size all the distraction Sasha felt she could take, she felt a wild surge of joy at this entirely new doubled form of pleasuring.

When John's tongue finally began to flick teasingly along Sasha's clitoris, she felt her orgasm commence, and when he closed his mouth around the liquid pearl and begin to suck at just the right moment, Sasha expelled Jack's finger from her mouth and buried her head in his thigh, sinking her teeth into the comfortingly rounded muscle and shuddering in silence as she rode out the crest of her climax. As she breathed out the last tremor of delight, still on her knees, her upper body resting on Jack's lap, Sasha dimly felt John come up from behind her and extend himself over her bent body, enfolding her in his arms and cupping her breasts in his hands. As he did so, Jack tenderly released the last few strands of Sasha's hair from her clips and spread it out over her shoulders, combing out the tangles with his fingers with the expertise of a salon stylist.

Eventually Sasha sat up, only the tiniest bit self-conscious, and, easing herself out of John's firm grip, turned to face him. She gazed into John's eyes, then reached out to wipe the last traces of her dew from his slightly smiling lips, which were still wet with her pleasure. She ran her finger along his mouth, rubbing away the wetness, then pressed her finger to her own lips, tasting herself on its tip. Still the men said nothing, merely waiting in companionable silence, while Sasha contemplated the decadent scenario the three of them had just played out. She arched a brow enquiringly at John, then looked back at the man in the chair before turning again to face the man seated naked in front of her on the floor, and at his nearly indistinct shrug and slyly complicit grin, she rose deliberately to her feet and walked as casually as she could over to her desk. She took out her handbag from her top drawer, and extracted a small tube of water-based moisturising cream and two condoms from her emergency mock-croc carrying case. She then turned back to the men and handed a small scarlet packet to each, then watched with anticipation as they deftly unrolled the sliver-thin sheaths over their still-rampant erections.

What a fantasy, Sasha marvelled to herself, as she seated herself once again between the two men. Whoever these two strangers were, whoever had sent them to her, whether by ghostly intervention or not, she was experiencing a deeper, darker thrill than she had ever thought possible, and she was eager to taste more. It didn't surprise Sasha at all to see that the men seemed to know her thoughts and to anticipate the

110

trajectory of her desire: they seemed to touch her exactly where she wished to be touched, even before she had articulated that wish to herself. It seemed in this mutual give-and-take of pleasure that her fantasies took precedence, and as she arranged herself now to face John lying full-length on the floor, she gestured to Jack to join them, knowing he had already foreseen her intentions.

'Come and lie behind me,' she whispered to him now, easing herself closer to John so that her face was directly in front of his. There seemed to be an unearthly glow about the man, she thought, then glanced over at Jack, noting the eerie luminescence that seemed to be radiating outward from his warm, live body, too. Perhaps it's just the lamp, Sasha thought, feeling the strangely familiar emanation of light from the two men flow over her body and enwrap her in its radiance. She gazed into the eyes of the man who lay quietly before her, and ran her finger over his lips before slipping the tip of it inside, stroking along the length of his tongue as Jack had done to her earlier.

'Kiss me,' she breathed, then met John's lips with her own, still keeping her finger inside so that she could follow the movements of their tongues as they rubbed playfully against one another. When she finally withdrew her finger, still keeping her mouth pressed to John's, she braced herself up on her hands and then rolled full-length on top of him, nudging him on to his back, her mouth slanted against his, and her hands following the curves of his strong arms as he tangled his fingers in her hair. As Sasha gave herself up to the pleasure of kissing this stranger, she manoeuvred herself into position over his cock, helped into place by Jack, who had silently come up behind her and was now guiding her sex so that it was tantalisingly poised over John's. Reluctantly, Sasha withdrew her mouth from his so that she could straddle his hips more effectively, again directed into place by Jack. She rose up on her knees, closed her eyes in heady anticipation, and slowly lowered herself on to John's waiting shaft. Once John was fully enclosed in her supple, clinging sheath, Sasha merely held herself still, ignoring her clenching vagina which was aching for friction, and waited patiently until Jack had settled himself behind her, kneeling between John's spread thighs and reaching for the cream Sasha had left lying discreetly by her desk. She didn't turn around, but simply bent as far forward as she could without releasing John's cock, so that the puckered rosy ring of her anal entrance was exposed. She flinched only slightly when she felt the first cold kiss of the cream as it was rubbed into her most secret space, and she held John's eyes with her own, feeling his penis pulse in expectation inside her as Jack finished lubricating the crease between Sasha's buttocks. Then, gently, carefully, with a kind of loving tenderness, Jack guided the head of his cock right to where Sasha wanted it, and paused motionless for a moment as if to gauge her reaction.

At the first push of Jack's cock into her back passage, Sasha let out a slight gasp of pleasure; she felt Jack stop as if in question, and silently shook her head, indicating that there was no discomfort, only the sweetest sense of tension and intense fullness. She pushed herself back firmly on to the staff shyly seeking entrance, encouraging it to pursue its journey into the dark valley of her anus. Sasha didn't feel it was necessary to assure Jack that she was no stranger to the backroads to sexual ecstasy, and that her rear passage was well used to the tight friction and delicious stretch of pleasure. He had obviously guessed as much, though, because, with a more determined thrust, Jack pressed his way fully inside the small space that was being offered to him, and then the three of them took a deep breath and paused as they sealed their odd bond of flesh, locked together in a weird triptych of desire.

At last Sasha began to move, trying out an experimental rhythm as she accommodated herself to the twin pressure of cock against cock, one lodged in her sex, the other throbbing in her anus. The two men gallantly held still as Sasha rose up on John's shaft, then back on to Jack's length, closing her eyes and blindly seeking her way to a form of fulfilment that would satisfy all three. Although she was well rehearsed in the joys of anal sex, Sasha had only ever been a participant in a one-to-one, and this was the first time she had ever been involved with two men simultaneously. She wasn't thinking of that now, however, but was concentrating instead on matching her rhythms to those of the men inside her, not even realising she was smiling a little as the delicious tumult began to fill her belly. As she slid downward on to John's up-thrust cock, she felt Jack withdraw slowly from behind, and as she pushed back on to the staff that filled the space of her anus, she lifted herself slightly off John, so as to increase the pressure when she slid back down. She could feel Jack's arms around her from behind, holding her tightly against the muscular density of his chest, and she gasped with delight when John's hands came up to cradle her breasts, rubbing against her nipples and adding to the confusion and complexity of her pleasure. Sasha also knew that Jack was wedged tightly between John's thighs, his knees practically under John's buttocks; the two heavy sacs of their scrotums pressed together as the men strained against each other, the motions of their

113

bodies arousing each other as completely as they were arousing Sasha, and she them. The three strove together as one, the arch of hip and buttock and thigh imitating one another until Sasha reached down to stroke her clitoris, feeling as though every nerve-cell she possessed had started to scream out in an agonising burst of intensity. With her sex and her anus both so deeply filled, she felt as though she might explode with the pressure.

As cock thrust against cock, and the hands on her hips and her breasts gripped her more tightly, Sasha began to lose any sense of control, feeling the confused rush of sensation overtake her. More than a climax, this was nearly a delirium which Sasha was swept into, and as she melted into the intensity of her orgasm, not bothering to know or care when or if the men came, she began to call out the name of the man who haunted her in a voice so hoarse and other-worldly she barely recognised it as her own. Streaming sweat, tears, and vaginal dew, with a tremble and a shudder Sasha clung to the men who surrounded and filled her, and the last thing she saw before the dizzy heights of rapture overwhelmed her was the face of Johnny Blakeley smiling tenderly at her, his hand raised to stroke her cheek. Then there was a fluttering, swishing sound, like the rustle of wings, a low roar, and, as Sasha felt the darkness overtake her, the sound of a woman weeping.

Chapter Seven

'*A*nd then they were gone.'

Xenia's forkful of Cobb Salad stopped halfway up to her mouth and her jaws momentarily ceased moving until, with a painful swallow, she digested Sasha's last sentence. Then she thoughtfully resumed chewing, concentrating on picking out the bits of bacon from her overloaded fork and dropping them on to Sasha's plate before finally lifting up her eyes to confront her friend.

'That's it? Just . . . gone?'

Sasha nodded miserably. 'I swear it, Xane,' she said, pushing away her plate, empty now save for Xenia's discarded pieces of bacon. 'It was bang-bang-bang, like firecrackers going off on the Fourth of July, and I felt like my head was spinning almost completely around; my whole body was shaking, and I was coming and coming and coming in a way I have never come before.' Sasha's eyes widened as she looked at Xenia and continued, 'And then there was this incredible noise, like the rustling of angels' wings, and then I guess I must have passed out because, like I just said, when I finally came to I was lying all stretched out on the leather chair, neatly dressed – even my hair was back in place! – and the two guys were gone.' She paused and mournfully contemplated her plate. 'Do you want some dessert?'

Xenia reached forward to place a comforting hand on her friend's. 'Sasha, I know you want to believe this whole amazing story really happened –' she began, but she was irritably cut off.

'I know it sounds crazy!' Sasha blurted out, pushing her hands distractedly through her loosely flowing hair. 'I know what you're going to say: that I've been working too hard, I must have drifted off in my chair after that long meeting, it was all some kinky kind of daydream, but I'm telling you, I know what happened was real!'

Xenia said nothing for a moment, only pushed her remaining food around on her plate, then said reasonably, 'Sasha, you always have had a vibrant imagination, you know: even when we were kids you were always making up outrageous stories about fairies you'd seen, and ghosts you'd heard, and remember that claim that you stuck to for years, that you were actually adopted and your real parents were descendants of some hush-hush royal offspring in Russia whose existence had to be kept quiet for the sake of international relations? I swear you began to believe those stories yourself!'

Sasha blushed. 'Yeah, I know,' she mumbled, reaching for her wine glass. 'I knew you'd find some rational explanation for everything, just like you always do. I don't know why I keep coming to you to tell you all this when I know you're just going to debunk it all and try to deflate me.'

'Come on, girl, you know it's only because I'm trying to protect you from your own wild self,' Xenia said, smiling, rolling up her napkin and tucking it neatly under her plate. 'You trust me to be truthful, don't you? You always are with me – painfully so! Anyway, honey,' she went on gently, 'if you want to believe that you were visited by an angelic pair of heavenly lovers, which it certainly sounds like they were, then I'm not going to try to convince you otherwise. I'm just trying to remind you that there may be a more, erm, ordinary, though undoubtedly disappointing, explanation.' Xenia turned to flag down a passing waitress. 'May we have the dessert menus, please?'

'And I guess you think I didn't really hear Amelia Asher's voice either,' Sasha said peevishly, glaring at her menu. 'You're probably going to say that the sound I heard was the wind or the rain or some other horribly clichéd response – except, of course,' she concluded triumphantly, laying down her menu, 'there was neither. It was a perfectly warm, sunny, mid-September day.'

'Let me look at that picture again,' Xenia said abruptly, ignoring Sasha's preceding statement. Sasha silently handed over the test shot of the two gorgeous young men she now thought of as John and Jack. Xenia gazed at it in silence for a moment. 'And you say this was left lying across your lap, and that you think it had been placed there by the two young men, because the last time you'd seen it, it had been tucked away in Charlotte's briefcase along with the shots of the other models?'

'And how do you explain that particular inconsistency, Ms Amateur Detective?' Sasha demanded, eyeing her friend. 'How did this picture transport itself up three flights of stairs from Charlotte's office to my lap?' She nearly snatched the treasured photograph

117

away from Xenia's elegant fingers, causing her friend to shrug and shake her head.

'Let's just order some dessert, shall we?' Xenia sighed in resignation. 'I give up. It's your mystery, and I guess I'll just have to respect that. How about if we split the Mississippi Mud Pie?'

'No way,' Sasha announced firmly. 'I'm having the Brownie Supreme with extra chocolate sauce, and I'm going to eat the whole thing myself.'

Sasha waited until the waitress had brought their desserts before she said to Xenia, sticking her spoon into the heart of her brownie, 'Paul's coming back to New York again later this week.'

'Again!' Xenia looked surprised. 'What does he want this time?'

'It's for work, silly,' Sasha rebuked her fondly, then said, looking a bit more serious, 'and it's just as well, because there's something I've been thinking about all weekend, ever since that night, and Paul might as well hear it from me, since it really affects him as well as Valerie.' She sucked the fudge sauce off her spoon and added, watching her friend carefully, 'And you too, in a way.'

Xenia looked immediately suspicious. 'Oh? And what might that be?' she asked, patently striving for casual indifference as she dug into her chocolate pie.

'Well,' Sasha began hesitantly, then looked bravely at her friend across the cluttered table for two and stated almost defiantly, 'I'm applying for a leave of absence from my job.'

Expecting a great show of disbelief from her eminently responsible friend, Sasha was perversely disappointed when Xenia merely speared cookie-crumb pie-base into her mouth and nodded her head as though she'd been expecting this. 'And do you want to tell me why?' she asked conversationally, dabbing delicately at her mouth with her linen napkin, as though Sasha's decision was the most sensible course of action in the world.

Sasha took a breath, closed her eyes, and said it. 'I want to go back to that hotel in London and see if there's anything else I can ... I don't know ... do,' she finished lamely.

'Do?' Xenia asked politely, with only a hint of an arched brow. 'About what?'

Sasha scowled at her. 'You know what!' she nearly barked, and then said more quietly, 'And don't make me feel a fool for doing this! There have been just too many peculiar things happening lately, and I want to return to the source of the mystery to see if I can figure out something I can do to lay this poor ghost to rest.' Her lips trembling, Sasha looked at her friend and said almost wheedlingly, 'Come on, Xenia, I know this idea of mine is a little off the wall, but I could really use your support on this. I want to take off just a week or two so I can go back to England, dig up anything I can find on poor Lady Amelia, and see if maybe there's someone I should try to contact – I don't know, a descendant or something – who can help me find some kind of clue about what I've been experiencing. Have I really been seeing ghosts? Have I somehow become involved in a centuries-old love-affair; have I been put in some curious way in the centre of it? Or am I going out of my mind, hallucinating, maybe?' She held Xenia's eyes with her own, as though asking for reassurance that she was doing the right thing, and she was not disappointed.

Xenia reached over and squeezed Sasha's hand. 'I told you,' she said firmly, comfortingly, 'of course I'll support you throughout this whole thing. If you want to go back to England to unlock a few mysteries, you go, girl! If it'll make you happy, and help you to sleep better at night, then of course you have my blessing. I only wish,' she added wistfully, as she smoothed Sasha's hair back over her ear, 'that I could take a vacation myself and go with you. I think I'm almost as curious as you are to see if you discover anything else about these two dead people!'

Sasha looked hopefully at her friend as she gripped her hands. 'Why don't you come with me?' she suggested, shaking her head so her hair flicked back into place. 'We could have so much fun! And I could really use your help and advice,' she added, knowing what the answer would be.

Smiling, Xenia shook her head. 'Sorry,' she said cheerily, though still clinging to Sasha's hands, 'but this is *your* thing. Whatever you're going over there to do, you've got to do it alone. I would just be in the way.'

'I know; you're right again, as usual,' Sasha grumbled affectionately, then glanced at her watch. 'And now I have to go: I'm already ten minutes late.' She reached to pick up the bill, but Xenia got to it first.

'Hey!' she said, playfully slapping away Sasha's hand. 'It's my turn this time; you got it last time, remember? And who knows?' she said laughingly, looking around for the waitress. 'You may be able to pay me back by bringing home an English stud for me; just make sure he's real, and not some flimsy ghost!'

Sasha walked back to her office that afternoon after her over-long lunch in a flurry of nerves, anxiously wondering how she was going to break it to Valerie that she was taking time off – and in the middle of the new campaign! She dawdled her way along Park Avenue, heedless of how late she was, reluctantly crossing over Madison on her way to Fifth while she tried out and discarded competing scenarios in her mind, as she'd been doing all day.

Having debated this issue continually with herself all weekend, ever since her encounter with the two darkly mysterious men in her office, Sasha felt sure that a leave of absence was the only viable approach, and she had convinced herself that it was the best thing for the office, considering how she had let her personal obsession take over her professional obligations. Even so, it was with an uneasy flutter in her stomach and a trembling of her knees that she tapped on Valerie's door that afternoon and slithered rapidly inside before she had even been invited in.

Valerie, in her usual obtuse way, seemed to take no notice at all of her colleague's nervous tremors.

'Here,' she said shortly, thrusting a sheaf of papers at the nonplussed Sasha. 'Look this over for me, will you, while you've got a moment? I need to get this signed and notarised ASAP in order to get it out in time for the evening mail.'

Not bothering to see what had been shoved her way so peremptorily, Sasha gently laid down the bulky whatever-it-was and took a seat across from her boss. 'Valerie,' she began in almost a whisper, but as the woman seemed to be taking absolutely no notice of her, Sasha's irritation grew, and she repeated, more loudly this time, 'Valerie!'

Her boss glanced up, not even bothering to stop writing as she did so. 'What?' she asked, rather rudely. 'What is it?'

'I need to ask you for a few weeks off as soon as possible,' Sasha said boldly, not at all afraid now. That certainly got her boss's attention.

'Excuse me? You what?' Valerie looked directly at Sasha at last, and asked, in a dangerous imitation of politeness, 'You need a what?'

121

Why does the woman have to be such a bully? Sasha thought crossly, but merely squared her shoulders and looked defiantly back at her. 'I have at least three weeks' vacation owed to me, as you know, and I would like to take them by the end of the month, ASAP,' she said, unable to refrain from childish mockery.

Valerie squared her shoulders in response and took off her glasses, a sure sign she was annoyed. 'You can't possibly be serious, Sasha,' she said in a teeth-gratingly patronising tone. 'You can't possibly expect me to allow you to leave at a time like this: not when we're about to launch the next line of products in the UK, and we're contemplating the new Face of Gripp campaign! And with Christmas practically around the corner –'

Sasha couldn't help a sneer: it was only just after Labour Day, for heaven's sake!

Unfortunately for her, Valerie saw the sneer and retaliated. 'I'm sorry, dear,' she said with exquisite condescension as she coolly replaced her glasses on her nose, 'but it's simply out of the question.' She paused to smile beneficently at her colleague. 'Perhaps in the new year we can talk. Now go on,' she said pleasantly, making a shooing gesture at the door, 'scoot on out of here. And Sasha,' she called out, indicating the pile of paper heaped on her desk as Sasha made her way to the door, 'don't forget to take that with you.'

Muttering sourly to herself as she sat in her office later that day, chewing frustratedly on some very old and dry Milk Duds, Sasha was so enwrapped in her own misery as she ploughed through the heavy legal document dumped on her by her boss that she nearly didn't hear Heather knock respectfully on her door, clearly unwilling to disturb her.

'Sorry, Sasha,' she said kindly, holding out a single sheet of paper, 'but this was just faxed through for you.'

Sasha grunted bad-temperedly at the poor woman and studied the wafer-thin page. It was a copy of Paul's travel itinerary, faxed over from Rollit in London, detailing his flight arrival and departure times. Now why was this sent over to me? Sasha wondered, puzzled, then noticed that actually the message was addressed to Valerie. She was just about to call her assistant back in when she decided, hell, why make Heather the unnecessary mediator: she might as well take the message over to Valerie herself. As she rose from her desk, however, Sasha noticed an odd discrepancy in the memo. That's funny, she thought: according to this, Paul is actually arriving a day earlier than the marketing team had been told. Has Valerie moved the meeting up a day: is that why Paul is due in tomorrow? she puzzled. She checked her diary, but no, according to her scrawled memo to herself, the meeting was still scheduled for Wednesday. Then why did the fax say that Paul's plane was expected in tomorrow afternoon, tomorrow being only Tuesday, when the rest of the Rollit team weren't due in until the following day?

The barest outline of an answer flickered across the edges of Sasha's consciousness, but, despite her attempt to chase it down, she was simply too preoccupied with her own problems to pursue the matter, so she merely tucked the curious memo under that day's edition of the *Wall Street Journal*, figuring she would hand it to Valerie later that afternoon. Paul probably wants to get in early to shop the post-Labour Day sales at Saks, Sasha shrugged, then turned back to her legal document and her Milk Duds.

* * *

As Sasha trudged her way towards Central Park later that day on her way home, being careful to stay on populated streets and on the outside of the sidewalk – this was, after all, New York – she was irresistibly drawn to a travel agent's office she had never noticed before on 58th Street. Stopping to look in the window, she gazed longingly at the advertised flights from New York to London. I've just got to get back there, she thought desperately to herself, practically pressing her nose up against the pane. There's got to be a way to make Valerie let me go; it's only for a week or two! As she stared intently at the posted fare of $350 round-trip, she suddenly gave a little gasp and jumped back a bit. Was someone staring at her from inside the travel agent's office? Sasha moved cautiously off to the side of the window and tried to peer back inside without being too obvious, and again she had the sense that someone was gazing back at her, but it wasn't someone from inside the building. Sasha forced herself to pull her eyes back a moment and refocus, suddenly realising with a jolt that whoever was staring at her must be standing behind her, for the man with the dark eyes and curling black hair was actually reflected *in* the glass, not standing somewhere *behind* it. For a dizzying moment, Sasha thought she saw the figure beckon, holding his hand out to her as though trying to pull her to him.

'Johnny?' Sasha wheeled around rapidly, half-expecting to find a flesh-and-blood man from late-eighteenth-century England standing before her on the New York City sidewalk. Of course, she saw no such thing. When Sasha looked back into the window, all she saw reflected back at her was her own pale expression, looking for all the world as if she really had just seen a ghost. I've got to get out of here, she thought miserably, leaning her head against the cool glass window; somehow I've got to find a way to get a leave of absence from my job so I can get back to England to try to restore my sanity.

Her chance came much sooner than she had expected, and it all hinged on that fax Heather had handed her by mistake.

'I have some good news for you today,' Valerie beamed at her assembled marketing team early the next morning. 'Well, actually it's bad news for us, but good news as well in a way.' She laughed fetchingly, her cheeks flushing a bright shade of pink and her cleavage trembling voluptuously in the sharp V of her rose-coloured jacket, which was buttoned up as far as it would go, but clearly revealed that she was wearing nothing underneath. 'It seems that the entire computer system on our floor is to be shut down this afternoon, so that the new millennium-bug-busting program we ordered – oh, months ago – can finally be installed. It seems that the contractor had a sudden cancellation in his schedule, and has generously offered to slot us in today, rather than come in next week, as originally planned. So I believe this means,' Valerie finished gaily, 'that we all get to take the afternoon off.'

A murmur of disbelief rippled through the dozen or so people seated around the conference table. The system being shut down! Since when did this happen on a busy Tuesday afternoon?

'Why weren't we told about this before?' Sasha demanded angrily. Surely, she thought, as senior marketing manager she should have been informed well in advance!

'Sorry, gang,' Valerie replied brightly, 'but we didn't find out that the contractor was available until late yesterday afternoon – honestly,' she added, wide-eyed and with palms outstretched and uplifted. 'The installation is due to begin at about one o'clock, and I've been promised that it will be completed by tonight, well in advance of our scheduled meeting with the ad people from Rollit, who are due to fly in tomorrow.'

Tomorrow morning? So that was it! Sasha thought, the forgotten fax now suddenly remembered. She peered closely at Valerie as she followed her out of the room. Surely not! Surely Valerie and Paul...? Well, Sasha thought, in a kind of startled triumph, let's just see what I might be able to dig up here.

'Oh, Valerie,' Sasha said, as if something which had slipped her mind had only just now returned to it. 'I was handed a rather puzzling fax by Heather yesterday which I believe was meant for you.' She smiled with insincere sweetness at her boss, noting the flustered rise of colour in Valerie's cheeks, and continued innocently, 'Something about Paul and his timetable?'

'Let me see it,' Valerie snapped, then, as though suddenly recalling herself, 'that is, if you've still got it.' And she smiled just as insincerely as her colleague.

When they reached Sasha's office and she was silently handed the fax Sasha unearthed from beneath yesterday's newspaper, Valerie's cheeks heightened a notch in colour, and she said hastily, crumpling up the sheet of paper in her fist, 'Oh – what a big misunderstanding this all is! Silly Paul,' she added with a forced laugh, 'what a muddle over timetables! Of course he's not due in until tomorrow!' She stared hard into Sasha's face for a moment, all apparent silliness gone, and said in a suddenly cold and steely voice, 'Let's just forget about the note now, shall we? In fact, Sasha,' Valerie said, almost warningly, as she turned towards the door, 'why don't you take the rest of the day off starting now, and go on home? I'll see you bright and early here tomorrow, all right?'

And without waiting for Sasha's reply, she stalked out.

Well, there's certainly no way that I'm going to leave the building now, Sasha thought fiercely: if I have to hide in the bathroom in order to pretend I've gone, then I will. I'm dying to discover exactly what's going on here!

And hide in the bathroom she did, before sneaking back to her desk later that afternoon, after she was sure everyone else had gone. Experimentally, she turned on her computer and was perversely disappointed when the screen remained blank, indicating that the system had indeed been shut down to facilitate the installation of the new software package. She'd been so sure Valerie was lying! Still, she mused, idly flicking over the pages of a sales report on her desk, something definitely doesn't seem right here. It's almost as if Valerie's trying to get rid of us for some reason. Perhaps I'd better see if I can discover anything lying around on her desk.

With numerous sinister scenarios playing themselves out in her mind, including a calculating scheme on Valerie's part to sabotage the new campaign for some nefarious reason, Sasha pushed her chair firmly away from her desk and strode determinedly to Valerie's office. She knew that the woman always scrupulously locked her office door when she left work at night, but Sasha was betting herself that her boss hadn't even left the building.

'Oh, yes, I have been a naughty girl!'

Was that – could that be Valerie's voice, that breathy, high-pitched, little-girl squeal? Was it possible that Valerie was engaged in some kind of sordid sex scene with the computer contractor? Resisting the temptation to squeeze her eyes shut, lest she unwillingly witness anything truly obscene, Sasha held her breath and shimmied her way around the half-open door leading to Valerie's spacious, plush office, took a deep breath, and peeked inside.

No way! Sasha thought, in outraged incredulity. For there, bent face-down over her desk, which was miraculously cleared of papers, was her boss, her rose-pink skirt hitched up around her waist, her jacket removed to reveal one of those lacy pink super-bras designed to create cleavage; Valerie's pink satin panties had been stripped off and lay rejected on the floor, and her lace-topped ivory stockings and frothy pink suspender-belt were revealed to the world. But what really caused Sasha's eyes to widen was the fact that Valerie's wrists and ankles were bound to the legs of her desk, her thighs were pulled apart, the plump curves of her bottom lifted in the air, and her gaping, honeyed sex was spread wide open in a shameless display of debauchery.

'Yes, you have been a naughty girl, haven't you?' came a familiar English voice, and emerging out of the corner of the room and into full view of Sasha's shocked and staring eyes was none other than Paul, fully dressed in a beautifully tailored light-grey suit, his hair gleaming, his shoes highly glossed, and only the slight flush in his cheeks indicating his own charge of excitement as he stepped up behind Valerie, smartly slapping a polished wooden ruler against the open palm of his hand.

Sasha immediately had to clamp her hand over her mouth in order to stifle a wild impulse to giggle. Surely not! she thought, as she pressed closer to the wall outside Valerie's office, desperate not to be seen. She knew Paul was a little on the kinky side, she could tell that from his excited response when she'd blindfolded him and teased him with the ice-cube, but she had always imagined him as far too elegant and impeccably mannered to engage in this sort of silly role-playing. But was it really that silly? Sasha bit her lip and leant in a little closer, craning her neck to get a better view.

'Who was the naughty girl who lied to her staff about the computer contractor's schedule?' Paul asked sternly, the ruler raised, ready to strike. 'Who re-arranged the date of the installation herself just so she could clear out the entire floor in order to begin her course of instruction in the proper means of discipline?'

'I did, sir!' Valerie squeaked out happily, waggling her buttocks suggestively, trying to attract his attention, as though Paul's eyes weren't already glued to the sight of that ripe and juicy peach-like backside.

'Who, in fact, invited me over early, illicitly and in secret, so we could establish our tuition as soon as possible?' Paul demanded, continuing to brandish the ruler.

'I did, sir, me, oh, it was I who did!' cried Valerie, trying vainly to thrust her buttocks out further, and, or so it seemed to Sasha, rubbing the front of her mound lasciviously against the desk as she did so.

'And who specifically requested that her chastise-ment be carried out in her place of business, so that the scene of her greatest power is also that of her most abject humiliation?' Paul intoned dramatically, though not particularly threateningly, Sasha thought. Valerie was never abject, nor was she ever humble, and this foolish game with bondage and rulers wasn't about to make her so. Still, there was no question that Sasha's boss was aroused by the playing-out of this perverse scenario: her legs quivered above the spiked pink heels she wore, her head thrashed restlessly from side to side, and she seemed to be trying to spread her legs wider as she desperately sought relief against the desk for her spiralling sexual arousal.

'Oh, sir!' Valerie cried out, trying to turn her head over her shoulder so she could look Paul in the face. 'Do chastise me now, so that I may be humbled for my sins of arrogance, deception and moral turpitude!'

Thwack! went the ruler, and Sasha jumped a little at the sound, then stepped as close to the inside of the office as she dared in an effort to observe the effects of that smack.

Why, that was hardly anything! she thought scornfully, as Valerie picked up her head and howled, more for effect than anything else, Sasha decided. Stop being such a baby! Smack! went the ruler again, but even from where she was standing, Sasha could tell that the sound was more dramatic than the contact it actually made with the woman's flesh. It must surely sting, but she doubted that Paul was striking Valerie with any real force, and it was clear that this game was not about pain or domination, but more about fantasy, about risk-taking, and about the ritual enactment of alternative personas. Sasha knew that her boss wouldn't stand for one minute to be hurt or humiliated for real; if anything, as Paul had hinted, she was just seeking a reversal of her usual accustomed position of power. Indeed, if it was indeed Valerie who had first suggested that they try a little fantasy play, or what Sasha was beginning to think of as SM Lite, then, although it was Valerie who was being bound and struck, it was, after all, her own idea: so who was really the one in charge?

Anyway, it seemed as though Valerie was getting tired of the game, for she began to struggle more determinedly against her bonds, and looked as though she was returning to her usual imperious self.

'Help me out of these, please,' she now said rather brusquely to Paul, who immediately dropped the ruler on the floor and complied. Once he had released her from her bonds, which were, Sasha now saw with amusement, old and worn-out computer printer ribbons, Valerie turned over and perched herself on her desk, rubbing at her wrists before hitching her skirt up even higher over her hips.

'Come here, you big, strong man,' she said with a throaty chuckle, spreading her legs lewdly apart and leaning back on her hands which were braced on top of her desk. 'Come here and let me give you your reward for being such a good master.'

Feeling slightly nauseous – this was, after all, her boss and her ex-lover – but unable to look away, Sasha watched in revolted fascination as Paul jerked off his suit jacket and tie, tossing them aside with a casual disregard for fine fabric that Sasha found more shocking than his expertise with the ruler. He wrenched at the buttons on his shirt, his gaze fixed all the while on Valerie's panting bosom, pushed together and up by her bra, and at the tangle of dewy curls which fringed the scarlet complexities of her sex. With a final kick at his shoes and a hasty strip-off of his trousers and shorts, stopping only to extract a condom from his wallet, Paul stood completely naked in the centre of Valerie's well-appointed, ultra-professional office, a totally incongruous and yet oddly thrilling contradiction. Sasha felt her own sex begin to heat and flow as she watched Paul come to stand before Valerie, who was poised on top of her desk, and the two stared at each other in silence, the traces of their mutual desire clearly evident in their expressions.

Now unwillingly aroused herself, Sasha pressed closer to the door and watched in breathless expectation as Paul dropped to his knees on the floor before Valerie and covered the lips of her sex with his mouth, splaying her legs even further apart with his hands and passing his tongue in slow, regular strokes up

131

and down the length of that clenching mound. With a low purr of satisfaction, Valerie lay back on her desk, the luxurious fall of her glossy black hair sweeping over the end, and scooped her breasts up and out of her bra, teasing and tugging at her stiff brown nipples with her long tapered nails. Sasha gazed almost in envy at the sight of her boss, decadently displayed on her desk, her fingers busy at her breasts while Paul was busy below at her sex. This was no play-acting now to which Sasha was an enthralled witness: this was real physical pleasure, and she thought she could even glimpse the shining end of Valerie's clitoris as Paul drew back for a moment, combing through the clutch of ebony curls before clamping his mouth firmly over that surely by now ecstatic little bud. Valerie's cries of rapture had only just started to ring out, however, when Paul swiftly rose to his feet and hurriedly pulled on a condom before deftly turning her back on to her stomach, into a similar position to that she'd been enjoying before, except that this time she wrapped her legs around his strong, lean thighs with a dexterity that surprised Sasha. Surely that position must be uncomfortable, she pondered, noting with almost clinical detachment how Valerie's legs twined around Paul's, her feet meeting between his thighs and her knees bent outward, pressing her clitoris against the top of the desk.

Unable to stop herself, while all the time acutely aware of the ludicrous impropriety of the scene, Sasha reached her own hand down under the snug elastic band of her control-top tights and slid her fingers over the soft froth of hair that guarded the apex of her mound. Biting her lips to keep back her cry of pleasure, she sought out the dew-heavy lips of her sex and gently, lightly, teasing herself with the briefest of brushes, she began to stroke her velvety folds, her eyes still glued to the happenings inside Valerie's office. Placed as she was just outside the door, Sasha was in a perfect position to witness the full back-and-forth movements of Paul's hips as he drove repeatedly in and out of that pleasured space between Valerie's thighs. His arms were braced far forward on the desk, his hands flat, his elbows bent, and his strong shoulders corded with muscle as he leant into the woman whose sex he was probing with rhythmic, lengthy thrusts. Valerie herself appeared to be in heaven: her eyes were squeezed shut, her head nearly hanging off the desk as she held on desperately to the outer edges, writhing and twisting beneath Paul as she ground her clitoris into the hard wooden surface. Even as Sasha's own fingers stole deeper and deeper into the hot depths of her vagina, and the penetrative bliss began to overtake her, she wished she had a camera handy just now: who knew what benefits she might have been able to reap? Just the thought of such a deliciously naughty scheme caused her to clench around her pumping fingers, and her orgasm seemed to coincide with that of her boss, who was squealing and squirming with exaggerated force, her stomach and hips bucking against the desk. Paul's buttocks were tensing and hollowing with his strenuous, driving rhythm as he, too, sought his peak. One climax didn't seem to be enough for Valerie, though, if her cries were anything to go by, for she was now apparently on her way towards a second, then a third, and long after Sasha's own internal vibrations had ceased and she had neatly rearranged herself, she continued to marvel at her boss's seemingly insatiable appetite. Paul's abrupt ejaculation and withdrawal, however, soon put a stop to Valerie's heaving pleasure, and when she finally turned over to sit upright on her desk, tossing her hair out of her face and delicately crossing her ankles, she appeared both sensually replete and ludicrously prim.

It was at that moment that Sasha chose to make her entrance. Paul, still standing nude before Valerie, was in the act of stripping off his condom, and Valerie herself was swinging her legs girlishly against her desk, fussing with her bra as she struggled to replace her full and glowing breasts into their cups.

'So,' Sasha said casually, leaning against the doorway and smiling full in the face of her hapless, startled boss, 'what was that you were saying about approving my leave of absence?' Flicking her eyes towards her ex-lover, Sasha said cheerily, 'Nice technique with that ruler, Paul: I never knew you had it in you.' She then looked back at her boss, who seemed oddly frozen: her fingers were still wrapped around her breast, her skirt hitched up around her waist, and her feet swinging against the desk.

'Well,' Sasha said brightly, as she turned to go, 'I guess I'll see the two of you first thing tomorrow morning. I trust that everyone's computers will by then be bug-free and ready for business as usual?'

Valerie had finally remembered to let go of her breast and stop swinging her feet, but was still gasping in shock as Sasha added, 'So I will be leaving for my vacation on Friday at five o'clock, Val, and don't expect me back for another two weeks.' Then she turned and nearly ran down the corridor, choking back her laughter until she had safely left the building and was standing outside in the warm September sun.

Chapter Eight

Sasha arranged herself more comfortably in her business-class aeroplane seat, waiting impatiently for take-off, and repeated her anxiety list to herself one more time. She'd wrapped up her work at ALM as securely as she could, leaving detailed instructions for her co-workers about projects left incomplete, client worksheets awaiting last-minute alterations, and notices about confirmation calls she was expecting from store buyers, as well as distributors who had to be chased up. She closed her eyes and sighed in exasperation, remembering the horrified expressions of dismay her colleagues had uttered on hearing she was taking her unannounced leave of absence. She was only going to be gone for two weeks, for God's sake! Surely the office could manage without her for such a short space of time!

She snickered quietly to herself as she relived yet again that triumphant moment when she'd coolly informed her boss that she was taking off, and pictured again that delightful expression on both Valerie's and Paul's faces – part outrage, part shame –

when she'd made her presence in the doorway of Valerie's office known. Well, she decided now, allowing herself one final chuckle at Valerie's expense, she refused to think any more about work until she returned to New York.

She continued with her mental itinerary of tasks she'd ticked off before leaving for the airport earlier that day. She had notified her cleaners, her mail had been stopped, her answering machine switched on, and she'd left Xenia the number of her travel agent, her flight information, and, most importantly, the address of the Asher Hotel in London. Nervously, Sasha fingered the memo which confirmed her booking arrangements at the hotel, faxed over from London late last Friday afternoon. It had taken her a few days to gather her courage in order to make that call; for some reason she refused to pursue, Sasha was reluctant to involve anyone from ALM in her travel plans, even though the obvious course of action would have been to ask Heather to make the arrangements for her. It didn't occur to her to ask her travel agent, the other obvious person to make the call; instead, Sasha felt it incumbent upon herself to book her own room at the Asher Hotel, but she had resisted the imperative for several days, partly because she was still a little astonished at her own daring in deciding to return to the source of the ghostly mystery that had been haunting her for so long. The other reason she had held back from making the call was out of a perverse sense of pleasure in delaying the delicious anticipation to which she constantly thrilled, waking up several times a night to fantasise about what she might discover once she set her feet back on English soil. For the last week or so, ever since Sasha had so deviously secured the approval of her boss for her leave of absence, she had felt her whole body hum with the vibrations of some kind of supernatural erotic impulse, and she felt closer to the spirits of Amelia Asher and John Blakeley than she ever had before.

As the Boeing 747 finally began its slow ascent into the heavens, the tremors of the heaving engines seeming to match the agitated vibrations within Sasha's belly, she stared unseeing out of the window and reflected on the sense of inevitability she felt about this journey. She felt as though this trip to England held a kind of symbolic resonance on a greater scale than a mere holiday trip: rather, Sasha felt that she was returning to an experience of a long-distant past, and that she would be relocating that past within her personal present. She considered retrieving Amelia's manuscript from the depths of her carry-on bag safely stowed beneath her seat to hold on to as some kind of talisman, but quickly rejected the idea, afraid to expose the fragile leaves to the claustrophobic atmosphere of the aeroplane. She had debated whether she should bring the journal with her at all, and shuddered at the thought of somehow leaving it behind in the airport or losing it in some way, but in the end she couldn't bear to leave it sitting forlornly in her apartment while she was away. It felt oddly right to Sasha that she should bring the manuscript along with her, since it certainly seemed so connected to the ghost of Lady Amelia, but she decided it was best for the moment to leave it in her bag. So, clutching instead the confirmation sheet from the Asher Hotel, Sasha leant her head against the window and gazed out at the evening sky as the aeroplane soared up above the inky-blue clouds, and she let her mind drift in fantasies about what might be awaiting her in England.

She must have dozed off almost immediately, for Sasha was rudely jolted awake by the cabin staff switching on the harsh yellow lighting and offering trays of warm cranberry muffins, fresh fruit salad, and steaming cups of coffee. The sky outside the aeroplane window was the peach and rose-streaked colour of early dawn, and with a flutter of excitement she heard the pilot's voice informing the passengers that they were due to land in less than two hours. As she impatiently counted the minutes, far too nervous to read, listen to music or watch any of the range of programmes offered on the minuscule television set mounted on the armrest of her seat, she tried to decide what she should do first once she'd checked in and unpacked at the hotel. For the problem was that she hadn't yet decided exactly what it was she should *do* once she'd arrived; she had no fixed plan of action, only a vague idea of wandering about the hotel, searching for clues – though as to exactly what she was looking for, she wasn't sure either.

It was this problem which preoccupied Sasha throughout the tedious process of disembarking from the plane, queuing at passport control, and waiting for her baggage by the carousel before finally registering for her hired car at the airport. She wasn't at all sure about how she would negotiate driving on the wrong side of the road, shifting with her left hand, and working out all the unfamiliar English road signs and what seemed to her perverse and dangerous rules of the road. However, after a few false starts and driving round the exit roundabout repeatedly before finally finding a way to turn off, she was quite pleased to discover that she wasn't yet ready to end up as a road-accident statistic, and that London drivers, rude as they were, generally chose to stay in their lanes and seemed pretty much to know what they were doing.

Sasha's self-satisfaction at her new-found ability to find her way along English roads rapidly evaporated, however, when she finally pulled up outside the

Asher Hotel a little after ten o'clock in the morning, and as she handed over her car keys to the smiling, morning-coated valet, she gazed up at the edifice before her and wondered why she'd never before appreciated the imposing Gothic style of the hotel. Even in the early daytime, the building was impressive: constructed out of dark grey stone, the front of the hotel looked remarkably ancient, with its sinister-looking crenellated turrets high up on the third floor. Sasha noticed, too, the distinctive design of the windows, some arched, some pointed, around which twined dark green ropes of ivy, and she gazed at the leaded panes of glass set in metal and stone. The remains of a portcullis hung, poised, over the gateway at the entrance, as though threatening to cut off entry to enemies. As Sasha dug out a crumpled five-pound note to tip the valet who carried her bags, she noticed another feature of the hotel which had apparently passed her by on her first visit to London: several of the battlements at the top of the building were peopled by curious-looking gargoyles, and she strained her neck upward to get a better look at the cunningly carved, certainly grotesque but also oddly endearing little creatures made of stone. She could just about make out a pointed ear here, a bulbous nose there, and one or two spiked tails, before she was courteously directed inside by the smiling valet who was heavily burdened with the weight of Sasha's overstuffed cases.

As Sasha entered the large and lavish reception area of the hotel, marvelling at all the finer points of detail she'd completely missed on her first visit here, she quivered with excitement at the thought of what other surprises might be awaiting her. She handed over her gold credit card in exchange for the key to her room, which was, as she'd requested, room 323, the chamber once occupied by Amelia Asher. Sasha felt an inexplicable thrill when the handsome young receptionist passed over the computerised card and said, smiling enigmatically, 'We've been expecting you, Ms Hayward. Welcome back.' She then made her way to the elevator behind the valet still carrying her luggage; she had hoped to catch a glimpse of Claire, the young woman who had first introduced her to Lady Amelia, but saw no sign of her. She entered the lift as though greeting an old friend, smiling in pleased recognition at the sight of the four volumes of *The Mysteries of Udolpho*, and ignoring the puzzled glance of the valet.

When at last she was shown to her room, her suitcases deposited on the window-seat in the corner and the valet duly tipped and taken leave of, Sasha jumped on to the bed and threw herself down happily, feeling not just as though she was now liberated from the commodity-driven and profit-motivated drudgery of the marketing world, but also as if she had, in some unexplainable way, come home. She debated with herself as to whether she should try to find her way back to Amelia's portrait by herself or wait for Claire to appear and guide her, but then decided to put off that particular pleasure for a while in return for the bliss of several hours' sleep in a lavishly sheeted and delicately scented bed. She stretched languorously, then rose and began to shed her clothes, anticipating the feel of those crisp, cool sheets against her naked skin; despite the criminally high expense of a business-class ticket, her rest in the airline seat had really been no more comfortable than a brief snooze in her desk chair at work. As she snuggled down amongst the soft pillows and luxurious counterpane on her bed, Sasha's last thought before sleep came was whether she'd recover from her jet lag sufficiently by supper-time to venture an excursion into the lawns and gardens at the back of the hotel, and find out whether Amelia's and Johnny's rose garden still existed, as well as the ha-ha in which Amelia had first discovered the joys of fleshly love.

When Sasha woke with a start, it was to discover that she had slept for nearly six hours; although it was still only late September, by four o'clock the sun had retreated quite noticeably from the sky, which was now overcast and darkening rapidly. As Sasha stumbled out of bed, aiming for the shower, a gnawing hunger intruded upon the fluttering in her stomach, and, with a shrug, she decided that a shower could wait: first she had to eat. Quickly, she pulled back on her travelling uniform of leggings and sweatshirt, shuddering a little in distaste at how grimy she was, and decided to simply pop downstairs to the bar and carry some sandwiches back up to her room. She could, of course, call down for room service, but she wanted to see whether she could find Claire.

She returned to her room shortly after, still having not seen Claire but bearing a tray laden with ham and cheese sandwiches, biscuits, fruit, and tea, and stopped in sudden bewilderment. How odd, she thought to herself in equal parts of surprise, eagerness, and anxiety. Where did this come from? Who on earth has been in my room? For although she had only been gone ten minutes, her bed was neatly made up, the curtains drawn, a lamp was burning brightly on the side table, and there was a white oblong box on her bed, graced on top by a propped-up envelope with her name spelt out in elegant, elaborate calligraphy.

In a daze, Sasha set down her tray and came forward to stare in befuddled stupidity at the envelope and box on her bed. It's happening! she thought in confused excitement as she reached out for the envelope. I knew I was right to come back here! I knew something like this would have to happen! She ran her finger over the slightly raised letters, the ink heavy and dark, and noticed the second 's' in her name looked a little like an 'f', as though written in an eighteenth-century hand. With shaking fingers, she unsealed the fold of the envelope and drew out a single, heavy, cream-coloured card, on which were written the following words in the same calligraphic style: 'You Are Invited to Attend the Michaelmas Ball at the Asher Estate, To Begin at Eight O'Clock in the Grand Ballroom. The Usual Rules of Fancy Dress to Apply.'

'Usual rules of fancy dress'? What the hell does that mean? Sasha wondered, but she knew that part of the answer must lie in the contents of the big white box. Hesitantly, with trembling fingers and shaking heart, she lifted the cover off the big box and reached through the rustling tissue-paper inside, shutting her eyes as her fingers closed upon the richest, softest, most sumptuous velvet she'd ever encountered. With a gasp of wonder Sasha opened her eyes, and nearly fainted when she beheld the dress in her arms. The deep lustrous rose of the fabric, the intricate lace ruching at the neckline and sleeves, the texture of the material, and the satin sash at the waist all identified this dress as a copy of the very same that Amelia Asher wore in her portrait in the back staircase of the hotel. Sasha held the exquisite gown to her face for a moment, stroking the plush velvet and breathing in its faint fragrance of lavender before reluctantly laying it tenderly on the bed and dipping back into the box to discover what other treasures it contained. There was a complete set of lingerie, though clearly not in the eighteenth-century mode: she pulled out a red velvet basque, the structured, boned bodice promising a greater uplift to her bosom than she had ever before

142

enjoyed, and the corseting at the back suggesting a loving attention to the curves of her waist and hips. The box contained no underwear, though Sasha searched everywhere: not even a thong bikini or similar tiny scrap of fabric, but she did discover a luxurious pair of elbow-length white satin gloves, a jet-black suspender-belt made of the finest, softest webbing of lace, and shockingly scarlet stockings, the tops of which were embroidered with an intricate pattern worked with what looked like little circles of rubies. Shoes, too, Sasha discovered in the box: buckled silver beauties with high-stacked heels, which sparkled like sequins. The only other item the box contained – besides a ribbon for her hair and a ridiculously small scrap of lace, presumably a lady's hankie – was a cats-eyed black velvet mask, fashioned on a stick and intended to cover the upper part of the face only. Experimentally, Sasha held the mask in front of her face and peered into the mirror; deciding that she looked not at all mysterious, only a little silly, she tossed it back on to the bed, resolving only to carry the thing in her hand for show, since to continually hold it in front of her face would be irksome in the extreme.

Well! Sasha sat on the bed and blinked hard. She certainly hadn't expected a mysterious invitation and a gorgeous costume as well, though she couldn't help wondering to whom the dress really belonged, and whether she would mind Sasha borrowing it for the night. She also hoped the clothes would fit; if not, would the hotel supply a ghostly tailor? She clapped a hand to her mouth in an effort to stifle an hysterical bout of giggles: this whole episode just seemed too far-fetched! Not at all hungry now, she forced herself to nibble on a juicy red pear, while she considered whether she would really have the nerve to put the clothes on and pull the charade off. What a terrifying idea! she thought, picturing herself moving mutely through a sea of costumed strangers, all of whom knew each other already and were dancing and chatting in elegant intimacy, while she wandered about, among them, but not one of them. Then Sasha glanced at herself in the mirror, and smiled. Terrifying, yes, but also an adventure of the kind which she might never see again. Why not dress up and join the ball? How could she possibly refuse?

Sasha was just towelling her hair dry as she stepped out of the shower an hour or so later when there was a slight tap at the door, and a familiar woman's voice quietly enquired, 'Are you ready for me now, Miss?'

Puzzled, but somehow not really surprised, Sasha pulled her robe tightly around her and edged the door open, to see standing before her the shining face of Claire, the hotel worker she'd been hoping to find all day. 'It's you!' Sasha cried happily, so pleased to see her that she nearly threw her arms around the girl to give her a hug, but stopped herself just in time.

'It's nice to see you again, Miss.' Claire smiled shyly, then said, 'I've come to do your hair.' She indicated her trolley of brushes, dryers, rollers and the like, and added, 'You're the next guest on my list.'

Sasha stared at her for a moment, taking in Claire's black lady's-maid costume, and felt just a little bit uncomfortable. 'What list?' she asked. 'Who invited me to this ball, and where did that dress come from?' She pointed to the bed, but Claire merely shook her head and put her finger to her lips.

'Sssh.' Gently but firmly, Claire pushed down on Sasha's shoulders, urging her into the chair in front of her dressing-table and skilfully beginning to brush through the heavy wet strands of her hair. She said, in a conversational tone, as though Sasha had never asked a question, 'Most of the guests are wearing wigs, but you have such beautiful brown hair, I thought you might just want it dressed up a bit.'

'Won't you at least tell me who else is invited?' Sasha asked, but at Claire's gentle smile and repeated shake of her head, she gave up and closed her eyes, trying to shut out all thought and simply revel in the feel of the girl's slim fingers massaging her temples and scalp, increasing the flow of circulation and leaving Sasha feeling blissfully relaxed and also, perhaps not surprisingly, a little aroused. In fact, as Claire dried, rolled and set her hair, Sasha found herself lulled into a kind of sensual daydream, imagining the textures of the silk and velvet of the stockings and basque against her skin, and fantasising about how it would feel to walk among a roomful of strangers wearing no panties. After all, she thought dreamily, as Claire loosened the rollers from her hair, drawers weren't even invented until the Victorian era.

'There,' Claire said in a satisfied tone, 'you're all finished. Open your eyes and have a look.'

Sasha did, and hardly recognised her own head of hair. Her usually straight, full mane had been expertly coiled into shining ringlets artfully piled all over her head, with a few tendrils pulled free to curl fetchingly around her face and throat. Claire had even threaded the red velvet ribbon through Sasha's elaborate hairdo, just as it appeared in the golden curls in Amelia Asher's portrait. Tentatively, Sasha reached up a hand to touch the glossy rolls on her head, but Claire smiled reprovingly as she packed up her styling things and made for the door. 'Be careful,' she said, one hand on the doorknob. 'Choose your positions well, or all those lovely curls will be ruined. I've pinned and lacquered them as securely as I could, but mind how you hold your head.' And, with this rather baffling advice, she was about to leave the room when Sasha stood up – a little unsteadily, unused to the weight on her head – and pleaded, 'Wait! I can't get into those things by myself!' She pointed unhappily to the basque and dress lying spread out on the bed, and, with a nod of her head, Claire came forward.

'OK,' she said comfortingly, 'I'll help you get dressed.'

Sasha only deliberated for a moment before she dropped her robe and strode, business-like though stark naked, over to the bed. 'I have no idea how this thing works,' she confided, struggling with the fastenings on the basque until Claire, clucking softly to herself, swiftly unclasped the hooks and gently eased the structured shape around Sasha's body, shifting and settling the thing until Sasha's breasts, belly and hips were comfortably enclosed in the rich red velvet.

'Bend over a little,' Claire whispered encouragingly, and Sasha obliged, shivering a little with shocked delight when Claire's fingers – accidentally? Or not? – brushed over the softness of her bare buttocks. Expertly Claire drew on the strings at the back, while Sasha exclaimed, 'Not too tight, please! I don't like constriction.'

'Of course not,' Claire said soothingly, and drew on the strings again until Sasha could feel the edges of the basque closing together, and she felt another rush of arousal at the tight velvet embrace. Her sense of erotic anticipation was heightened still further when Claire unexpectedly reached around and slipped her hands inside the front of the garment, closing her fingers around Sasha's breasts and lightly caressing the puckered pink nipples inside as she lifted up the creamy curves, so that Sasha was now the proud owner of a truly impressive, deeply shadowed cleavage.

'And now for the stockings,' Claire announced,

withdrawing her hands and kneeling at Sasha's feet to help her ease the lengths of silk up her legs. Sasha felt a momentary twinge of embarrassment, as Claire's head was nearly level with her naked sex, and she stammered, 'Perhaps I should put on some underwear,' but, with a small shake of her head, Claire laid a long finger along the dewy softness of Sasha's lower lips and gently stroked back and forth along the glossy channel. 'Don't be silly,' she murmured, and, reaching up, she trailed a sweet wet path with her tongue along the grooves of Sasha's rapidly moistening sex.

Startled, Sasha moved hurriedly back against the bed, shy and unsure about how to react. She desperately wanted to feel more of the girl's mouth on her; she wanted to spread her thighs wide apart and open herself with her fingers, inviting the young woman's kiss right up inside the heart of her sex. Her clitoris ached to be sucked, the protective hood of flesh pulling away to reveal the eager little bud seeking the urgent pleasure of lips and tongue. But she was also a little uncomfortable about demanding sexual services from a woman she barely knew, and she wasn't about to return the favour. So instead she reached for the other stocking, busying herself with attaching it to her suspender-belt and trying desperately to appear casual.

'That's OK,' Claire said laughingly, helping Sasha into the dress and easing the heavy material up around her body. 'You want to be pleasantly aroused when you go into the ball, not already satiated and fulfilled.'

Sasha arched a brow at her as Claire adjusted the lace ruching around Sasha's shoulders and throat. What was she talking about? But Claire merely shrugged, as though Sasha had spoken the question aloud. She rapidly fastened the mysterious workings at the back of the dress, then silently stepped back and handed Sasha her shoes.

'Can't you stay while I put on my make-up and come to the ball with me?' Sasha asked the girl pleadingly, but Claire, looking a little regretful, shook her head and made her way to the door. 'You look lovely,' was all she said, and Sasha, looking in the mirror, knew she spoke truthfully. Claire looked at her again, then said, turning the knob on the door, 'Don't worry, Miss: you'll soon see me at the ball.' Then she touched her fingers to her lips, blew a kiss goodbye to Sasha, and trundled her trolley out of the room, shutting the door behind her.

Sasha slipped on her shoes, noting with delight that, like everything else, they seemed to fit perfectly, then seated herself again at the dressing-table and began to apply her make-up. She hoped she wouldn't be expected to wear lashings of white powder and several well-placed patches to resemble beauty marks, as she had seen in period dramas and read about in books; instead, she went through her usual ritual of matte foundation, blusher, eyeliner and lipstick, though she applied it all with a heavier hand than usual, opting for more drama and heightened colour, and she even daringly stroked her blusher brush along the deep swells of her breasts. When she had finished, she stepped back to admire her unfamiliar image: her hair, dress and theatrical make-up all added to her sense of dreamlike unreality, as if she couldn't really believe this was happening to her. As she pulled on the opulent white gloves, Sasha smiled ruefully at her reflected image, wondering what it was she was getting herself into. Then, with a determined lift of her shoulders, she tucked her teensy handkerchief into the cleft of her now-substantial cleavage, picked up her mask, opened the door to her room and stepped out into the corridor, preparing herself to join the party.

Chapter Nine

*T*he hall was eerily silent as Sasha clacked her way nervously towards the lift, the shoes not fitting quite as perfectly as she'd initially thought. The dress, too, was more cumbersome to wear than she had suspected: the heavy velvet trailed along the floor behind her, though the front of the gown ended just above her ankles, so that her pretty silver shoes could clearly be seen. Sasha plucked anxiously at the constricting basque through her dress, wondering uneasily who the clothes really belonged to, and whether their owner would approve of their temporary wearer. Now that she thought about it, Sasha was glad she hadn't found any underwear in that big white box, and she certainly wouldn't have worn any if there had been: the thought of laying another woman's intimate garments against her own private parts gave her a little twinge of discomfort – as well as, she was surprised to admit, a more pronounced twinge of arousal. That brief moment in her room when Claire had pressed her tongue along the moist crevice of Sasha's sex had left her with an after-thrill of sensual

149

delight, but before she had time to pursue that puzzling thought any further, with a clang and a whirr, the lift arrived, though Sasha had pressed no buttons to summon it.

As she stepped into the open embrace of the elevator, Sasha wondered whether, in some curious way, the lift remembered her: ever since her arrival at the Asher Hotel that morning, the building had seemed, in some uncanny and inexplicable way, almost sentient, nearly alive. Indeed, as the doors slowly wound shut and the lift made its gradual descent, again without any directions from Sasha, she saw with a smile that an elegant crystal flute of champagne sat fizzing lightly away on the bookshelf, just below the mirror on the wall. She saw also that there was a card placed in front of the glass which was written in the same hand that had inscribed her invitation, and she stared at the two simple words of greeting: Welcome back.

Sasha sipped gratefully at the delicate drink, shivering a little in pleasure as the gentle bubbles slipped smoothly down her throat. She had nearly emptied the glass when the lift ground to a halt, the doors slowly wound back, and she found herself facing the entrance to a dimly lit though sumptuously appointed corridor on a basement floor that she hadn't even known existed in the hotel. Puzzled, she glanced at the panel of buttons on the wall inside the lift; none were lit up, which made the situation even more disturbing. Cautiously, she made her way out of the lift, clutching tightly to the mask she now thought best to hold in front of her face, the heavy velvet of her dress rustling loudly along the floor as it trailed behind her. Nervously, Sasha dawdled down the pale pink carpet towards a half-opened set of gilt-trimmed white double doors which ended the long narrow passage. As the lift quietly closed behind her and made its way back up, Sasha glanced from side to side at the high white walls around her, adorned with perfectly aligned rows of oil-painted portraits depicting a variety of ancient-looking personages, none of whom Sasha recognised. There seemed to be no electric lighting in the hallway, but there were many candles held in elaborately constructed sconces, their flickering light partially illuminating and partially shadowing the aristocratic faces on the walls. As Sasha neared the heavy double doors, drawn by the golden light spilling through the gap between them, she could hear the strains of a string quartet competing with a ceaseless stream of chatter and laughter, though she could discern no identifiable voices or words.

When she had finally reached the doors, and could go no further unless she went in or turned back to the lift, Sasha shut her eyes tightly behind her black mask, gripped a door-handle in one gloved and sweating palm, and pulled it slowly towards her, just enough to allow her to slip inside, expecting to hear her name boomed out into the crowded room.

Disappointed, she opened her eyes behind her mask, then pulled it entirely away from her face, as no one seemed to notice her at all. She gazed around in wonder at the huge, beautiful ballroom, hardly knowing where to look first, so struck was she by the impressive visual impact of this mysterious Michaelmas Ball.

The room looked like the set of a costume drama: there were enormous chandeliers hanging from the ceiling, which were bedecked with a multitude of glittering white candles. The ceiling itself was an elaborately domed affair, ostentatiously adorned with gilt trimmings and odd little rococo embellishments: intricately carved fretwork, artificial clusters of flowers

and fruit, smiling cherubs, and densely hued mytho-
logical scenes. The walls, too, were hung with richly
coloured tapestries and paintings depicting a bewil-
dering variety of naked bodies – women's, men's, and
some of indeterminate gender – all cavorting about in
an endless and ingenious series of anatomical impos-
sibilities. And the guests themselves! Sasha scuttled
over to stand beneath the dangling genitals of a marble statue of some incredibly handsome, incredibly
naked man or god – Mercury, perhaps? – who stood
braced in the upper corner of the room, as though
supporting the weight of the ceiling on his carved
shoulders. Sasha wedged herself tightly into the corner and stared at the most astonishing collection of
individuals she had ever observed in her life. There
were powdered and bewigged ladies and gentlemen
who seemed to be dressed in clothes of the same era
as she: breeches, buckled shoes, patches, silk stockings
and cleavages seemed to dominate the room, as well
as other curious styles of dress she couldn't easily
identify. Certainly the costumes weren't confined to
the style of the eighteenth century: there were flappers
from the 1920s, Victorian gentlemen in mutton-chops
and top-hats, Roman gladiators with menacingly
clanking swords at their sides, medieval ladies in
impressively beaded gowns, and even, Sasha was
surprised to see, some nuns and priests drifting about,
their long black robes flapping against the more ornamental costumes of their fellow guests. Sasha also
noted that, like herself, not all of the guests had chosen
to wear their masks, though many who had opted for
the disguise had hidden their features behind ornate
and unearthly facades: some animal, such as owls and
bats, some human, including harlequins and clowns,
and some altogether unnerving – what looked to
Sasha like demons, devils, and fiends, as well as some

resembling the gargoyles who were perched atop the battlements outside.

Emboldened by everyone else's apparent uninterest in her, Sasha ventured a little farther into the party, observing the coiffed and sweating quartet players who were sawing vigorously away at their instruments, and she admired the grace and immaculate timing of the few guests who were performing the complicated patterns of the quadrille in time to the music. She could also see little clumps of guests clustered around several heavily laden buffet tables, and, mindful of the fact that she hadn't eaten in several hours, Sasha stepped closer to get a better look at the food. There were huge platters of ducks, geese, chickens, and some other kinds of fowl she couldn't readily identify, as well as curious-looking cuts of meat which didn't look at all appetising; nor did the entire suckling pig, complete with apple in its mouth, whose carcass a white-coated chef was busily carving up. There were candied fruits, mounds of odd-looking vegetables, tureens of soups, and heaps of rolls and intricately plaited loaves of bread, as well as piles of delicate-looking confections, pastries, and sweetmeats of all kinds. There was so much food, in fact, of types both familiar and foreign to Sasha's dazzled eyes, that she felt no longer hungry at all, but rather quite ill. Indeed, some of the guests – particularly those dressed in the costumes of much earlier times – were eating in a manner that to Sasha seemed positively revolting; they were standing up and cramming in food with their fingers, deliberately eschewing the valuable-looking silverware, and some were even feeding tidbits to tiny dogs, birds, cats and other animals they were carrying tucked into their sides.

Whew! This was stranger than any Halloween party Sasha had ever been to, and she'd been to some pretty wild ones. Intrigued, enthralled, excited, and a little overwhelmed, she moved about the room, weaving her way among the guests, who paid absolutely no attention to her, not out of rudeness, she surmised, but simply because there were so many other people worth attending to.

As Sasha moved farther into the room, she also began to notice little curtained-off alcoves set into the far walls, and various suggestive sounds could be heard emanating from some of them. Indeed, she noticed small groups of people clustered around some of these private little areas, and, with her stomach fluttering violently, she picked up her skirts and moved closer to join a fascinated pair of women, elegantly clad in Grecian dress, who were clutching each other as they peered intently into an alcove whose black velvet curtains had been partially pushed aside.

The two women barely looked at Sasha as she sidled over to join them, but they did move away slightly, enough to allow her a fraction of space so that she too could peer into the curtained-off cubicle.

Now this was a sight to be seen! Sasha caught her breath and nearly dropped her mask. She stood alongside the two women and gazed at the pair of naked lovers embracing on the floor, apparently blissfully oblivious to their audience, writhing against each other with exquisite sensuality. Both performers were women, and they had their heads between each other's thighs, their mouths on each other's sex, with their tongues working in unison as they licked each other to climax. One woman lay on her back, her face only barely visible, as it was buried in the glistening pink mound pressed against her face; Sasha had a better view of the face of the woman on top as she braced herself on her hands and knees above the prone body of her lover. The woman's eyes were closed in what Sasha assumed was sexual ecstasy, as she kissed her way along the juicy pink folds clearly exposed to view. Then, just as her partner on the bottom started to tremble as though on the verge of a powerful orgasm, the woman on top drew back and slithered off the body of her friend, reaching around for something Sasha couldn't see behind the black velvet curtain. Then, with a smile at her partner, the woman produced quite the oddest looking instrument Sasha had ever seen. She had no trouble guessing its function, however, as the shiny leather straps, the double sets of buckles, and the two alarmingly large protuberances identified it as a double-headed dildo. Fascinated, aroused, and a little repelled, Sasha moved even closer to the little room, avidly watching the two women as they eagerly strapped the device around their waists and positioned themselves so that they sat facing each other, their legs open and outstretched, the one woman's legs enclosing the other's as they aimed the artificial phalluses into their no-doubt pulsating vaginas.

Once both prongs had been duly inserted, the women were seated even closer together than before, so that their clitorises rubbed against each other as both women began to grind themselves on and off their dildoes. They wrapped their arms around one another, kissing each other rapturously and undulating against each other as they rose and fell in perfect harmony, drawing themselves up and down the glistening artificial shafts. Then the woman whose legs were enclosed by the other's urged herself backward, still clinging to her lover, so that they lay again on the floor, the one atop the other, their breasts pressed together and their two mounds working urgently against the doubled pleasures of phallus and flesh: sex

155

against sex, clitoris against clitoris, woman against woman.

Whew! Sasha needed a break from this decadent scenario of lust, and she was just about to move away and leave them to it when the woman on top lifted her head and – quite deliberately, it seemed – looked Sasha full in the face. Sasha blinked and took an involuntary step backward, her eyes wide with the thrill and shock as the woman, never ceasing her friction against her partner, winked at Sasha and slowly, lasciviously, ran her tongue along her upper lip, shifting her gaze downward to the hidden area of Sasha's sex, naked but concealed beneath her dress.

The message was unmistakable, and not one to which Sasha felt equipped to respond. Hastily, she turned away and walked unsteadily back towards the centre of the room, towards the mass of people and the food, trying desperately to ignore the warm trickle of arousal that was beginning to flow from her heated and open sex. What kind of party was this? she thought wildly, unable to reconcile the difference between her presence here, at this surreal ball, and her life up to twenty-four hours ago, when she'd been just another New York working woman. As she made her way towards the drinks table, however, the image of that professional modern Manhattanite was beginning to recede further and further away, and her presence at this bizarrely erotic masked ball increasingly seemed like her only reality. She reached out a gloved hand and accepted a crystal flute from a passing server, and stood sipping her champagne and glancing around at the milling, dancing, chatting crowd, before spotting a small arched wooden doorway set into the far wall on the left and a crowd of people clustered outside it, apparently queuing to get through. She was just about to make her way over to join them when she felt a strong grip on her forearm, and a low, husky voice whispered in her ear, 'Lady, are you quite sure you are prepared to enter there?'

Sasha nearly choked on her drink as she took in the handsome, seductive appearance of the man at her elbow who seemed to have suddenly come from nowhere. Like her, he was unmasked, about her age, and he also was clothed in eighteenth-century garb, his clothes indicating a similar rank to her own. His hair was neither powdered nor a wig, as far as Sasha could tell, but was long and pulled smoothly back from his nape, tied with an elaborate blue velvet bow which contrasted favourably with the rich mahogany brown of his hair. He was dressed in an elaborate blue embroidered frock-coat which reached nearly to mid-thigh, and his copiously ruffled white blouse couldn't conceal the masculine solidity of his chest. The lines of his fawn doe-skin breeches flowed along clearly defined thigh muscles, and the sheer white stockings from his knees to his black buckled shoes showed off strong, shapely calves.

But it was his face that drew Sasha's eyes most forcibly. Damn, but he was handsome! Eyes of the darkest blue, delicately arched brows, skin so smooth – and that mouth! Sasha gazed longingly at the artful curves of his lips, neither too full nor too thin, and she could nearly feel how they would press against her own as she parted his mouth with hers.

To her shame, she realised she must have been puckering up in anticipation, because the man gallantly bowed as he laughed, saying with refined politeness, 'I rarely kiss a lady who has yet to utter a word.'

'What? Oh! Sorry!' Sasha blurted out rather gracelessly as she leapt a little backward, releasing herself from the hand that had continued to grip her arm. 'It's just that you're the first person to speak to me here!' she said hastily, and drank to cover her confusion.

The man bowed again. 'Surely so charming a lady should never be ignored,' he said, removing her empty glass from her hand. 'Would you allow me to be your escort for the evening, and introduce you to the pleasures of the night?' He smiled at her good-humouredly and added, as he effortlessly lifted another glass from the tray of a passing server, 'If you'll forgive me, you don't seem entirely familiar with the rituals of the Michaelmas Ball.'

This guy was really getting into character! Sasha thought, as she allowed the stranger to grip her elbow in his palm and steer her towards the little wooden door.

'Where are you taking me?' she asked a little sharply, and the man chuckled low in his throat as he replied, 'Why, where it is you wish to go, of course.'

She noted that he was smiling and nodding familiarly to many of the people they passed, as though almost everyone here was known to him.

'Wait a minute,' she said crossly, 'I don't even know your name!'

The man smiled darkly, and put a finger to her lips. 'Hush,' he said softly. 'No names here.' And in a gesture that was coolly, intentionally, deliberately sensual, he traced his forefinger gently over the lines of Sasha's mouth, smiling as he felt her lips tremble before parting slightly to allow him to brush lightly at her smooth moist tongue.

'Ah,' the man murmured to himself with half-closed eyes, withdrawing his finger from between Sasha's lips and licking its tip, as though to taste her tongue with his. When he opened his eyes and smiled directly into hers, it was as though Sasha could feel that tongue sweeping between the blushing lips of her sex, and

158

she frowned at him suddenly in an effort to redirect her desire from yearning to irritation.

'Where is it you think I want to go?' she demanded as rudely as she could, though she was reluctant to be left on her own again.

'I saw you were looking this way,' the man replied as they drew up to the crowd at the door. 'You are not allowed in uninvited, and you, my sweet,' he added – almost mockingly, Sasha thought in annoyance – 'are obviously in need of an introduction.'

Sasha now saw that the door which they had approached was being guarded by a pair of medieval knights, complete with armour and breastplates, who were barring the door against many of the guests gathered around clamouring for entrance. When they saw Sasha and her escort, however, they immediately leapt aside, bowing respectfully and touching their visors to the pair of them while they opened the studded wooden door and allowed them to pass.

'What is this place?' Sasha asked, now in real trepidation, but the man merely shook his head and whispered, 'Hush. All will soon be revealed.' And he indicated that she should bow her head as together they passed through the low, small door.

Not another mysterious passage! she thought: for indeed, as soon as the door had closed behind them, Sasha found herself standing in the dark, huddled closely to her escort for protection, although from what, she wasn't quite sure. The man took her gloved hand in his.

'Come,' was all he said, and she followed him, stumbling a bit, along a narrow corridor, at the end of which she could dimly make out some light which grew brighter as they headed towards it. There were sounds, too, which seemed to grow louder: strange, almost mechanical sounds that Sasha couldn't identify, and suddenly they were standing at the top of a set of stairs.

'Go down,' the man urged her, pressing her securely against himself. 'Go ahead: I will assist you.'

'Where are we going? Down into some labyrinth or crypt?' Sasha asked, but the man merely urged her further down the stairs and said, 'Hold tight to your mask: you might choose to put it on once we arrive.'

And as Sasha neared the bottom of the steps, she came into full view of the spectacle that awaited her below. As she stood and stared, she wondered dimly if they were still within the confines of the Asher Hotel, or whether they had left it through some underground tunnel and were now in some perverse dungeon of pleasure in the bowels of the London urban sprawl. She would never have dreamt that, while she and her ALM colleagues had been hammering out the advertising deal several floors above, this sordid arena of sexual excess existed and was operating somewhere far below!

Everywhere she looked, Sasha could see couples and groups of people engaged in various sexual practices, but not all of it was sex as she knew it. There were whipping benches and trestle-tables, mirrors set in recessed walls so lovers could watch themselves perform; there were restraints, chains and fetters of all sorts, as well as some more sinister-looking equipment: spikes, body-bags, clamps, and hoods, whose meaning Sasha shuddered to decipher.

There were also, she was pleased to discover, activities with which she was a little more familiar: women and men, men and men, women and women, in pairs, threesomes and groups, all shapes, sizes and patterns, and it was all so thrilling and new she hardly knew where to look first.

'Come,' the man beside her said again, tugging at

160

her hand as he guessed at her confusion, 'let's begin with the more mundane.'

He drew her alongside him to observe a naked woman and man, the man lying flat on his back on a bench, while a woman sat astride him, riding him energetically, both their faces contorted with pleasure, and the man's hips writhed and bucked beneath his partner, his hands reaching around her waist to grip her bouncing buttocks.

Sasha gazed at the couple in silence for a moment before turning away to consider a more intriguing tableau towards the centre of the room. Here were two men, one completely naked and lying face down along a rough wooden trestle, barely wide enough across to support his body; his wrists and ankles were bound to the frets, his head turned to one side, and his eyes shut tight. Behind him stood a scary-looking man with a whip; Sasha jumped a little and looked at her escort in fright, but he merely smiled and shook his head, gesturing to the whip-man in a reassuring manner. Nevertheless, Sasha put her mask to her face, though neither participant before her seemed to pay her the slightest attention; she moved closer to her companion, off to the side and well away from the evil-looking man, who exuded menace with his bald head and his leather soldier's dress which Sasha would have found ridiculous on a man less big and imposing. Instead the costume seemed to suit this bald man, his great hairy legs in their laced-up sandals and his bare, heavily muscled arms shown off to great advantage. Sasha looked again at the face of the man laid out before his tormentor. He didn't look at all frightened, she decided: rather, he appeared to be in a state of heightened sexual arousal and anticipation, though she couldn't see his penis to determine whether it was erect. Certainly his buttock cheeks were clenching and releasing as though in lustful expectation.

Crack! went the whip, and Sasha clung to her escort, noting despite her fear the comfortingly firm bulge of his biceps beneath the rich cloth of his coat. Absently, the man patted the hand which clutched his arm, the two of them still staring intently at the spectacle before them. The whip-man drew back, raised his arm and struck again, but though the sound of the whip was loud, the lash left barely a mark on the man's rounded cheeks, though he shivered and moaned aloud, with pleasure, Sasha hoped, rather than pain.

'It's latex, not leather,' whispered the man at her side – the only hint he had given so far that he really was of the modern world. 'It makes an impressive noise, but lacks the true sting of the hide.'

Well, that's certainly a relief, Sasha thought, her eyes still glued to the theatrical display before her. She was tensed and waiting for the lash to strike again when the gladiator-man abruptly dropped his whip and strode around to the front of the trestle so that his pelvis was jutting aggressively forward into the bound man's face. With a quick wrench of his wrist, the man freed his penis from whatever was confining it beneath his skirt and bared the proudly erect stalk, its prodigious thickness and size making Sasha feel quite faint. Ignoring his audience, the man aimed his cock straight at the bound man's mouth, a pre-ejaculatory drop adorning the bulbous purple crown.

'Suck it,' he directed hoarsely, and Sasha watched in amazement as the man on the trestle eagerly opened his mouth and drew in that throbbing red shaft, swallowing practically the whole of it, until his nose was buried in the other man's dense pubic bush, the tormentor's plump, raised testicles nearly bumping against the prone man's chin.

How can he breathe? Sasha wondered, simultaneously repulsed and engrossed, while the dominant one slowly drew his stiff and engorged cock back out, his shaft shining wet with his lover's saliva, until only the head was lodged in the slave's mouth. The man frantically sucked at that great round plum before, with a growl, the gladiator-man drove himself back into his sex-slave's mouth, gripping the man's head and grinding his hips against the other man's face.

Sasha was feeling genuinely concerned for the slave, bound and gagged with his dominant lover's cock, and she glanced anxiously at her guide, but again he simply shook his head and put his finger to his lips, indicating that she should stay silent. Curiously, Sasha tried to get a look at her escort's groin, to ascertain whether there was a vertical bulge to indicate his aroused interest in the homoerotic tableau before him, but she couldn't tell. Instead, she turned back to look at the man on the trestle, who was wriggling his hips with desperate urgency against the wood underneath him, as if seeking the blissful relief of friction against his own erect cock.

The man before him saw this too, and, with a lusty laugh, he withdrew from the man's mouth and repositioned himself at his rear, sliding his massive penis, slick with the other man's saliva, into the impossibly tiny hole of the man's puckered back passage. Sasha held her breath and nearly dropped her mask in uncertainty, concerned that that huge cock would never fit all the way into that small space, but, amazingly, the whole of the thick, veined shaft began to disappear, inch by inch, into the other man's anus, until they were fully joined, the big man's balls pressed tightly against the hollowing cheeks of the man on his stomach. With a great howl, he withdrew slightly, then slammed himself back in, the man on the trestle bucking wildly against his bonds and moaning uncontrollably. Again and again the big man pulled out and pushed in, the man beneath him arching his back with each withdrawal, and urging himself backward with every re-entry, striving to meet his partner's thrusts with every evidence of delight. Finally, with a tremendous shudder and a roar, the dominant one withdrew himself fully, and, gripping his pulsating cock tightly in one hand, roughly palmed it as he ejaculated, spraying thick white jets of cream all over the quivering buttocks of the man lying face down.

When at last he was finished, he silently bent down and, with infinite tenderness, unfastened the bonds restraining his fettered partner, who, once freed, stood up, full-length and fully erect, and held out his hand. The bald man dropped to his knees before him, pressed a fervent kiss into his palm, then solemnly handed him the whip.

'Strip,' commanded the man whose backside still bore the milky traces of his lover's recent spasms. The big man silently divested himself of his leather dress and arranged himself, face down, on the trestle, just as his partner had so recently done. Sasha turned and walked away as the now-dominant man was adjusting the cuffs and restraints around the wrists and ankles of his tormentor.

'Yuk,' Sasha said, wrinkling her nose in distaste at what she had just witnessed. 'What was that about?'

Her escort stopped a wandering minstrel and slipped another flute of champagne into her hand. 'Think of this as a public arena of people's private pleasure,' he advised her, indicating the complementary pairings of lovers on display and the audiences who observed them. 'Some people come here to watch, some come to play, and for some, watching is a form of play,' he continued, indicating a man masturbating enthusiastically as he watched a young woman being taken from behind by a handsome black fellow. 'You see why entry to this room is by invitation only.' Sasha's companion smiled, watching while she downed her drink in unladylike haste. 'Admit it,' he teased her, gesturing to the room at large, 'you were fascinated by what you saw happening between those men.'

But Sasha was already making her way towards a tableau which had just caught her eye. Now this was more her scene, she thought, standing at a distance, yet close enough to enjoy the view. A woman was seated on what looked like a velvet throne, a confusion of frothy white petticoats and a rustling jade-green silk dress ballooning about her hips, her head thrown back against the cushioned top of her chair. A man was kneeling between her spread thighs, and another man was bending over her naked breasts, the bodice of her dress having been pushed down almost to her waist, so that her pretty pink nipples were readily available to her lover's fingers and lips. In one hand she clutched a glass of wine; in the other she held a luxurious-looking blue suede whip, with which she was absently stroking the bare back of the man who was kissing her naked breasts. Now that's what I call arousing, Sasha murmured to herself, half enviously, as she gazed at the woman's shut-eyed joy at being simultaneously pleasured by two devoted men. In fact, Sasha realised, stepping a little closer to get a better glimpse of the man's tongue sweeping across one pert, luscious bud, that woman looks like – it is! It's Claire! she realised, delighted to see that the young hotel employee was being properly serviced herself.

'See something you like?' whispered the stranger in

her ear, and with a start Sasha turned to face him, her eyes drawn again to his beautifully tempting mouth.

'Let's get out of here,' she murmured, tracing her fingers over the shape of his lips. 'Let's go somewhere . . . a little more private.'

The man gazed into her eyes for a moment, the hint of a smile playing around his mouth as he gently sucked on the tip of one gloved finger, before clasping her other hand in his and leading her away from the dungeon of pleasure. Marvelling at his knowledge of this subterranean labyrinth, Sasha followed along beside him, her long velvet dress sweeping over the ground, feeling as though she were walking in a dream. Surprisingly, the man didn't lead her back up the stairs the way they had come, but instead took her down a confusing number of corridors and what looked like secret passages until she found herself in an eerily familiar part of the hotel.

'Where are we?' she whispered anxiously, straining to see in the gloom.

'Sssh,' her guide replied, placing his finger against her lips. 'Just follow me.'

With an uncanny sense of familiarity, Sasha allowed the man to lead her to a staircase set way back in an unused part of the hotel, with grimy dark walls and an old, decaying carpet, and, as they climbed the staircase together, Sasha knew that Amelia Asher's portrait would be waiting for them.

Sure enough, there was the lady in the painting looking just as she had in Sasha's memory, her dress in the portrait matching the very one Sasha was wearing herself, and, as her escort closed in on her, backing her up against the opposite wall so he could press his mouth and body to hers, Sasha looked over his shoulder at the dimly figured image of John Blakeley,

his indistinct features taking clearer shape and defini-
tion in her mind. She continued to gaze dreamily at
the portrait as her lips met those of her lover, and her
mouth opened rapturously beneath his, feeling the
heady delight of the pressure of his tongue against
hers. Then she closed her eyes, no longer needing to
look at the portrait, as she untied the ribbon at the
nape of the man's neck, sliding her fingers through
the heavy silk of his hair and sighing in pleasure as
his mouth slid from her lips to her shoulder. Gorgeous
as this man was, he was no Johnny Blakeley, but he
would suit her just fine. His mouth slid down the
length of her arm, pushing down the sleeve of her
dress; he stopped to admire the pretty black swan
tattooed on her shoulder, before slipping Sasha's
white satin glove off the hand which had now
dropped the black velvet mask.

Stepping back a bit, his eyes on hers, the man drew
the long glove off Sasha's other hand and arm as well,
then raised that hand to his lips, his tongue seeking
out the groove at the base between her second and
third fingers. Sasha closed her eyes and leant back
against the wall, her belly shimmying as she felt the
tug and pull of the man's mouth between her fingers
as though he was stroking her between her thighs.
Slowly, the man kissed his way back up her arm to
the pulse that beat at the base of her throat, and he
pressed his mouth for long blissful moments against
the creamy smoothness of her neck and shoulders.
Finally, his mouth moved lower to nestle into the
temptingly deep cleavage of Sasha's upthrust breasts,
finding the silly little hankie she had placed there
earlier that night and slowly drawing it out with his
teeth, dropping it carelessly on the floor before returning to the pleasures of her bosom. Sasha clutched at
his shoulders, grateful for the hard support of the wall

behind her back that was helping to prop her upright, for so urgent was her need that she felt herself growing quite weak in the knees. She tugged restlessly at the heavy fabric of the man's frock-coat, sliding it off him, then fluttering her fingers helplessly at the impossible intricacies of his cravat and tightly fastened blouse.

He seemed to be having no such difficulty with the mysterious clasps at the back of Sasha's dress, however, for as he captured one swelling pink nipple between his lips, he was reaching behind her back and slipping the maddeningly small fastenings through their tight little enclosures.

As Sasha felt the folds of her dress loosen and fall away from her, she redoubled her efforts at the man's shirt, craving the feel of his flesh against her fingers. With a smile, he released her nipple from his kiss and swiftly undid the garments himself, leaving his shirt on, but his neck and chest were now gloriously bared. With a shiver of delight, Sasha buried her mouth in his chest, gently scraping her teeth against the firm curve of his breast and sliding her tongue against the tiny tight puckerings of his nipples. She stepped out of the overly cumbersome dress, still clad in the red velvet basque, black lace suspender-belt, red silk stockings and, of course, her high silver shoes.

'How delightful of you to wear no panties tonight,' the man murmured as his fingers sought and found the sweetly wet lips of her sex. He stroked lightly along their unfurled edges, circling round her hard moist bud and tracing the path to the entrance of her clenching vagina. At last he inserted one, two, three fingers into that hot, moist haven, and he drove inside her with such pressure and strength that Sasha was pressed even harder against the wall, although she worried momentarily about the damage she might be doing to her elaborate hairdo as her head rubbed against the musty old wood. She closed her eyes and clung to him, her fingers working fruitlessly against the fastenings of his breeches, unable to release him from the constricting fabric until, with a muffled groan, he pushed her hand away and released himself, then clasped her hand around his satisfyingly hard and heavy shaft.

'Ah, yes, love,' he sighed softly into the rolls of her hair as she, with his help, stroked and tugged at his cock. 'Lady, yes,' he sighed again as she circled the head with her thumb, feeling the silky moisture of the single drop of fluid that trembled at its tip. She smoothed that rich wetness over the soft thick cowl that enclosed the firm length which pulsed so enticingly in her palm, emitting another opalescent drop, its fragrance so musky and sweet that Sasha had to taste it on her tongue. She moved a few steps down the staircase, while the man still stood on the landing above her, so that she was level with his cock; before she took him in her mouth, she looked up to see the man looking down at her, his desire for her so clearly evident in his face.

'Yes,' was all he murmured, patiently waiting for her kiss, and Sasha did not delay in drawing him slowly between her lips, kneeling a little on the stairs as she urged more of him into the warm cavern of her mouth. Ah, but it was satisfying to suck him! she thought in a haze of dreamy pleasure, savouring the salty, male taste of him and running her fingers over the peachy textured sac which enclosed his round and tight balls. She withdrew from his cock slightly so she could run her tongue under the soft folds of his foreskin, but as she did so he pulled away completely, leaving her feeling oddly bereft.

'I don't want to spend too soon,' he murmured in

explanation, but Sasha was barely listening as she urged him down on to the steps, and, ever mindful of the weight of her hair on her head, pressed down on her lover's hips, nudging him on to his back on the stairs. She then lay fully on top of him, rubbing the soft velvet of her basque against the smooth hardness of his chest, naked beneath the flowing fabric of his opened shirt. She wrapped her legs around his hips and positioned herself over his rampant erection.

'Look at me,' Sasha breathed, as his eyes threatened to close. 'Open your eyes and look at me.'

Her gaze met and held his as she raised herself slightly then eased herself downward, the opening of her sex meeting smoothly with the rich plum of his penis, and as she took the rounded head inside her, she saw the man's eyes widen a little with the fullness of pleasure, though he remained silent. She could hear no noise, only the sound of their breathing as she eased herself further down on to him, slowly, slowly, until the base of his cock was flush against the dewy softness of her sex. The two of them held together, still staring into each other's eyes as they both assessed their mutual fit. Then, at an exquisitely tantalising pace, trying to wring as much satisfaction from this moment as she could, Sasha moved herself up the pleasing length of her lover's shaft, reluctantly letting go of that sweet, intense fullness, before sliding herself back down, the increase in pressure drawing a soft sigh from her lips. With every rise up on the man's cock, Sasha increased the tempo until, in tacit accord, they were matching the pace of their rhythms, woman against man, flesh against flesh, bodies rocking together. Sasha leant forward and buried her face in the stranger's neck, feeling the strength of his hands as they tenderly caressed her back even in the midst of their driving hunger. As the man pushed himself deeper into Sasha's sex, and she pressed down as hard as she could to meet him, she was startled to feel, though the depths of the pleasure, a warm trickling on the back of her left shoulder. As she and her lover simultaneously climbed to the peaks of their passion, and the climactic heights began to overtake them, Sasha felt again that moist, warm flow, and, as her orgasm swirled around her, she realised what the drops were that were dampening her skin. Tears were falling on to her body. The portrait of Amelia Asher was weeping.

Chapter Ten

Sasha awoke the next morning feeling disoriented, yet at the same time oddly euphoric. It took several moments of blinking her eyes repeatedly to clear her thoughts before the memories of the night before came flooding back to her, causing a heated rush to soar to her cheeks and her eyes to dart wildly around the room, searching for tangible evidence that the events of the previous evening had actually occurred. Yes, there was the gown she had worn, lying in regal splendour across the padded armchair in the corner, carefully laid out in all its full-length glory, looking eerily as though it was inhabited by some ghost-thin female form. Sasha stared at it for a moment, then reached up a hand to tentatively finger her hair: the heavy rolls so expertly lacquered into place by Claire had dissolved into Sasha's usual morning disarray. Dimly, she remembered flinging the pins from her hair before falling into bed, and loosening the elaborate curls, for there was no way she could possibly have slept on that tightly pinned coiffure.

Naked, Sasha rose from her bed and stumbled

across the room to lovingly caress the sumptuous fabrics heaped on the floor by the dress: the silver shoes, silk stockings, black suspender-belt, red velvet basque, white satin gloves and black velvet mask. She gathered up the entire bundle of clothes and pressed them to her face, inhaling their mingled scents, which seemed almost embedded in the textured garments: she could still smell the lingering traces of perfume and smoke that had tinged the atmosphere of the Michaelmas Ball, as well as, more beguilingly, the denser scents of the Pleasure Dungeon; the musty, slightly stale air of that mysterious back staircase; the elusive trace of the handsome stranger she had embraced so fervently; and the rich, honey-sweet musk of her own womanly fragrance.

Sasha buried her face a little deeper into the heavy fabrics she was cradling in her arms and, eyes shut, she tried to piece together the series of events which had led her from that intense coupling on the stairs back up to her own room. She still couldn't quite believe that the dampness on her skin had come from the tears sliding down the painted face of Amelia Asher, but she could vividly recall her final shocked confrontation with the weeping portrait. She also remembered her hurried insistence on returning to her room, terribly anxious that the man on the stairs beside her should not see the sorrowing face on the wall, as though for him to witness the mystery of the weeping portrait would be in some way a violation of the privacy of Amelia Asher's sufferings.

Sasha recalled being escorted to the lift by her nameless lover, who seemed to effortlessly find his way along the labyrinthine corridors of the back pass-ages of the hotel, gallantly carrying Sasha's discarded mask, gloves, and dress as she scurried along beside him, clad only in her elaborate underwear and shoes.

When they finally re-entered the main part of the hotel, the lift was expectantly open in the lobby, its doors wound right back as though it had been patiently awaiting her return. With a silent press of his lips to the palm of Sasha's hand, the stranger had smiled tenderly at her, then handed her into the lift before standing back to watch as the doors slowly wound shut. Sasha was then gently carried upward as, unbidden, the elevator had ascended to the third floor, and that had been the end of last night's adventure.

Reluctantly, Sasha laid her precious bundle of clothing back on to the chair and made her way to the shower, wondering if she'd be allowed to keep the exquisite finery or if someone would come to collect it – Claire, perhaps? But Sasha's more immediate concern was food: well aware that she'd eaten almost nothing since her aeroplane breakfast the day before, and too impatient to wait for room service, she scrubbed herself quickly in the shower, dressed casually in a pair of well-worn Levis and cosy fisherman's sweater, and raced down the curving central staircase to the breakfast room on the ground floor.

As Sasha sat at her table for one in the corner of the elegantly pretty restaurant, happily replete from her full English breakfast, complete with porridge and smoked kippers, she sipped at her third cup of excellent coffee and surreptitiously observed her fellow diners, all sitting quietly reading the paper or speaking to each other in hushed tones. She gazed at the other guests curiously, trying to determine whether she recognised anyone from the night before, but none of the breakfasting people looked in the least bit familiar to her, nor was Claire anywhere to be seen. With a dismissive shrug and a satisfying rumble in her tummy, Sasha pushed her plate away, intending to take the stairs back up to her room, but a little more slowly this time, freighted down as she was with the weight of her breakfast.

It wasn't until she had placed her Reeboked foot on the lowest step of the staircase that she turned, puzzling, towards the main door, and spied a slick brown pony-tail partially obscuring the collar of a man's impeccably tailored navy-blue business suit. As Sasha turned away from the stairs towards the man, hoping to stop him before he left the building and was swallowed up by a waiting taxi, he actually turned her way and flashed her a sly smile. Her heart in her mouth, Sasha watched while her lover of the night before – if it was really he – turned back to the other dark-suited men who accompanied him and, exiting the hotel, was soon gone from view.

Giggling girlishly to herself, Sasha turned back and headed up the stairs, narrowly dodging a tray-laden maid on her way. When she returned to her room, breathless and flushed from the exertion, she stopped in sudden disappointment and gazed around the room. Oh no! she wailed to herself. Not the dress! But it was sadly true. The dress, the shoes, the basque, even the silly little hankie and the ribbon from her hair: all were gone, including the suspender-belt and velvet mask. Distressed, Sasha stared at the glaringly empty chair where her borrowed finery had so recently lain, barely even noticing that the bed had been made, the room freshly aired, and a sweet little basket of chocolates and fruit sat temptingly filled on top of the pile of clean towels on the dressing-table.

Not even the shoes! Sasha thought grumpily. Couldn't they at least have left me the shoes? Who will believe me now when I try to tell them about the ball, if I've got nothing to prove I was actually there? Frantically, she searched around for her beautifully

175

printed invitation, but was unable to remember whether she had brought it downstairs to the ball or had left it in her room. Her frenzied search proving fruitless – after all, there were just so many places it could be – Sasha left her room in disgust and strode back to the lift, determined to explore the hotel on her own in order to locate the mysterious ballroom.

She jabbed at the bottom button on the panel, and the elevator obligingly retreated to the basement of the building, taking Sasha along with it. However, when she stepped out of the lift a few minutes later, after it landed with a thump, she was cross – but not surprised – to discover that she was, indeed, in the basement of the hotel, but nowhere near where she'd been last night. This was obviously a part of the hotel guests were not supposed to see: a passing waiter glared angrily at Sasha as he rushed on to the dumbwaiter in the corner, and Sasha could smell the sharp sweetness of laundry detergent, and hear the rumble of machines. The boiler room was also down here in the bowels of the building, but, as far as Sasha could make out, there were no exits or entrances to this basement floor other than the dumbwaiter and the lift.

Disappointed, but not about to give up, Sasha rode the lift back up to the ground floor and strode out into the main reception area. She looked around for a moment, and a thought struck her. She had yet to visit the hotel library, though she'd passed by it on her way to the breakfast room and peeped in: perhaps that might be a good place to start. Encouraged, she entered the leather-and-wood interior and took a good look around. As was only to be expected, the room was full of books, oak panelling, heavy damask curtains and worn leather armchairs, but no readers at all. Determinedly, Sasha walked around the perimeter of the room, though she wasn't at all sure what she was looking for: but as soon as she saw it, she knew.

This part of the wall was clearly not seriously intended to deceive: the books were fastened into place and couldn't be removed, as in the lift, but this, of course, would be self-defeating in a library. The little alcove was the only part of the room set back into the wall, its artificial status immediately calling attention to itself. Sasha assumed that most visitors to this room would simply admire the artfulness of the facade, considering it to be just a charming ornamental addition to an otherwise functional room. Sasha, however, knew there had to be something more intriguing about it; experimentally, she ran her fingers along the row of empty spines, noting that the covers were simply hollow facades with no pages in them at all. Suspecting that this part of the wall might also be hollow, she rapped lightly against a fake copy of *Tristram Shandy* and listened intently, but felt a little foolish, since she didn't know what a hollow wall would sound like anyway.

'Miss? Can I help you?'

Sasha wheeled around. A stern-looking bell-boy stood facing her, indicating the wall with his eyes. 'Is there something I can help you with?' he enquired icily.

Sasha knew she could expect no help from this hotel employee, so instead she smiled weakly and murmured, 'I was just admiring your wall here.'

The bell-boy stood pointedly aside to let her pass, and Sasha smilingly walked towards the ladies' toilet, daring him to follow her inside. She waited a few minutes in the very bathroom where she and Valerie had primped themselves before joining the ALM-Rollit team just a few months ago. Was that all it was?

Sasha wondered in amazement. What a lifetime ago it seemed!

She waited until she was sure the pesky bell-boy had gone, then darted back to the library, pressing her fingers frantically along the backs of the fake books, sure that there must be a catch or something. Her fingers, however, discovered nothing: no knobs, buttons, or springs, and she stepped back in dismay to stare at the false wall, until suddenly something clicked in her mind. With a mischievous grin, she spied a copy of Horace Walpole's *The Castle of Otranto*, and, hardly believing this was actually happening, but chalking it up to all the other uncanny events she'd been experiencing lately, she slipped her fingers inside the empty volume and, unbelievably, closed them around a cold metal ring. Trembling with excitement, desperately willing no one else to enter the room, Sasha closed her eyes and pulled. Nothing happened. She waited, took a breath, and tried again, and felt the slightest sense of something give way, as though the ring was attached to a chain or a rope which had been fastened into place through disuse. Come on, come on, Sasha urged silently, and tugged gently on the ring again, terrified that if she pulled too hard the chain might suddenly snap and break in two. But no: with a slow, steady pull, Sasha felt the wall of fake books she was leaning against slowly swing inward, and when she had released the ring enough to cause a gap to open up between the edge of the door and its frame, she slipped quietly through, careful not to let it swing all the way back into place, lest she might not be able to get back inside.

Sasha now found herself in a short stone passageway, the small slice of warmth and light from the library behind her and an imposing solid door of wood before her. With a shaking heart, Sasha approached the door, reached out her sweating hand and laid it on the chilled metal bolt that fastened it. Slowly, gently, she tried to turn the latch to unlock the door, but it seemed firmly bolted into place. With greater force now, Sasha wrenched fiercely at the sturdy length of metal, heedless of how her fingernails were scraping against the wood, but after five minutes of exhausting wrestling with the door, she sagged helplessly against it, fighting back tears of frustration.

'Amelia,' she whispered, hardly aware of what she was saying, 'please, Amelia, help me.'

Feeling foolish, and a little ashamed of herself, Sasha nevertheless dared to give it one more try. Taking a deep breath of courage, she wrapped her fingers around the cold metal bolt and tried one more time. She nearly wept again as the bolt yielded to her touch and the heavy wooden door slowly opened outward.

Sasha slipped outside into the cool late-September air and shivered. No wonder that door stays locked, she thought to herself, uncertain where to step. For it was obvious that she was standing in a private grave-yard, an impressive plot of land bordered by trees and wild bushes with a view of a small, ancient-looking chapel perched a little further away on a hill. In stunned silence, Sasha made her way slowly among the sites of repose for the dead, stopping here and there to read an inscription or note a date, many of which stretched back to the early seventeenth century and none, as far as she could see, extending into the eighteen hundreds. There were beautifully wrought statues of cherubs and saints among the graves, and Sasha admired the stark simplicity of the crosses, as well as the elaborate carvings on some of the blocks of marble. There seemed something wonderfully appro-priate about wandering around a private churchyard secreted behind a hidden door in the chill of early fall, the leaves already beginning to turn glorious shades of orange, crimson, and gold. Sasha forgot all about her quest for the mysterious ballroom, so caught up was she in the compelling aesthetic pleasures of this quiet little churchyard.

But why had she been led here? For she now had no doubt that her quest for this hidden graveyard had been aided by supernatural forces, and, as she pored over the inscriptions on the tombstones, she could see that many of those buried here were of the Asher family, though not all. After a bit of a search, she was finally able to locate Amelia's tombstone, which stood beside that of Lady and Lord Asher's graves, and Sasha stood for several moments in respectful contemplation of the simple, sad inscription: 'Here Lies Lady Amelia Asher, Beloved Daughter, 1776–1795.' She gazed at the carved image of a kneeling saint, the hood of her gown nearly covering her face, which graced the side of Amelia's tombstone. Sasha felt tears prick her eyes, and she wept unashamedly as she stood by the grave.

At last she turned to go, for she felt that the purpose of her being led here had now been made manifest, when a sudden gust of wind blew quite close by her, and, startled, Sasha looked up as though her name had just been called. Eyes widening with surprise, as well as a sense of fright, Sasha beheld quite clearly a figure standing by a grave some way in the distance, and though it was simply standing still, she intuitively sensed it was beckoning her. She drew closer to it as the wind swept fallen leaves around her feet, and her hair was lifted and blown about her face.

He was dressed just as he was in the portrait and as she had seen him reflected in the windows outside her bedroom and the New York travel agent's office:

coarse broadcloth shirt, leather waistcoat, loose brown breeches, heavy workman's boots. As Sasha came to stand as close as she dared, however, she could also clearly see what had been so heavily shadowed in the painting. No, he wasn't quite like the two strange models in her office, she mused to herself as she gazed at his face: his lips were a bit fuller, his hair a little darker, his eyes not quite so deeply set. He was looking at her quite calmly, almost, it seemed, smiling a little, and as her eyes met his, she felt all her shock and fear melt away, and a strange sense of inner peace descended upon her. She gazed at him, aware of little else other than the wind and the leaves, for what seemed to be hours, but when a bird suddenly swooped down from a nearby tree and squawked angrily at her, Sasha jumped and looked behind her, and the spell was broken. When she looked back to where he had been standing, she saw quite clearly that he was gone, and she now felt free enough to walk up to where he had just been.

He had been standing, she saw, near a small battered tombstone, one quite different from the others. This one had no ornate carvings or marble statues to adorn it, and the writing engraved on the stone seemed somehow rougher and less precise than on the others, as though wrought by a less skilled hand: Maria Blakeley, Hopewell, 1702–1745.

Sasha gazed thoughtfully at the engraving for a few more minutes, then slowly made her way back to the heavy wooden door and the cold stone passage. Her mind was ticking over while she pulled the door firmly shut behind her, bolted it back into place, and slipped back through the fake wall of books, still thankfully left open for her. When she was once again safely inside the hotel library, Sasha brushed a few dead leaves off her sweater and walked slowly and calmly to the hotel bar, where she quietly sipped at a double shot of whisky and planned her next move.

She had just accepted a refill from the bartender when someone came up to stand noiselessly behind her, causing her to jump before she turned around to see who was there. Sasha was delighted to see that it was Claire, her hotel employee's uniform all in place, a shy smile on her face.

'Hello, Miss,' Claire half-whispered, all traces of last night's enthroned debauchery completely erased. 'I was hoping I'd see you today.' She ducked her head and gently enquired, 'Did you enjoy last night's ball?'

Sasha had all but forgotten about last night in her deep concentration on the events of this morning. Now, however, she blushed happily at Claire's question and nodded a quick 'yes.' She wanted to ask about the location of the mysterious ballroom, but was so consumed by this latest enigma that she instead asked the girl, 'Claire, what's Hopewell?'

The smile vanished from Claire's face. 'Who told you about Hopewell?' she asked anxiously, lowering her voice even further and glancing around the room as if to make sure no one else was listening.

'Why? Is it a secret?' Sasha asked warily, beginning to feel a little fed up with the cloaked workings of this place.

Claire held her eyes in a steady gaze. 'You've been in the library, haven't you?' she asked in a tone of faint reproach. When Sasha bravely nodded her head, however, making it clear what she'd discovered there, Claire actually smiled, and said simply, 'You've seen the churchyard.' She didn't need to tell Sasha she had entered forbidden grounds: that much had been obvious from the start.

'But what about Hopewell? And who was Maria

Blakeley?' Sasha asked again, reluctant to divulge what else she'd seen there. It didn't seem appropriate to say his name aloud, but Claire said it for her.

'John Blakeley's family lived in a tiny village on the Yorkshire moors named Hopewell,' Claire answered her, fidgeting with the keys at her waist. 'Johnny's grandparents, Samuel and Maria Blakeley, came down to London in the early eighteenth century to go into service, because their sheep farm in the north had been destroyed in a fire. After Johnny was banished from the Asher estate,' she continued, her voice so low now that Sasha had to strain to hear it, 'they say he returned to his grandparents' farm to rebuild it. No one from London ever heard from him again, though, so it might have been just a rumour.'

Claire shrugged, and looked so expressively into Sasha's face that the older woman was momentarily seized by the urgent desire to describe to the girl everything she had experienced since her first visit to the Asher Hotel. She was just about to open her mouth to do so when Claire jumped guiltily to her feet and glanced around her. 'I shouldn't really be here,' she said apologetically to Sasha. 'I have to get back to work. I really just came over to say hello.' She smiled again bashfully at her, and seemed so young and vulnerable Sasha wanted to enfold her in her arms and take her away with her. But instead she merely smiled and said with great tenderness, 'It was wonderful to see you again, Claire.'

Claire blushed, and before she hurried away she squeezed Sasha's hand and murmured, 'Good luck to you on your journey, Miss. I hope you find what you're looking for.'

After she had gone, Sasha thought deeply to herself for a moment. 'Good luck on your journey'? At first she'd thought Claire had simply been referring to her trip back to New York, but the more she thought about it, the clearer it seemed to Sasha that she was somehow intended to find this village Hopewell – if it still existed. Perhaps, she mused, that's why I was led to the churchyard, and that's why he appeared to me by his grandmother's grave; I've got nothing to lose by trying.

She asked for a road atlas of Britain while she ate her ploughman's lunch in the bar, and consulted the multicoloured layout of the arterial roads of Yorkshire over her blackberry crumble and custard. Unfortunately, search as she might, Sasha could find no mention of any town named Hopewell, but figured that instinct and luck – and perhaps more unearthly aid – had got her this far. I'll just have to trust to them a little longer, she told herself firmly.

She went back upstairs to her room, having decided that she might as well leave for the north as soon as possible. She quickly repacked her bags, checking to make sure Amelia's manuscript was still safely tucked away, and finally admitting to herself that she had really overdone it – why on earth had she packed two business suits? She was just about to go downstairs to pay her bill and check out, when she saw the silver shoes she'd worn last night sitting quietly on the armchair in the corner. Delighted to see that she had been allowed to keep them after all – though she still couldn't find her invitation to the ball – she paused to fondle their high-stacked heels and elaborate black buckles before quickly stashing them in her case, half afraid some hotel employee would suddenly appear at her door and demand them back. No such person appeared, however, so Sasha went downstairs and regretfully handed back her computerised card to the receptionist, who said courteously, 'We hope you enjoyed your stay here, Ms Hayward, and we look forward to seeing you again.'

While waiting for the valet to bring round her rented car, Sasha gazed up at the crenellated turrets and grinning gargoyles of the Asher Hotel, wondering where the next phase of this adventure would lead her. She wasn't at all nervous, just very excited, and as she slid into the driver's seat of her car, she whispered a promise: 'Don't weep any more, Amelia: I'll find your Johnny for you.'

Sasha spent the rest of the day driving, heading north up the M1, and frowning in irritation when the congestion forced her to slow to a tortoise-like rate of fifty miles per hour. Once out of London, however, she was able to pick up speed, and she marvelled at the opportunity to cruise between eighty and ninety miles an hour, a welcome change from the New York State limit of sixty. She passed on to the A1, following the signs and her notes to Yorkshire, and stopping only once in Leeds to go to the bathroom and refill the car. At last, by five o'clock, she found herself nearing the outskirts of the moors, haunting images from the books of the Brontë sisters beguiling her mind as she drove.

By the time she arrived at a town called Helmsley, it had started to grow very dark indeed, and Sasha was beginning to feel a little bit anxious when she considered her position as a woman travelling alone at night in a hired car, unsure of where she was going. She decided to stop at the first pub she saw to ask if anyone knew anything about a town called Hopewell.

Well, no one at the Fullback and Firkin had heard of it, nor had anyone at the Froth and Elbow in Carlton, the Queen's Head in Low Mill, or the King's Arms in a town that seemed to have no name. As she headed into the heart of the moors, discouraged, weary, and longing for food and a bed, Sasha decided to drive for another fifteen minutes only before calling it quits for the night – and, of course, once she'd made that decision, she spied a small white sign on the road, nearly obscured by the trees which overhung it: Hopewell 5 Miles.

Elated, Sasha pressed her foot to the floor and drove, narrowly missing a herd of sheep as they bleated their way slowly across the road in the gloom. She swore when the sharp bends in the road forced her to slow down, but she knew she was finally at her destination when, with a beating heart, she read the sign announcing the dates of the Hopewell Village Fair.

Sasha drove carefully along the narrow road which rose steeply, closely bordered by rows of houses huddled tightly together, cars lining both sides of the street and making it nearly impossible in places to get through. By now she had been driving for over six hours, and she was sore, stiff, and hungry, no longer even interested in searching out whatever it was she was looking for, but only in hot soup, cold beer, and TV in bed. There! she decided, as she swung her car sharply off the road: I'll spend the night there at that pub called the Swan and Rose. She pulled into the half-empty car park, noting the sign advertising rooms vacant, and walked up to the door of the pub. She passed through the small outer room of smoke, music, and pool and into the main area of the inn, where a red-haired young bartender was simultaneously counting change, pulling pints and bantering good-naturedly with the handful of people at the bar.

'Excuse me.' Sasha coughed politely, waiting to be noticed. When the bartender looked enquiringly her way, she asked, 'Do you have any rooms available for the night?'

The bartender paused to stare at her a moment, as did all the other patrons at the bar – startled, no doubt, by her American accent – before turning back to one another and picking up the conversations they'd left off.

'Twenty-five pounds a night, including full breakfast and VAT,' the bartender said briskly. 'How many nights do you need?'

'Just the one,' Sasha said quickly, feeling a little uncomfortable and out of place in this pub. A kind of desolate loneliness threatened to overtake her as she waited for the woman to bring her the key to her room. She hadn't been back in the country forty-eight hours yet, and here she was, in the middle of nowhere, in a town that wasn't even on the map, not knowing a single person, on some crazy paranormal errand, the point of which she didn't even know herself. The absurdity of her situation had nearly caused the tears to form in her eyes, when the bartender thrust a half-pint of some evil-looking brew at her and ordered her a little roughly, 'Here, drink this. You look like you need it.'

Gingerly, Sasha accepted the proffered drink, reminding herself to mutter a self-conscious 'thank you' before taking a hesitant sip of the stuff.

'Go on, lass,' one of the older men said to her, nodding encouragingly. 'That's good Yorkshire ale: that'll soon perk you up.'

Aware that everyone's eyes were upon her, Sasha took a tentative sip, then opened her mouth wider and took a deep drink. 'It's good!' she said breathlessly, tipping her head back and draining the mellow golden-brown brew. With a satisfied wipe across her foamy upper lip, she set the glass back on the bar and said, swallowing back an unladylike belch, 'Thank you. You're right, I did need that.'

The bartender gave her a friendly smile and handed her the room-key. 'Top of the stairs and turn left,' she directed. 'Number 3. It's the only room with en suite.' Then she gestured to the menu chalked on the blackboard. 'Hot food served till nine o'clock,' she said, then added, 'but I could do you sandwiches until closing time.'

With a grateful smile, Sasha turned towards the stairs and started to lug up her heavy cases. One of the younger men who'd been clustered at the bar raced to her side to offer assistance, and Sasha followed thankfully behind him as he hoisted her bags up the stairs. With a brief nod of his head, the gruffly kind stranger set Sasha's bags on the floor outside her door and disappeared back down the stairs.

Sasha leant her head against the door and sighed. Tomorrow, she vowed silently to herself. Tomorrow I'm going to find what I'm looking for.

Chapter Eleven

*D*espite her firm resolve of the night before, Sasha awoke in her bed at the Swan and Rose the next morning still awaiting inspiration about what she should do next. Last night, after eating a warm, satisfying supper of parsnip soup, shepherd's pie and chocolate gateau in her room, she had shyly brought her empty dishes back downstairs to the crowded bar, bid the bartender a hasty thank-you and good-night, and scurried back up to her room. After a deliciously hot shower and achingly comfortable bed, thoughtfully warmed by some unseen good fairy with a charmingly old-fashioned hot-water bottle, she had slept long and well. Now, however, as Sasha stretched languorously and then looked blankly at the ceiling of her room, she wished she'd lingered downstairs at the bar the previous evening to absorb some local gossip and even perhaps some hints as to why she'd been guided here – if, after all, she had.

Determined to do some sleuthing around town straight after breakfast, Sasha rolled out of bed, stood under another gloriously strong and invigorating

189

shower, and dressed hurriedly in a knee-skimming black suede skirt, waist-length cream cotton sweater, and a warm pair of black opaque tights. She slid her feet into black lace-up calf-high boots with chunky heels, applied some blusher, mascara and lipstick, and clipped her way slowly downstairs and into the empty bar.

'Good morning,' she said a little bashfully to the red-headed bartender who was briskly polishing glasses.

''Morning,' the woman said crisply, barely looking up. 'Sleep well?'

'Yes, thank you.' Sasha slid on to a stool at the bar and asked politely, 'Am I too late for breakfast?'

The red-head stopped polishing and looked at Sasha with a smile. ''Course not,' she said, whisking out a little notepad and pen. 'What would you like, my love?'

'Sausage, bacon, scrambled eggs, mushrooms, grapefruit juice, brown toast, and tea, please,' Sasha answered, then added, 'and a local telephone book, please, if you've got one.'

The bartender's eyebrows raised at that last request, but she said nothing, merely bustled off to the kitchen to return a few minutes later with an impressively heaped tray and a disappointingly small phone book. Ignoring her food, Sasha flipped eagerly through the pages of the telephone directory, unsure of exactly what she was searching for, but there was no 'Blakeley' listed, though she even looked under 'Gardeners' in the yellow pages: nor, as was only to be expected, were there any 'Ashers.' Disappointed, Sasha pushed aside the book with a frustrated grunt and poked listlessly at her eggs, suddenly no longer hungry.

'Couldn't find what you wanted, hmm?' asked the bartender, clearly struggling to disguise her curiosity, and when Sasha shook her head, she said with a shrug, 'Listen, love, I don't know who you might be looking for, but have you considered going through one of our local papers?'

Sasha couldn't see what good that would do, but she was too polite to indicate she thought the suggestion was pointless. 'Do you have any lying around?' she enquired, biting unhappily into her toast.

She nearly choked on that self-same mouthful a moment later, however, when she knew she had found exactly what she'd been looking for in the wrinkled pages of the *Hopewell Herald*. The advertisement was tucked up in the top right-hand corner on page seven, but the sketch of an elegantly carved chest of drawers caught Sasha's eye right away. It read:

Local Family Company
Hand-carved Furniture Made to Order

And down below, almost as an afterthought, was the name of the shop: J. Blakeley, Carpenter.

'Something the matter?' the bartender asked in concern as Sasha, white-faced, had to cling momentarily to the bar as the room threatened to spin and whirl around her. Her nerveless fingers dropped her toast, and she was so shaky that when she pushed away the plate of food before her, it fell to the floor with a deafeningly loud crash.

'Oh, no . . . oh . . . I'm so sorry,' she stammered and tried to stand up, but her legs refused to support her and, like her plate, Sasha slid to the carpeted floor of the pub with a sickening thump.

She must have fainted then, because the next thing she knew, Sasha was being cradled against the comfortingly rounded bosom of the young bartender, who was attempting to lay her out full-length on the floor.

For a few minutes, Sasha's mind let go of its shock as she burrowed contentedly into the womanly softness and warmth that surrounded her; then she attempted to pull away and release herself from the bartender's ministering embrace.

'Slowly there, lass,' the woman coaxed, as Sasha, a bit nauseous from her sudden movements, struggled to sit up, only to find that made her dizziness grow worse. Obediently, she allowed the woman to gently prop her up against the wooden base of the bar where she sat, limply, for some moments with her eyes closed and her legs splayed out before her in a most unladylike fashion.

'There now,' the bartender crooned, while she applied a damp flannel to Sasha's pale and sweating face.

'Sorry about the mess,' Sasha murmured as, eyes still closed, she leant her head back and allowed the woman to tenderly press the cool cloth against her arched and twitching throat. She sat there in contented silence for another few minutes until, with a reluctant move upward, she opened her eyes and gently pushed away the woman's attentive hand.

'Thank you, but I think I'm all right now,' Sasha said, rising gingerly to her feet. She grimaced at the sight of the remains of her breakfast strewn along the bare tiles behind the bar. 'Wow, I really did make a mess; I'm so embarrassed. Let me help you clean it up.'

With a smile and a restraining hand, the woman urged Sasha back on to her stool. 'Don't be silly, love. You sit there and I'll get you another cup of tea. It's two sugars, isn't it?' Once she'd returned with the milky drink, she said a little carelessly, as she knelt to sweep up the mess, 'You must have taken quite a fright there.' She glanced up at Sasha, who was wrapping her hands tightly around the warmth of her cup, but who said nothing, merely looking away a little. She felt a little foolish about blabbing out some absurdly unbelievable story about ghosts and weeping portraits and mysterious hidden passages to this kind and obviously quite clear-headed young woman, although, Sasha thought, she would probably just nod her head and at least appear to take Sasha's story quite seriously.

'My name's Rose,' the woman said after a moment of awkward silence, and she extended a strong wide hand, giving Sasha's rather sweaty palm a cheeringly firm shake. 'Are you feeling a bit better now, my love?'

'Yes, much, thank you,' Sasha replied, feeling oddly bereft once Rose had released her hand. 'And I'm Sasha.' A thought struck her, and she looked into the china-blue eyes of the woman across from her. 'Rose, like in the name of this pub?'

'Rosie, actually,' the red-head responded, laughing a little as she poured Sasha more tea. 'My mother swears that I was conceived in the back garden of this very pub twenty-five years ago, and I was christened in honour of that joyous moment.'

For some reason, Rosie's name seemed to tug at the edges of Sasha's memory, but she was unable to figure out why, and so she simply shrugged and showed the bartender the ad which still caused her heart to pound so thickly in her ears. Sasha asked a little hoarsely, 'Do you know where I can find this shop?'

An indecipherable expression crossed the other woman's face for the most fleeting of moments – was it sorrow? Anxiety? Or just a keen interest? – before her face once more cleared into its customary kind good humour, and she nodded her head of bouncy auburn curls. 'Sure I do,' she said briskly, and

193

sketched out a few simple directions on her pad. 'Left out of the carpark on to the main road, left at the turning by the garage, straight for another mile or so, then right at the fork in the road.' She stripped the paper off the pad and held it out to Sasha. 'It's on the left-hand side,' she finished, in a curiously husky voice. 'You won't miss it.' She then stepped back a bit from the bar and asked, 'Can I get you another plate of breakfast?'

'No, thank you,' Sasha said quickly, the mere thought of food now making her throat swell and close up. 'I'll just finish my tea and let you get back to work.'

She drained the rest of her cup in silence, then stood to go back up to her room. 'Rosie,' she began a little awkwardly, unsure about what to say. 'Thank you for – well, you know,' she ended lamely, blushing a little at the recollection of how she had burrowed her head down into the softness of the woman's breast as she had held her.

'It's fine,' the woman replied casually, resuming the polishing of her glasses. She looked intently at Sasha for a moment, as though she'd been about to say something quite important, but then simply shook her head and asked in a business-like way, 'Will you be needing the room for another night?'

'I'm not sure,' Sasha began uncertainly, but something in the woman's eyes made her nod her head and say, 'Yes, actually, if that would be all right.'

''Course it would,' Rosie replied with a curt nod of her head, then added as Sasha turned to go up the stairs, 'We'll be seeing you later, then.'

Once Sasha had repaired her make-up and was preparing herself to locate this mysterious carpenter, however, she had such a strong feeling of panic that she frantically considered either staying in and not daring to go at all, or somehow cajoling Rosie into going with her. This, of course, was a ludicrous impossibility, and so there was nothing for it but for Sasha to pull up her tights, resettle her skirt and check her lipstick in the mirror before heading back down the stairs. As she passed through the bar, she looked longingly around for a glimpse of the curiously comforting bartender, but there was no sign of her, and Sasha knew she would have to do this alone.

Rosie's simple instructions were accurate and easy to follow, and it took Sasha a mere five or ten minutes before she saw the little furniture shop standing all on its own on a nearly deserted road, its wooden sign swinging in the breeze in its wrought-iron frame, the words painted on in elegant black script: J. Blakeley, Carpenter. Sasha looked around. The parking lot was empty save for one very battered-looking pick-up truck, so she pulled up nervously alongside it, forced herself to shut off the engine, and, knees quaking and belly shimmying with equal parts of hope, joy and fear, she approached the open door of the shop.

She paused before going inside, not simply out of nerves, but to take a good look at what she saw. It was a small two-storey building, the upper floor boasting only two windows, across which the curtains had been drawn, in contrast to the cluttered array in the main window of the shop below. Sasha stepped closer to examine the oak, cherry, beech and mahogany pieces clustered in the window before her: a traditional-looking chest of drawers, a pretty little table with spiralled pedestal base, a sweet red-painted rocking-horse, and a stately, cunningly carved desk of deep, dark wood.

Timorously, Sasha peeped inside. The shop appeared to be empty of people, though it was certainly full of objects, all made of wood, in various stages of completion. The interior of the shop was almost eerie, despite the strong September sunlight streaming in through the uncurtained windows at its sides and front. The unvarnished tables, upended chairs minus their legs, and stripped-down dressers and desks all looked oddly ghost-like, their unfinished surfaces and amputated forms giving Sasha a slight case of the shivers.

'Something I can help you with?'

As soon as she heard that voice, Sasha knew that this was what she had come for. She willed herself to take a steady breath, clenched her fists tightly before reminding herself to release them, and then slowly turned around to finally confront the man she had travelled all this way to find.

Yes, he was exactly as she'd imagined, with one startling distinction: he seemed to be a bit younger than she, perhaps not even yet thirty, but that black curly hair, that rich, husky voice, that tall, powerful-looking body and those beautifully shaped lips – all, all were precisely as she had seen them in the portrait, by the grave, reflected in the windows, on the floor of her New York office, and in her dreams. All but the eyes: with a shock, Sasha saw that this man's eyes weren't dark at all, no, not the merest hint of black or even brown, but instead were blue, blue with the keenest, sheerest intensity – huge, sparkling eyes of blue with such inky thick lashes, that fluttered ever so slightly as he gazed at her, that Sasha felt herself grow quite weak and faint at the sight.

'Johnny?' was all she could say, breathing the name in a voice of such hushed intensity that it seemed to her the effect must be as sonorous as if she'd shrilled it at the top of her voice.

He stood there, staring at her. 'Aye.' He nodded his head, his arms – bare despite the autumn chill –

crossed over his chest, his elbows clasped in his palms. The white short-sleeved T-shirt he wore hinted at the strong curves of the firmly chiselled chest and laddered stomach beneath, and his sawdust-covered jeans clung loosely to his slim hips and fell in straight lines around his long, lean legs. Sasha gazed at this man in flushed, trembling silence, before taking a step closer to him and whispering aloud, her fingers of their own accord reaching out to clasp his naked arm, 'You have haunted me for so long.'

At the contact of her fingers on his flesh the spell was broken. Quickly, but not rudely, the man took one step backward, away from Sasha, and she realised in horror what she'd done. Clearly this man had no idea who she was. She snatched her fingers away and loudly cleared her throat, fanning her still-flaming cheeks with her hands and trying to laugh to cover her embarrassment.

'Whew,' she panted, wishing she could be air-lifted right out of there, 'sorry about that. For a minute there I thought you were someone I knew.' She tried to flash a bright smile at him, but he was clearly unmoved by her elaborate show of gaiety, for he simply rubbed at his roughly shaven cheek and asked again, ignoring her flustered state, 'Is there something I can help you with?'

Sasha couldn't help herself: she just had to say his name. 'Are you John ... John Blakeley?' she choked out, feeling the tremors start all over again as she said his name out loud.

'Aye,' he said again, looking not in the least bit puzzled, curious, or even angry, merely a little bit bored. 'Is there something that you need?'

Yes, there certainly was, but she knew she wouldn't be receiving any supernatural aid just at that moment, so Sasha, casting her eyes frantically around the little

197

shop for a different source of inspiration, immediately found it nearly hidden away in the corner.

'Yes, please, I'd like one of those,' she said loudly, hoping for firmness but instead overwhelmed with the need to cough. While she hacked away for an agonisingly embarrassing moment, Mr Blakeley's eyes followed where Sasha's finger had been pointing, lighting on the full-length cheval-glass mirror set in a beautifully wrought wooden stand and frame.

'This? The mirror?' he asked a bit brusquely, crossing the room to stand next to it, though Sasha feared he simply wanted to put more distance between him and herself. At the determined nod of her head, John Blakeley straightened himself up a little and said, 'I'm sorry, that's impossible. This mirror has been commissioned by another customer.'

'Well, then, make me another one,' Sasha blurted out, desperate for an excuse to claim his attention for one moment more.

He shook his head and said again, 'I'm sorry, Miss, but that's impossible. I'm overbooked as it is until well into next year, and I'm not accepting any more commissions at the moment.'

'Please,' Sasha heard herself saying, stepping a bit closer to the man, but alarmed at the way he seemed to shrink from her. 'I've come all this way: I'm only going to be here a short time, and I've experienced far too much to just let it go like this!'

Now he did look puzzled. 'Excuse me?' he said a little gruffly, but there seemed to be a hint of something almost softening in his demeanour. 'What did you say?'

'Look,' Sasha said more quietly, forcing herself to speak slowly and summing up all her experience in the competitive marketing world to add weight and authority to her words. 'I've come all this way from

New York – surely you've noticed my accent! – and I'm looking for something very special for my . . . for my friend. I've heard a lot about you – about your work, I mean,' she stumbled quickly, 'and I would be willing to pay the full fee for this mirror in advance – right now, in cash – if you'll only go on and sell it to me.' Well, it wasn't exactly a lie. She held her breath and awaited his response.

Maybe it was her suddenly rational stance, perhaps it was the impressive calmness which she was suddenly exhibiting, but John Blakeley seemed to relax as he regarded her in thoughtful silence.

'All right,' he finally said, coming back towards the centre of the room where she stood. 'This is what I'll do. I can't give you this one –' he indicated the mirror in the corner '– but I can make you another one in, say, a week or so. It might not be as grand as that one –' he nodded again at the mirror '– since I'll have to work on it in a bit of a hurry, as you say you won't be here long, but I'll see what I can do. Would that suit you?'

As Sasha excitedly nodded her head, the tension in the air seemed to dissipate, and she now felt marginally more in control of herself. She started to reach into her handbag for her wallet, quite sure she didn't have nearly enough money to pay for the mirror in full, when, with a smile verging on kindness, the man said gently, indicating her purse, 'No need to pay me now, lass. The bill won't come due until the commission has been completed.'

There seemed to be nothing left to say. Sasha stared stupidly at the man before her, painfully aware that she was running out of excuses to be near him, though he clearly seemed to be waiting for her to make some kind of move or say something important. Finally, with an impatient gesture, he said, 'You'll need to tell me where you'll be staying. So I'll know where to send the bill,' he added, at her look of blank incomprehension.

'Oh!' It took her a moment to adjust, but Sasha finally realised what he had said. She hastily scribbled down her name and address in New York and handed it to him, saying brightly, 'This is so you can deliver it to my home in the States.' She looked at him uncertainly for a moment. 'You do deliver overseas, don't you?'

He smiled at her rather indulgently. 'I know this is just a small village, Miss, but we do have international parcel post here.' He then repeated, 'But I will need to know where you'll be staying while you're in town so I can notify you when I've finished the mirror.'

'Yes, of course,' Sasha gabbled nervously. 'I'm staying at the Swan and Rose.'

There was the merest flicker of the thick fringe of his lashes, and the slightest lift to his arched brow, but the man merely nodded his head and said, 'Well, then, I guess I'll know where to find you, won't I, Miss . . . Mrs? . . . Hayward.'

'Please, Mr Blakeley, call me Sasha,' she said, extending her hand.

'John,' he said, clasping her hand in his in a brief, firm grip. Their eyes met. With a pounding heart, Sasha gazed into the face of this man who bore such an uncanny resemblance to the figure in Amelia Asher's portrait, as well as all the other places Sasha had seen him, or, at least, versions of him. Ah, but this man was real, the trace of his hand in hers even after he'd removed it still lingeringly warm and alive, and Sasha knew that however questionable the reality might be of the other images of John Blakeley she'd encountered up until now, this man was the one she had somehow been destined to find.

'Well,' she said now, nearly in full possession of herself again, 'I'll look forward to hearing from you soon about my mirror.'

'That you will do, Sasha,' he said, and she wondered if he could almost see the strong arrow of delight that thrilled through her body at the sound of her name on his lips. She gave him one final full look before reluctantly turning for the door, wishing there was something else she could say, something she could do that would give her an excuse to stay longer in his presence, but of course there was nothing. And so, still shaking a little from the realisation that her journey had finally brought her here, to this place, to this man, Sasha left the shop of J. Blakeley, Carpenter, and let herself back into her hired car in the carpark.

Unwilling to return to her room in the pub just yet, Sasha decided to simply drive around for a while and perhaps find a place for a secluded walk on the moors, while she contemplated the remarkable events of the past hour or so. After ten or fifteen minutes of driving aimlessly about, she found a relatively isolated place by the side of the road where she could park. She got out of her car and began to walk, undaunted by the harsh, uneven ground of the moors, inhabited only by sparse clumps of brown and purple heather, odd, craggy rocks, ominous-sounding birds, and one evil-looking ram that Sasha was sure was about to gore her to death with its horns.

As she picked her way carefully amongst the rough hillocks and low plains of this unfamiliar territory, continually anxious not to lose her bearings or stray too far from the road, Sasha half-expected to see the ghosts of Cathy and Heathcliff come bounding over to greet her, or to hear Edward Rochester's voice as he cried, broken and blind, for his dear Jane to come home. By now Sasha had nearly convinced herself that she was actually living out some kind of uncanny Gothic fantasy, and she smiled at the thought of what ideal subject matter her experiences would provide for a book or a film. As she wandered about in the variable climate of this unearthly territory, shivering as unexpected clouds threatened rain, only to just as surprisingly disappear under suddenly strong sun, she wondered how she would ever be able to return to the New York life she had known. The curiously changeable atmosphere of the moors, an environment like no other Sasha had ever seen, seemed to epitomise her distance from the woman she had always thought she'd been: here on the irregular terrain of the Yorkshire moors, there seemed to be no place for the old Sasha concerned with market shares, frequent-flyer miles, the newest ways to reduce fat-to-muscle ratio, and all the other unnecessary concerns of contemporary New York life. Instead she felt as though she were participating in a different kind of culture and history, not timeless or mythical but quite the opposite: this tiny village in the rural north of England presented Sasha with a compelling vision of other lives she could be living, seductive alternatives to the now suddenly meaningless compulsions of her other life back 'home.' Sasha smiled. She contemplated telephoning Xenia, one of the only people from New York she missed, but decided to wait, to see where else this adventure would bring her before it was finally played out.

She returned to the Swan and Rose well after dark, having driven into one of the larger towns in the area to have lunch and do some shopping. After a wonderfully filling meal of beef stew with dumplings, and vanilla pudding with banana custard for dessert at a delightful country pub, Sasha had dawdled through the town centre, studying the clothes in the shopwindows and admiring the killingly stylish shoes the young teenage girls were wearing with their traditional school uniforms. She spent the greater part of the afternoon wandering from shop to shop, before finally driving back to the Swan and Rose pub. When she finally unloaded her purchases from the boot of her car and staggered under the weight of them up to her room, several hundred pounds poorer but laden with bags from the most fashionable names on the High Street, she surveyed her efforts with satisfaction. Admiringly, she studied her new ankle-length wool skirt, mock-leopard-print coat with matching hat and gloves, sweet little cocoa-coloured handbag with short double handles, and low-slung, skin-tight, moderately flared black stretch trousers she doubted she'd ever have the nerve to really wear. She admired the other treasures she'd bought as well: the breezy fresh scent of a new brand of shower gel, some enticingly scented aromatherapy candles, several boxes of luxurious Belgian truffles, one of which she was nibbling at now, and a couple of sets of wickedly extravagant lingerie, including an intricately detailed bra in black lace with gold thread, and a matching set of transparent lace bra and panties with built-in suspender-belt.

Sasha glanced at the clock, then back at the items on her bed. She picked up her favourite purchase of all: a body-hugging black velvet dress of thigh-skimming length, with a scoop neck and long sleeves that ended at the wrist in petal-like flares, very retro, very hip, and completely unlike anything Sasha had ever worn before. She then looked thoughtfully at the high silver shoes she'd been given at the hotel, holding them against the dress and measuring their suitability. Well, why not, she decided with a shrug, and, picking up her new ocean-scented shower gel and the freshly laundered towels arranged on the rack by the sink, she made her way to the shower to indulge in some well-deserved pampering.

When she came down for dinner, intending to eat at a table for one, she felt self-consciously aware that she was somewhat overdressed compared with most of the other patrons: many of the customers looked as though they had come in straight from work, which clearly hadn't been conducted in offices. So instead, Sasha sat at the bar by the corner, feeling her short black dress riding up provocatively over her thighs, and waited patiently for Rosie to finish pouring drinks for some particularly raucous customers before coming over to bring Sasha her supper.

'So how was your day?' the red-head asked amiably, nodding approvingly at Sasha's vamped-up appearance. 'Did you find what you were looking for?'

Sasha ached to unburden herself to this friendly young woman who looked at her with such kindness and sympathy as she picked miserably at her food. 'I think I made a pretty big fool of myself today,' she finally confided to Rosie in between bites of baked potato. 'I've come all this way to meet some strange man I'd never heard of before, only to make a jerk out of myself by practically scaring the guy away.' She paused to swallow some bean soup before adding, 'I'm sorry, I know that sounds ridiculous, but trust me, the whole story is pretty unbelievable.'

The bartender sighed. 'Oh, that Johnny Blakeley,' she said, in what was almost a lament. 'He's a real heart-breaker, that one.'

Sasha looked up sharply. 'How did you know?' she demanded in astonishment, draining her half-pint of beer.

Rosie smiled. 'You asked for directions to his shop,

remember?' she said good-humouredly, deftly pulling Sasha another.

'Oh, that's right,' Sasha replied, and started to take a sip before adding, 'Could you please make this a full pint?' She glanced at the other woman's face. 'How well do you know John Blakeley?' she asked, a hint of suspicion beginning to take shape in her mind. Of course! No wonder they had both reacted when Rosie saw the ad and when Sasha told John where she was staying! This lovely young woman and that darkly handsome man were obviously lovers.

'Oh, Johnny and I have known each other since we were kids,' Rosie said slowly, measuring out two double brandies for a pair of women at the bar. 'I guess you could say we've grown up together . . . in all kinds of ways, really,' she added once the women had gone back to their table. She leant her elbows on the bar, close to Sasha's face. 'Never you mind about me, my love,' she said sympathetically. 'If John Blakeley is the man you want – if he's the reason you came up here – you go right ahead and do what you have to do. That's one man who will never tie himself to one woman. He's broken his fair share of young lasses' hearts around here, I can tell you that.'

Sasha was astounded at the woman's generosity. 'You and he are . . . um . . . a couple,' she began delicately, 'but you don't mind if he sees other women?'

Rosie smiled – a little sadly, Sasha thought. 'We have an understanding,' she said simply, with a little shrug. 'Eventually he always comes back to me.' She nodded at the door. 'You'll see. He usually comes in here every couple of nights.'

But he didn't come that night, though Sasha's eyes were riveted to the door at first, but as Rosie continued to pay solicitous attention to her while she finished her supper and drank her beer, it almost seemed to stop mattering. Sasha found herself becoming more and more fascinated by the pretty young red-head: partly, it was true, because she now knew that Rosie knew Johnny, but there was something else, something new, in the way Sasha began to regard her, something different from the way she'd ever felt about a woman before, though she'd felt a suggestion of it several nights ago in her London hotel room when she was being dressed by Claire.

Now, as Sasha drank her beer and studied the figure of the woman before her, she began to imagine, first, how Rosie would look pictured in bed with John Blakeley, his lips and hands on those rounded breasts, hips and buttocks, and then, more daringly, she began to imagine her own hands and mouth in Johnny's place, and she fantasised about how Rosie's body would feel pressed against her own. She watched while Rosie paused to brush away some tousled red curls that were dancing along her forehead, the clinging fabric of her dark blue top stretching across those voluptuously full breasts as she then arched forward, placing her palms on the small of her back and stretching to ease the strain of pulling too many pints. As her body curved outward, Rosie caught sight of Sasha's eyes lingering intently on her body, until, with a fierce blush, Sasha looked up at her face to see Rosie smiling openly at her with a look that on a man would have seemed one of invitation. Was it also so with this woman? Sasha blinked in surprise. She had never desired the feel of a woman's body against her own like this before. She dropped her eyes from the bartender's and gulped hastily at her beer, hoping the bitter, salty taste would drown out the increasingly strong urges of her body. Surreptitiously, she glanced at Rosie again, while the woman's back was turned as she fetched some crisps from a high shelf for a customer. Rosie's body stretched upward as she groped on the shelf for the elusive packet, her legs and buttocks tensed in their tight casing of denim, and Sasha could almost imagine the feel of those full thighs wrapped around her own, the fluid weight of Rosie's buttocks as they would fill Sasha's outstretched hands.

Burning with embarrassment, but no longer willing to deny the demands of the burgeoning desire inside her, Sasha allowed her gaze to linger on Rosie's well-shaped mouth, and she wondered whether kissing a woman's lips would feel the same as kissing a man's, and how it would feel to actually press her mouth against the wet, melting heat of a woman's sweetly opening –

Horrified, Sasha realised that Rosie was staring straight at her again, and was actually coming forward tenderly to enquire, 'What are you thinking about over there, my love? You do have the most curious look on your face, you know.'

And as Sasha looked up into the clear blue eyes of the woman in front of her, she knew that her desire was not only clearly expressed in her face, but was being just as clearly answered in Rosie's. 'How long until closing time?' Sasha asked huskily, daring herself to reach out one finger and run it along the knuckles on the back of the bartender's hand.

The woman smiled suggestively at Sasha. 'Not too much longer now,' she murmured, and stopped Sasha's roving finger in her palm before bringing it up to her warm, full lips, pressing the finger closely to her mouth and flicking lightly at its tip with her tongue. When she finally released Sasha's hand, smilingly placing it back on the bar as she turned to another customer, Sasha found herself trembling with passion and a little fear, as she wondered whether she really understood what she was offering.

Soon after, the last-orders bell was rung, and a few minutes later the lights flicked on and off as a not-so-subtle suggestion that it was time for people to leave. By this time Sasha had drunk several pints of the smooth Yorkshire ale, but she knew that the effervescent bubbles inside her had less to do with any after-effects of the beer than with what was about to happen between her and Rosie.

When at last Rosie had shut and locked the door on the final departing patron, tidied away the glasses and locked the cash-register drawer, she turned to face Sasha with a meaningful look on her face, and lifted her eyebrows enquiringly towards the stairs.

'Are you going to bed now, my love?' she said softly, coming around from behind the bar to stand perilously close to where Sasha was perched unsteadily on her stool.

'Only if you'll come up with me,' Sasha whispered, blushing furiously at her own daring, uncertain exactly what it was that she wanted to do, but desperate to lay her hands on the creamy promise of this young woman's skin.

'Are you sure about this, my love?' Rosie murmured, and, at Sasha's shy nod, she moved closer still to where Sasha sat, wrapping her arms around her waist and urging her off her stool so that the two women stood pressed together, arms enclosing each other's bodies, each simply holding the other close to herself.

The two women were nearly the same height, though Rosie was perhaps an inch or so taller, so that Sasha had to hesitantly tilt her head upward in an invitation to a kiss. In the moment before the other woman's mouth closed upon her own, Sasha had the briefest of pauses to remind herself that what she was about to embark upon could not be revoked, that she was promising to carry through with all that this kiss implied. And so with a shiver of delight, she met Rosie's lips with her own, closing her mind to all else but this most pleasurable of sensations, the feel of the softness of a woman's mouth against hers. At first, it was only their lips that met, sliding against each other with gentle pressure until, eager for more, Sasha parted her mouth slightly, her tongue slowly easing forward to lap shyly against Rosie's lips. As their tongues made contact, Sasha's grip on her lover tightened, her hands flattening out to run enquiringly over the contours of Rosie's strong shoulders, back and waist. Sasha bent her head a little backward under the increasing pressure of Rosie's mouth against hers, their tongues now fully engaged as the two women familiarised themselves with the structure and shape of each other's bodies. It was Sasha who broke away at last, releasing herself from Rosie's tender embrace to look into her eyes and murmur, in a voice that seemed to come from deep within her throat, 'Come upstairs. I want to kiss you all over.'

Arms entwined about each other's waists, the two women made their way together up the staircase to Sasha's room, breaking apart as Sasha turned to shut and lock her door before leaning against it to gaze longingly at the woman before her.

'Strip for me, Rosie,' Sasha whispered hoarsely, no longer feeling at all nervous or shy. 'I want to see you naked.'

Rosie said nothing, merely smiled a little teasingly and turned her back on her audience of one, glancing coyly over her shoulder before sliding her hands lasciviously down her sides to rest at her waist, where she grasped the edges of her dark blue shirt before starting to lift it over her head. In a tantalisingly slow move, she divested herself of her top, still with her back to Sasha, who admired the smooth ivory curves broken only by the thin strip of Rosie's bra. With another saucy glance backward, Rosie reached her hands behind her to unclasp the scrap of blue lace, bending forward a little to slip the straps off her shoulders so that Sasha now knew that Rosie's breasts hung naked and free, though she couldn't see them. With a teasing wiggle, Rosie suddenly tossed the confection of wire and lace over her left shoulder, aiming it with uncanny accuracy so that it fell against Sasha's face, who eagerly pressed the cups to first her lips, then her nose, inhaling the woman's sweet fragrance of roses and musk. Still clutching Rosie's bra, and rubbing it seductively over her cheeks, lips and throat, Sasha gazed at Rosie's bare back, breathlessly waiting for more.

With her arms coyly crossed across her breasts, Rosie turned around, the suggestion of ripe curves slyly peeping over her forearms.

'Drop your arms, Rosie,' Sasha huskily instructed her. 'Show me.'

With a little laugh, Rosie raised her crossed arms above her head, lifting up the round orbs tipped with small circlets of scarlet which pointed provocatively at Sasha. Then, with a little shimmy of her shoulders, she dropped her arms and turned around again to unzip her jeans, which, with a slow, sensuous sway of her hips, she slid down her smooth white thighs. Sasha caught her breath at the sight of the proud curves of Rosie's voluptuous buttocks, watching with eager eyes as the woman kicked off her sneakers and rolled her jeans down to her ankles before delicately stepping out of them. She then stood up tall, clad only in a brief pair of blue lace panties, and, with the precision and grace of a ballet-dancer, she extended her arms and bent forward slowly from the waist, the strong muscles in her thighs and the high rise of her buttocks clearly exposed to Sasha's view.

Sasha longed to rush forward, fall to her knees and press her lips to those temptingly full cheeks, but she forced herself to hold back and wait, while Rosie swung herself back upward, then placed her fingers on the sides of her hips to slowly peel down the remaining scrap of fabric that shielded her body from sight. As the naked beauty of her backside was revealed, inch by sweet inch, Rosie swayed her hips enticingly, standing first on one foot, then the other as she stripped off her panties with her feet. At last she turned around, fully nude, and simply stood, allowing Sasha to absorb the impact of her gloriously bared body.

By now Sasha felt she was melting inside. She pressed herself flat against the door to her room, the shoulder-straps of Rosie's bra still draped around one finger, watching in awed silence as the naked woman came towards her to stand, breast to breast, thigh to thigh, in front of her.

'And now you,' Rosie whispered in Sasha's ear, reaching behind to slowly unzip the back of Sasha's pretty velvet dress. With a shudder of lust, Sasha felt the garment slide down her shoulders and legs to fall in a sumptuous heap on the floor, and she closed her eyes in wonder at the feel of Rosie's wet, open mouth on the deep valley between her breasts, pushed into place by the constricting grip of her underwired bra, which Rosie soon unclasped and let drop on top of the dress. Sasha moaned aloud as she felt Rosie sink to her knees and gently release her feet from the black buckles of her silver shoes which were now beginning to pinch, something the other woman must have guessed, for she tenderly pressed first one foot, then the other to her mouth, kissing away the angry red marks left by the shoes. She then rose up a little to expertly unhook Sasha's suspenders before rolling down each silky black stocking, leaving Sasha naked now save for the lacy froth of her transparent panties. She then paused, and waited.

Sasha stood, trembling, desperate to feel Rosie's fingers on her flesh once more, but the woman did nothing, and when Sasha finally opened her eyes and stared down at her, still kneeling on the floor, Rosie merely grinned and said, in a voice that was husky and low, 'Say please.'

'Please,' Sasha urged, her eyes shutting again tight. 'Oh, yes, please.'

At last she felt Rosie's fingers slowly strip away her panties until Sasha was as naked as she. Rosie then stood up full-length against Sasha and, pressing her back even more firmly against the door, she kissed her full on the mouth, while her fingers sought the slick crevice of Sasha's open sex, heavy with dew and craving sweet friction. Her own curly auburn bush pressing against Sasha's darker pubic thatch, Rosie slid her fingers over the full, plush petals, clearly intent on a slow tease, until Sasha moved her mouth away from Rosie's to whisper in her ear, 'Oh, please, now, I can't wait.'

At the same time she reached down to guide Rosie's thumb to the knot of her clitoris, the round, hard bud so acutely sensitised that all it took was one, two, three sweeps of Rosie's finger and Sasha went off like a rocket, her body racked by strong spasms of delight.

Finally, with a slight push, Sasha nudged Rosie away from her to walk, shakily, over to the bed.

'Wow,' she blinked as she sat, 'this is really a first for me.'

Rosie looked concerned. 'I haven't made you uncomfortable, I hope,' she said anxiously as she seated herself beside Sasha. 'I thought this might be your first time with a woman.'

Sasha looked at her, a little surprised. 'You mean, it's not your first time?'

At Rosie's gentle shake of the head, Sasha found she felt strangely dismayed, as well as oddly aroused. She turned to gaze at the naked woman next to her on the bed, and reached out a finger to trail it suggestively down the bare planes of Rosie's stomach. 'Well, I hope I won't disappoint you, then,' she murmured, urging Rosie backward on to the bed. She then straddled Rosie's body with her own, swinging her legs over the other woman's hips and lying down full-length upon her, experiencing the unfamiliar sensation of naked nipples against her own, the strong curves of waist and hips under hers, and the crisp entanglement of pubic curls as she began to arch her pelvis against Rosie's. The pressure of vulva against vulva was rich and intense, but Sasha didn't want Rosie to come too soon. She sensed that this woman liked a bit of delay, that she wanted to prolong her pleasure, and that orgasm was only one of the multiple joys of women's erotic contact. So Sasha rolled off Rosie's body to lie alongside her, running her fingers hesitantly over the pink tightness of her pert nipples.

'Mmmm,' Rosie sighed, propping herself up a little against Sasha's pillows so that her breasts retained their full and buoyant weight. 'That's nice.'

No longer timid in the slightest, Sasha bent over and closed her lips firmly over one puckered bud, marvelling at its fullness and its slightly smoky taste, and she rolled Rosie's nipple around in her mouth for

213

a moment before drawing back slightly to flick her tongue over the pert little tip. She licked quietly at Rosie's nipple before bending back over her breast, taking as much of it into her mouth as she could, sucking gently on the one while she palmed the nipple of the other, fingers and mouth full of the wonder of a woman's breasts. Her own sex felt heavy and moist with desire, and she felt sure that Rosie's must be feeling the same. Enquiringly, she placed her hand first on Rosie's thigh, then, more daringly, directly on the pulsing softness within, with its complexities of texture, shape and size. There were the plush, velvety outer lips, the satiny, smaller inner ones, the deep groove of pleasure, and, as Sasha snuck one, then two fingers into the rippling centre within, the contracting, meltingly warm haven that felt satisfyingly similar to her own. Experimentally, she worked her fingers inside Rosie's sex, trying out different speeds and pressures, varying the thrusts and strokes in the ways she had always pleased herself, hoping they would please Rosie and taking care not to neglect her clitoris. As Rosie's liquid pearl vibrated beneath her thumb, Sasha began to inch her way downward, brushing her mouth along Rosie's breasts to the dip and swell of her stomach, pausing to plunge her tongue into the perfumed well of her lover's navel.

'Mmm, yes,' Rosie murmured above her, urging Sasha's head lower with her hands. 'Please don't stop now.'

And so, with trembling heart and shaking fingers, Sasha lowered herself to the floor by the bed, sliding her lover along with her so that the woman's feet were flat on the floor, her thighs widespread and the rich fruit of her sex poised at the edge of the bed, directly in front of Sasha's mouth. Sasha gazed for a moment in silence at this part of a woman's body she had never seen up close before, and her heart swelled with pride to know that this was what she, too, looked like when viewed from this angle. And was this what she would taste like as well?

With a breathy sigh, Sasha leant in close and pressed her mouth against the musky warmth of Rosie's sex, so trustingly spread out before her, and as she began to lick softly and gently at that rosy vagina, savouring the salty-sweet taste of a woman's pleasure, Sasha thought to herself that it was rather like kissing a mouth, only far more interesting. She ran her tongue, shivering with joy, over, around, and inside all the delightful little grooves, ridges, and furrows, feeling as though Rosie was kissing her back, only using her sex instead of her mouth. She thrust her tongue inside the satiny recess, feeling it clutch and pull, and then drew back to suck gently on Rosie's clitoris, which rippled and thrilled beneath her tongue. She suspected that by now Rosie had climaxed several times, though each orgasm was more a shudder of delight than a volcano of rapture, and she sensed that Rosie's capacity for pleasure was infinitely more complex and diffuse than she was used to. And so, Sasha discovered, was her own, for as she kissed Rosie's sex she felt answering tremors of pleasure in her own, and when Rosie finally nudged away Sasha's mouth, temporarily sated, Sasha too felt sexually replete. And as the night wore on into the early grey hours of the dawn, as the two women finally settled down to sleep in each other's arms, Sasha felt that a part of her had truly come home, and she silently thanked Amelia Asher for bringing her so far on her journey.

Chapter Twelve

'So, my love, how are we going to get the handsome Johnny Blakeley into your bed?'

Sasha looked at Rosie and blinked. The two women were sitting at a table in a quiet corner of the pub at a shamelessly late hour the next morning, sipping coffee and gazing dreamily at each other the way new lovers often do the morning after the night before. Sasha had nearly forgotten about John Blakeley in her pleasure at discovering the velvet intimacies of Rosie's body, although there had been an insistent little voice at the back of her head reminding her that she was perhaps retracing the paths of Johnny's hands and lips on the body of his lover with her own. Now, however, she jumped at the mention of his name when Rosie spoke it, and she looked at her a little guiltily, fearing that Rosie might suspect that Sasha had merely been exploiting her as a way of getting closer to the mysterious carpenter.

'Oh, Rosie, I don't ... well, I don't know,' Sasha stammered, unsure about how to deal with the woman's generous offer.

She needn't have been concerned. Rosie laid a comforting hand on Sasha's arm and gave her a reassuring squeeze. 'Listen, lass,' she said warmly, 'I told you last night that I have no problem with John Blakeley bedding other women; after all,' she added, laughing, 'given what we two got up to last night, I can hardly complain if Johnny goes elsewhere for some fun! Besides,' she went on, with a tender glance at Sasha, 'for some reason you still haven't explained, this man obviously means something special to you, and if getting him alone is what will make you happy, then I want to help you make that happen.'

Sasha gazed at Rosie with gratitude and surprise. 'I wouldn't do anything to hurt you, you know that, Rosie,' she said tremulously, 'but I seem to have developed a real craving for this man.'

'Well then,' Rosie said firmly, leaning back to finish her coffee, 'why don't I invite the two of you up to my flat for a drink after closing tonight?'

'Oh, no,' Sasha said with haste, thinking that that particular scenario might be just a little too uncomfortable. 'That won't be necessary. Didn't you say he often comes into the pub?'

'That he does,' Rosie said thoughtfully, fingering a cold slice of toast. 'It's been a while since we've seen him here, actually, so perhaps he will step in tonight. But Sasha,' she added, coaxingly, 'you still haven't told me why this man is so important to you.'

Sasha looked at Rosie and considered. The urge to tell was too great: the secret had sat with her too long, and she felt burdened with the need to finally confide fully in another person. 'Are you sure you've got the day off?' she asked, toying a little nervously with her napkin.

'I told you, I'm not due behind the bar until the five

o'clock opening tonight,' Rosie reminded her a little impatiently.

Sasha stood. 'Let's go up on the moors,' she said abruptly, tossing her napkin on to the table. 'It doesn't seem right to talk about it here.'

Rosie smiled. 'I know just the spot,' she said, with confidence.

They headed out to the moors in Rosie's charmingly old-fashioned Volkswagen Beetle, complete with rattling muffler and erratic heating system which Sasha figured must be a dreadful inconvenience in the cold Yorkshire winters. She watched admiringly as Rosie guided the car with skill through odd little avenues and curious deserted byways, until she finally pulled over at a lay-by off the road and shut off the motor. Rosie leant across Sasha's lap, pushed open her door and prodded her out of the car. 'Come on,' she said. 'Let's go find my secret place.'

Stumbling a little, Sasha followed the younger woman as she strode familiarly over the uneven terrain, pausing to lay down a rough tartan blanket before seating herself on a great grey slab of rock which extended out on to the deserted plain. She dug out a flask of fresh coffee and a warm woollen shawl from her rucksack.

'Sit,' she invited Sasha, patting the space on the blanket beside her. 'Talk.'

Sasha accepted the soft, heavy shawl held out to her and wrapped it around her shoulders, contemplating the situation with bemusement. Here she was, in the middle of the Yorkshire moors with this woman, the taste of whose musky rich pleasure was still lingering on Sasha's tongue, yet who was so generously offering to assist her in seducing her own lover, just as one might offer assistance to a friend who needed a favour. As a kind of recompense, Sasha was about to volunteer her own story of ghostly visitations, a mysterious masked ball, a secret manuscript and a weeping portrait, a story of which even her own best friend at home was only partially aware. Yet there was no question that it felt right to Sasha that Rosie be the recipient of her strange tale, for it was beginning to seem as though Rosie was no disinterested outsider to Sasha's narrative, but instead was somehow directly implicated in the story herself.

And so Sasha began to talk, seated on that rock on the moors in the watery grey daylight: she started with her arrival at the Asher Hotel in the summer to meet with the advertising team from Rollit, and continued with her story on up to the present. When she got to the part about finding the hidden manuscript in the lift, she carefully slipped the fragile sheaf of papers from her handbag and handed it to Rosie, who silently read it through, eyes darkening curiously at certain places, and then returned it to Sasha, who continued her story. She told Rosie about how the manuscript had moved around in her house, about the two strange models in her office whose bodies glowed in the lamplight and who made sounds like the rustling of wings; she talked about the pony-tailed lover she'd met at the ball, and about seeing the vision of the dead Johnny Blakeley standing on his grandmother's grave. Rosie listened to the whole wild story in silence, nodding companionably at moments when Sasha's voice seemed to falter, and at one point reaching out to hold Sasha's hand tightly as she described her feelings at standing by the grave of Lady Amelia Asher. When Sasha was finally finished, ending her story with her feeling of debt to Amelia for leading her here, not just to the present-day John Blakeley but to Rosie herself, the younger woman sat silently, sipping at her coffee and staring out at the silent moors.

'Wow,' she said finally into the silence. 'That's really some adventure.' She said nothing else for several moments, while Sasha, who had talked herself hoarse, was content simply to sit huddled in the warmth of the shawl and sip her coffee, marvelling at the harsh beauty of the moors in the chill of early autumn.

'I'll tell you something else that will add to your sense of destiny,' Rosie said slowly, not looking at Sasha. 'You know how you have that pretty tattoo of a black swan on your shoulder? And you say that John and Amelia used to meet in the rose garden?' Sasha nodded, but looked a little blank. 'I'm not saying that this means anything: maybe it's just a strange coincidence, but I can personally confirm that Johnny Blakeley – our Johnny, the carpenter – has a lovely tattoo of a black rose on the lower part of his stomach, right about here.' Rosie ignored Sasha's sharp intake of breath as she indicated the spot on her body where John Blakeley bore his tattoo. She went on to say, in a tone of honest dismay, 'I always thought that his rose maybe had something to do with me, you know, it being my name and all –' she turned to look at Sasha '– but considering everything you've just told me, maybe it has more to do with you and him, although I do seem to be involved in some way with your story.' At Sasha's continuing blank look, Rosie sighed, and went on, 'Don't you remember how Amelia talks about her maid Rosie, who helped to find ways for her and Johnny to get together?'

At Sasha's stunned but excited nod, Rosie continued, 'Well, don't you see? Doesn't that seem like another strange coincidence? And I'll tell you something else,' she went on, in a rather subdued voice. 'They say that it was Johnny's great-great-great-grandfather, going way back to the end of the eighteenth century, who bred a new kind of rose, a rose that's only grown in Yorkshire, and you'll never guess what it's called.' She glanced over at Sasha, who seemed to be holding her breath, and slowly nodded her head. 'Yes, Sasha, it's called the Amelia Rose,' she said softly, and then sat in silence with her eyes downcast.

Sasha said nothing at first, then leant over to place a warm kiss on Rosie's half-opened mouth. She shuffled over to sit as close to the other woman as she could, placing her arms around Rosie and holding her close against her breast. The two women sat like that for a while, bodies pressed together in silence before, with a half-embarrassed laugh, Rosie disentangled herself from Sasha's grip. 'Hey,' she said, smiling sweetly as she smoothed away a lock of chestnut hair from Sasha's cheek. 'It's bloody freezing out here. Let's go and find a pub somewhere and have a drink to warm us up.'

'You know, Rosie,' Sasha said carefully as they picked their way through the clumps of heather on the way back to Rosie's car, 'I don't know quite how to put this, but I really don't think that I'm . . . well . . . meant to stay up here for very much longer.' She glanced at her companion, who said nothing, before continuing, 'Whatever happens to me in the next couple of days, I don't think it's supposed to change my life in any really drastic way.' She stopped walking for a moment and turned Rosie's shoulders so that she faced her. 'This carpenter man is going to make me a mirror, send it back to the States for me, and then I'm going to get on an aeroplane and go back home. Yes,' she said softly, noting the look on Rosie's face, 'New York is still my home; I'm not here for good, only for now. And I certainly didn't come all this way to change the way things are – for anyone.'

A silence of understanding passed between the two women before Rosie said, stepping away and breaking the mood, 'Come on.' She tugged at Sasha's hand, and started back to the car. 'Let's go and drink some fine Yorkshire ale and you can tell me all about New York.'

By the time Sasha and Rosie returned to the Swan and Rose, it was nearly five o'clock, and Rosie had to dash off to get ready for opening up the bar, promising Sasha that she would find some time to sit with her while she ate her supper later on that night. Feeling suddenly quite weary, and impressed by Rosie's continuing ebullience after a virtually sleepless night, Sasha trudged upstairs for a long, restful sleep, feeling the weight of delayed jet lag suddenly settling on her shoulders. She had only been back in the country a few days, she reminded herself, and two of the three nights she'd spent in England so far had involved a lot of sex, but not a lot of sleep. If she really was somehow fated to meet John Blakeley that night – as she was beginning to be more convinced than ever that she was – Sasha decided that she had better rest up in preparation.

So it was nearly nine o'clock when she finally came back down the stairs, after a refreshing nap and a soothing, warm shower. She met Rosie's eyes with a merry grin and said, seating herself at the bar, 'Just some salad and sandwiches tonight, if you don't mind.'

Rosie grinned at Sasha, indicating her black velvet top and new skin-tight hipster trousers with approval. Sasha hadn't been too sure about the trousers when she'd pulled them on after her shower, but she did think they looked rather flattering in the mirror in her room, more so than they had in the shop, and she decided that she looked rather fetching. Rosie's good-humoured leer seemed to confirm Sasha's own assessment, and she was pleased that she'd dared to wear something that she had thought really only suited teenagers.

It was when she had just finished the last bit of cucumber in her salad and was pushing her plate towards the bartender, when Rosie's eyes suddenly darted towards the door; she leant towards Sasha and whispered with an enigmatic smile, 'He's here.'

Sasha's eyes flitted towards the door. He was there, in zippered black leather jacket and battered blue jeans, his curly black hair tumbling over his startling blue eyes, his cheeks slightly flushed with the cold as he looked around the pub, before nodding in recognition to an unseen someone in the corner. As he made his way over to his companion, Johnny's eyes turned towards Rosie at the bar: he gave her a slight smile and a nod, and then his glance settled momentarily on Sasha. She caught her breath and froze, then flashed him a bright smile, but he merely looked at her and frowned, as though trying to remember who she was, before continuing on his way into the corner. Rosie caught the look of despair on Sasha's face and smiled sympathetically.

'Don't worry there, lass,' she said quietly, as she slid a shot of whisky across the bar at her. 'He can be a bit of a bastard at times, can our Johnny.'

Sasha sipped gratefully at the mellow sting of her drink, her stomach fluttering wildly and her palms beginning to sweat. Nervously, she looked to Rosie for support. 'What do I do now?' she whispered. 'Maybe I should just forget this whole thing.'

But Rosie was already leaning across the bar, her whole demeanour exhibiting the casual warmth one extends to an old and intimate friend. 'We haven't seen you around here for a while, John,' she said archly, as he approached the bar. 'Where have you been, man?'

Sasha's stomach did another double-flip as the tall stranger came to stand beside her, reaching into his wallet to extract money for his order.

'Is it the usual for you?' Rosie asked, already reaching for the wooden handle to release the flow of bitter. 'And is there anything else?'

The man's eyes flicked again to Sasha, just as they had when he'd first entered the pub. 'Two pints, Rosie,' he said gruffly, counting out some change. 'And the same for Charley.'

Rosie chortled. 'Don't tell me he's still trying to get you to invest your money in that crazy old scheme!' she exclaimed, while Sasha sat, mystified and once more ignored, slowly sipping at her whisky and hoping she could make it last the length of the friendly banter between Rosie and John. As she watched the two of them converse about people and events so obviously familiar to them and so completely alien to herself, Sasha wondered again exactly what she was doing here. She didn't know this man standing next to her at the bar! she reminded herself sharply, although Rosie clearly did. She tried not to stare at the way Johnny's eyes gazed so intimately into Rosie's, and she turned away so as not to behold the wild flush of pink that bloomed on the porcelain-white surface of Rosie's cheek. And yet, even as Sasha was confronted with the reality of the bond between Johnny and this other woman, her body yearned towards him: her thighs trembled at being so close to his, her nipples tightened into pinpoints of desire in the lacy cage of her bra, and her heart hammered painfully against her chest. Yes, she felt a loyalty and kinship to Rosie, but didn't she also owe something to Amelia Asher? Hadn't she been sent up here for the very purpose of finding this man, John Blakeley, and – what? To do what with him, exactly?

Even as the pulse beating damply in Sasha's sex was throbbing out the answer to that question, the carpenter's eyes turned to hers and he said with an almost friendly smile, 'Your mirror's coming along just fine: I'm expecting the glass early tomorrow, and I've already finished part of the frame.'

So he did remember her! Sasha's cheeks flamed with pleasure at this simple courtesy, but the moment didn't last: with a brief nod, John Blakeley picked up the tray with the four pints of bitter and headed back to his corner with the invisible Charley.

Rosie watched him go with a sigh, an unmistakable expression of longing on her face which she made no attempt to disguise as she turned to Sasha and said, 'Yes, he's a heart-breaker, that one.' Catching the look in Sasha's eyes that seemed to mirror her own, Rosie reached across to lay one hand against her still-burning cheek. 'Never you mind, love,' she said firmly. 'I told you not to worry about me. If you want that man over there, then that man you shall have. He'll soon be on his own, you'll see: Charley never stays for long in this pub. Two pints, that's his limit, and he'll be off home to plan more impossible money-making schemes. You just sit there and drink your whisky, and let me take care of the rest.'

And sure enough, after a little while Sasha saw a grey-haired, slightly hump-backed man of about sixty or so cross the crowded room to the bar, where he carefully set down two empty pint glasses, traces of foam still clinging to the sides.

'There you are, my girl,' the man said fondly to Rosie, then turned politely to Sasha. 'And how are you tonight, lass? Still drinking our good Yorkshire ale?'

Sasha recognised the man as the one she had met at the bar on her first night in the pub. She blushed shyly at the man now, while Rosie said cheerily, 'We'll see you again here tomorrow night, eh, Charley?'

Together she and Sasha watched the older man limp his way slowly to the door. 'He lost his house and his wife when the last pit closed up here in the eighties,' Rosie said softly as Charley left the pub. 'Ever since then he's been dreaming up one wild money-making scheme after another as a way of spending his time.' She smiled at Sasha, her eyes clouded with pain, but her face suddenly cleared as John Blakeley approached the bar and placed his empty pint glasses in front of her. With a silent nod, he moved to zip up his leather jacket, apparently intending to leave, a gesture which filled Sasha with panic. Rosie caught her eye and nodded.

'Hold up there a bit, Johnny,' she said abruptly, pointing to the empty stool beside Sasha. 'My mate here is sitting all alone. She doesn't know anyone else here, and I've got to rush off to the storeroom for a bit: won't you stay and mind her for me for a few minutes while I'm gone?'

With what seemed to Sasha to be a great show of reluctance, John Blakeley sat down heavily beside her and said to Rosie, with only a trace of a smile, 'It'll cost you, girl: another pint for me, and whatever the lady here wants.'

'Oh, I'll have a pint too,' Sasha said breathlessly, shamelessly aglow with the thrill of being once again so close to this man with the curling black hair and effervescent blue eyes. Damn, but he was handsome! she couldn't help thinking, and she had to sit on her hands to stop herself from reaching out to touch him, to lay her fingers along his hide-covered sleeve and thrill at the thought that his bare flesh was separated from hers by a mere few layers of fabric.

Get a grip on yourself! Sasha thought, willing her

internal tremors to cease. Striving to appear calm, she picked up her pint and turned to face the man. 'So,' she began uncertainly, struggling to make conversation, 'how long have you been a carpenter?'

He laughed at that. 'Checking up on my credentials, are you?' he asked in quite a friendly tone. 'And I thought you said you'd heard about my work from all the way over in New York.'

'Oh . . . well, I . . .' Sasha stammered uncomfortably, wondering how to get out of this one, but Rosie saved her.

'Go on, answer the girl!' she instructed Johnny. 'Tell her about the business.' And with that she whisked off to the storeroom, leaving the two of them alone at the bar.

After that, conversation was easy. Knowing absolutely nothing about carpentry, or joinery, as she was charmed to hear Johnny call it, Sasha drank her beer and listened to stories about braces and bits and awls, paying little attention to what he said, but staring instead at his blue eyes, his finely chiselled mouth, his broad shoulders and his elegantly long, artistic hands. When he in turn asked her about her work in the States, Sasha spoke with great animation, not because she was fired up with enthusiasm about her job, but because the presence of this man beside her filled her with such a strong sense of passion and excitement. She was so engrossed by his nearness that she didn't notice Rosie had returned to behind the bar, and she barely registered that her pint glass had been refilled, though she continued to drink from it absentmindedly.

In fact, as the evening wore on, they both drank quite a bit, and it seemed to Sasha that John Blakeley was certainly thawing out and becoming more friendly as the night progressed, though whether that was due to her or to the beer, she couldn't tell. She noticed with gratitude that Rosie for the most part left them alone, seeming to sense that Sasha no longer needed her, until, with a jolt, she heard the bell ring for last orders, and soon, too soon, she saw the lights flicker as a warning that it was time for the customers to leave.

Oh, no! Sasha wailed to herself. Now what should she do? How was she going to convince this man to stay?

She needn't have worried. Once again Rosie came to her aid.

'I'd best be getting on home,' John said as he stood, reaching for his jacket. 'I'll just be off to the gents' first.'

'Sorry, mate,' Rosie interrupted him briskly. 'Toilet's overflowed.'

Johnny stared at her. 'What, both of them?' he asked in surprise.

'I know,' Sasha hastily interjected, inspired by Rosie's obvious ploy. 'Come upstairs and use the bathroom in my room.' She looked at Johnny and held her breath.

He cocked a suspicious eye at Rosie, who made a shooing gesture with her hands. 'Go on, then, man,' she ordered him, 'get up those stairs before you make a mess on my carpet!'

Well, it wasn't the most romantic of plots, but it worked. With a wink at Rosie, Sasha followed Johnny upstairs to her room, unlocked the door with a trembling heart, and let him inside. Feeling a little embarrassed, she coughed politely and said, 'I'll just wait in the hall until you're done.'

'Don't be silly, woman!' John grunted in response. 'It's your room; I'll only be a minute.'

She watched while he disappeared into the bath-

228

room and allowed herself to indulge in the fantasy of what his cock would be like when he'd released it from his jeans. Would it be long and thick? Reddish-purple or more pink? Would he be circumcised or would his cock be shrouded in a spongy cowl of foreskin? She tried to picture the expression on John's face as he handled his staff: would it be pleasurable for him, or would he regard it as merely another appendage? And what would he do if she suddenly appeared in the bathroom and offered to hold it for him? Would he allow her to do it, or would he think she was some kind of pervert?

Just then the bathroom door was pushed open, abruptly intruding on Sasha's blissful fantasy, and with the most unerotic sound of the toilet flushing in the background, Sasha turned and faced this man she craved so fiercely, knowing this was the time.

'Wait,' she said huskily, coming forward as he stepped into the middle of the room. 'Don't go: not yet.'

His blue eyes met her brown ones as she came to stand before him, as close as she dared. The two of them stood motionless for a moment, their breathing the only sound in the room. He was tall, so tall, she thought to herself with a dizzying sense of rapture: he's so tall, he's going to have to bend right over to kiss me.

And kiss her he did, as Sasha's hands slid up under the leather jacket he still wore, urging it off his shoulders and hardly noticing as it fell to the floor, concentrating instead on the width of his shoulders, the soft curls of his hair, the smooth shaven feel of his jaw as she grasped his face in her hands to bring it closer to hers. He had his hands on her waist, holding her loosely against him as his mouth explored hers, his lips parting to allow Sasha's tongue access so that it rubbed delightfully against his, and this moment felt so strong, so precious to Sasha, that she opened her eyes to be sure it was real.

She saw that his eyes were open too, gazing into her own with a startling blue intensity as he gripped her waist and held her tightly to him, running his hands up over the planes of her back and slipping them under her black velvet top to feel the warmth of her skin. Then, with an abrupt movement that left Sasha feeling bereft, he released her and stepped away.

'Is this what you want, Sasha?' he asked her quietly, and she rejoiced at the heavenly sound of her name on her lips.

In answer she came forward to him again and, saying nothing, she merely gazed up at him as she slowly began to unbutton the rough cotton of his shirt, releasing with every flick of her fingers the honey-gold glory of his strong chest, the strongly muscled curves flecked with crisp black curls which Sasha twined around her fingers before continuing to undress him. He stood there in silence until the final button had been undone and she had pushed his shirt off him. Sasha gazed at his bare stomach and gasped, beholding the tip of the black rose tattoo that Rosie had described to her when they had sat on the moors. She could only see the very topmost part of a black petal, its rounded shape peeping up over the top of the waistband of his jeans. She raised her eyes to meet his, stepping up on tiptoe to kiss him again, opening his lips with hers and pressing her hands flat against the hard roundness of his bare chest, his small nipples puckered and erect beneath her palms.

'You now,' he growled softly into her ear, easing up the soft fabric of her top and pulling it roughly over her head to fling it away to the floor. He then wrapped his arms around her body, urging her to arch backward as he stooped to run his mouth along the exposed column of her throat and the creamy tops of her swelling breasts, only partially revealed by her pearl-encrusted bra. Johnny bent her nearly double and pressed his mouth against the ivory lace, his tongue teasing out the spaces of the openworked material to tantalise her nipples, which were straining against the confines of her bra. When at last he moved back upright, it was to release the single hook at Sasha's back with a casually studied finger, and, through the haze of her pleasure, Sasha felt a bolt of envy at the thought of the countless other women upon whose lingerie he had perfected his obvious expertise.

At the feel of her naked stomach against his, however, Sasha lost all thought of anything else but the shivers of delight that coursed through her, and, with luxurious ease, she tasted the textured roughness of his chest, burying her face in his ebony curls before locating one of his taut pink nipples and sucking gently at it, relishing its coppery taste. As her mouth played along the firm contours of his chest, her hands reached lower to unbutton the waistband of his jeans, the ridged planes of his stomach tensing beneath her fingers.

When at last she had undone all the buttons, Sasha dropped to her knees to examine at close range the black rose which graced Johnny's stomach: it began below one hip and extended upward to end just next to the deep well of his navel. She drew back and studied the rose, drawing first her finger, then her tongue along the thorny stem and single leaf before coming up to press her whole mouth against the head of the rose, a tightly packed bud only just beginning to open. As she worked his hips, buttocks, and thighs free of his jeans, Sasha jutted her tongue into the furrowed grooves of Johnny's navel, feeling the thick curls at his groin tickle her throat and his heavy cock prod impatiently between her naked breasts, as though trying to aim at her mouth.

She pulled away to look up at him as he gazed down at her, his hand knotted in her hair, his eyes like shards of blue flame. She then bent down to untie his clumsy workman's boots, stripping off his socks and easing off his jeans so he stood gloriously rampant and entirely nude before her. She drew close again to wrap her lips around the rich round head of his cock, the glossy smoothness of the skin as it slid into her mouth feeling exquisitely delicate against her tongue. At first she simply sucked on the very tip of his shaft, running her tongue around the sensitive ridge and sampling with delight the fragrant drop that eased out from the tiny opening. Then, sliding her mouth further downward, Sasha reached between Johnny's legs as he stood, feet apart, his cock in her mouth and her fingers gently stroking that silky, sensitive place behind his weighted scrotum, and she pressed lightly against the yielding little pad before edging even further back to scratch teasingly at his anus. No, he wasn't circumcised, she thought dreamily, as she tested the softness of the fleshy cowl before turning her attention to the hardness of his shaft. Johnny groaned quietly, widening his stance still further as Sasha slid her mouth off his cock then ducked her head lower to enfold the tense sac of his scrotum into the warm cavern of her mouth. Her hands tightly gripping his buttocks, Sasha toyed with his balls with care, filling her mouth with the precious sac, marvelling at the intimacy he was allowing her. Finally, with another stifled groan, Johnny pushed her away almost roughly and, bending down, lifted her up in his arms, apparently intending to carry her to the bed, when, with an urgent hand against his chest, Sasha stopped him.

'Condom?' she asked breathlessly, while he stared at her, almost smiling, his eyes gripped by hers. 'Oh, never mind!' she said almost brusquely, turning away from him to point towards her new rectangular handbag on the top of her dresser. 'I've got some in my bag.'

Gently, Johnny lowered her to the floor by her dresser, but while Sasha rummaged hurriedly through her bag, searching for the elusive packet, John came to stand behind her to unfasten her hipster trousers, and, before she had a chance to respond, he knelt behind her to deftly strip them away, along with her boots and her panties. Sasha now stood completely naked, her body pressed against the cool painted wood of her dresser, the packet of condoms clutched tightly in her hand.

'Don't move,' Johnny muttered from somewhere on the floor behind her; then, with a muffled gasp, Sasha gripped tightly on to the edge of the dresser as she felt his fingers parting her thighs, so that she stood straddling the floor as he had done earlier, and then she felt him softly stroking his way along the damp fullness of her lower lips. Sasha hung on to the dresser and moaned as Johnny's fingers found the hard round bud of her clitoris, and then, knees trembling, she felt the wet heat of his mouth as he licked along her sex, his fingers holding her open to allow his tongue greater access.

Sasha's quick, fierce, climactic spasm took her a little by surprise, but before she had time to recover, Johnny had moved his mouth away from her sex to kiss along the deep crease leading, Sasha realised with a delicious sense of horror, to the tight opening to her anus. No one had ever done this to her before! she

233

thought in breathless amazement as she bent over as far forward as she could, exposing her puckered anal rose to Johnny's questing tongue. She stood, nearly fainting with delight, as he plunged his tongue in and out of her anus, his hands gripping the cheeks of her backside and holding them apart for this, the most intimate kiss Sasha had ever experienced.

'Enough – please, no more!' she cried out at last, staggering away from his mouth to stand with her back against the door to her room.

He moved away to grin down at her, looking quite pleased with himself, before gently taking the packet of condoms from Sasha's limp fingers, extracting a single disc and holding it up to her with a questioning arch of his eyebrow.

Sasha understood that he was tacitly asking whether she was now ready for a different kind of pleasure, and she nodded, barely able to speak, as he ripped the packet apart, rapidly unrolled the sheath over his blushing, swaying penis, and came to her to hold her in a tight embrace.

'Are you ready for me, lass?' he murmured in her ear, and to show him that she was, Sasha reached out to grip his cock, opening her thighs and guiding him towards her so that the tip of his shaft nudged temptingly against the entrance to her sex.

'Come inside me now,' Sasha whispered, her eyes locked with his. 'I want you now.'

And then, pressing her back against the door, Johnny positioned himself between her thighs, gripping her hips and lifting up her legs. Bending slightly at the knees, he lowered her on to his length and slid smoothly upward so that their bodies were joined, her arms around his shoulders, his face nearly level with hers, their mouths a heartbeat apart.

'Now,' was all he said, and he lowered his mouth

to her throat as he began to lunge roughly inside her, Sasha's hips arching down to meet his upward thrusts, the two of them working together, matching their rhythms and coordinating the pace in mutual erotic harmony. Impatiently, Sasha nudged Johnny's mouth away from her throat, cupping his cheek in her hand as she gazed at him, and struggling a little for balance while never ceasing to grind against him.

'Kiss me, Johnny,' she breathed, and he covered her lips with his, their mouths slanting against each other with the urgency of appetite, his eyes nearly dazzling her with their startlingly blue luminosity. The pressure of his body against her own rocked her hard against the door, and she thrilled to the strength and the depth of his body driving into hers. With every stroke of his cock within her, she answered with a clench of her inner muscles and an arch of her hips against his, feeling the hardness of his bare chest, stomach and thighs as they rubbed so delightfully along the length of her body. When at last Sasha's climax shattered over her, she broke her mouth away and shamelessly howled out her pleasure, barely even noticing Johnny's own climax when he erupted inside her. As he gently lowered her to the floor, releasing himself with a reluctant but abrupt withdrawal, the two of them simply stared at each other in silence, before Johnny turned away to dispose of the condom in the bathroom.

Panic clutched again at Sasha's heart. Would this be it? she wondered frantically. Was he going to leave her now?

When Johnny came back into the room, he appeared to be as indecisive as she. They circled one another hesitantly, each still fully nude, until Sasha decided such uncertainty was unnecessary, and she moved to lie on the bed.

'Come here, Johnny,' she whispered invitingly, patting the space beside her. 'Come and lie with me.'

Johnny approached her slowly, and cautiously lay down beside her. She moved over to lay her head on his chest and, after a pause, he placed his arm around her and began to gently stroke her hair. There was another silence. At length he spoke.

'You know that Rosie and I have an understanding,' he began, but Sasha laid a finger on his lips and silenced him.

'Hush,' she said softly, placing a kiss against his jaw. 'I know.'

There was silence again as the two of them lay there, Sasha running her fingers down the length of his chest and stomach, and tracing the pattern of the rose that broke the symmetry of his body.

'What did you mean when you said in my shop that I haunted you?' Johnny asked at last.

Sasha turned to look at him. What could she say? She said the only thing she could think of. 'I've had a vision of a man like you,' she said quietly, then, when he was about to speak, she went on before he could interrupt, 'and I needed to know whether he really existed. That's all I need to know. I'm not going to do anything crazy, like move up here to be near you, or anything like that.' She looked at him and smiled. 'You and Rosie belong together: I'm not about to intrude.' She shrugged, and smiled again. 'I just had to find out for myself whether you really existed or not.' She paused, then asked, not quite believing she was daring to, 'Have you ever heard the name of Amelia Asher?'

Johnny's hand in her hair stilled. 'How do you know about that?'

She looked at him and said nothing, so he sighed and said, apparently unwillingly, 'There's some kind of legend in my family, something about an ancestor from hundreds of years ago who worked in the gardens of the estate of some big important family in London.' He looked at Sasha as though deciding whether or not to trust her, and continued, 'The story is that he fell in love with the daughter of this family, but her father wouldn't allow them to marry. In fact,' he said, with a bitter smile, 'the father banished the poor bloke from his estate, so he came back up here, started a sheep farm, and then somewhere along the way the family turned to joinery.' He shrugged. 'I guess there wasn't much of a need for gardeners around here. Eventually he married some nice Yorkshire lass, settled down, and had some kids.'

'And that's it?' Sasha persisted, sure there had to be more. 'That's all you know?'

Johnny paused, then added, 'Well, I say there wasn't much of a need for gardeners up here, but apparently it was this ancestor of mine who bred a new variety of rose called –'

'I know,' Sasha breathlessly interjected. 'The Amelia Rose, right?'

Johnny smiled. 'That's why I have this tattoo,' he said proudly, clasping his hand over Sasha's as it pressed against the rose on his stomach. 'There is one other thing, though,' he said thoughtfully, fingering Sasha's hair. 'There have been rumours that this dead ancestor's ghost will occasionally appear to certain members of the family, and some people claim they've heard him calling out the name of a woman called Amelia.'

Sasha stared at him. 'Have you ever seen or heard this . . . this ghost?' she asked almost fearfully, feeling some inexplicable sense of relief when Johnny shook his head.

'No, I can't say that I have,' he said almost sadly,

then, after a brief moment of inner struggle, he admitted, 'but my dad claims he has.'

Sasha regarded him in silence, and debated whether she should tell him what she knew. Probably not a good idea, she decided, leaning over to kiss him on the mouth. There's no need for him to know. And as Johnny rolled her on to her back, covering her body with his, she decided that this was all she needed, that it would be enough for her just to know that he existed.

She fumbled with a condom for a moment before finally easing it down over Johnny's impressively erect cock, then wordlessly guided him into her, her sex so slick with dew and so pliant with pleasure that he slid fully inside then lay motionless, propped up on his elbows, their hips pressed together, his face gazing down into hers.

'Ah, Lady,' he murmured as she arched up beneath him, urging him to move, 'if you stay here much longer, you'll soon be haunting me.'

Yes, she could love this man, Sasha thought, as she wrapped herself around John Blakeley, the two of them driving against each other, his cock pressing hard against her as she clenched around him. But he wasn't hers: Sasha wasn't even sure he was entirely Rosie's. She would have to be content with this one moment of completion, this final fleeting glimpse of fulfilment. As Sasha urged Johnny deeper inside her, feeling herself tremble with the fullness of her pleasure, she listened out for the now-familiar sound of Amelia Asher weeping, but there was only silence.

Chapter Thirteen

Sasha awoke early the next morning, disappointed, but not surprised, to find herself alone in her bed. She had been dimly aware that sometime in the night, during the silent lucidity of near-sleep, the man beside her had eased himself out of her arms, risen from the bed, and dressed himself quickly and silently before leaving her room, shutting the door noiselessly behind him. Sasha's awareness of his movements had hovered on the edges of her consciousness, but she had chosen not to force herself further awake to try to prevent him from leaving.

Now, in fact, once her initial disappointment at finding Johnny gone had evaporated, she was rather relieved she didn't have to face him in the early light of dawn: she didn't want to admit to unspoken expectations, or try to pretend that their encounter last night had been the start of something momentous and committed between them. It wasn't that she felt that it was Rosie who belonged with Johnny, although that certainly seemed to her to be true: it was more that Sasha knew, as she had known all along, that she really had no intention of staying much longer up here in the remote north of England. She had no place up here: she belonged back in the familiar urban sprawl of modern-day New York. She no longer felt herself to be an eighteenth-century Gothic heroine or a character in a Brontë novel; she had come up here with the purpose of seeing Amelia Asher's sad story through to whatever conclusion she could reach, and she had found it in the arms of John Blakeley, the twentieth-century descendant of Lady Amelia's eighteenth-century lover. Amelia's spirit had stayed silent; there had been no weeping last night. Sasha's quest was now over, and it was time to return home.

But she mustn't forget her mirror! And there was Rosie to see to. Humming happily to herself, Sasha picked up her towel and walked into the bathroom, but then paused. She buried her nose in the crook of her arm and inhaled, absorbing the lingering scent of Johnny's flesh on her own, suddenly reluctant to wash off this fragrant imprint on her skin. Still, she did have to get dressed, and so she showered quickly, slid into her favourite black leather skirt, and topped it with a slinky peach-coloured shirt, which contrasted favourably with the deep rose-coloured lipstick she used to slick her lips. Once dressed, she headed downstairs, a little nervously, to the bar, wondering what Rosie would say about her adventure of the night before.

But the bartender was nowhere in sight. Instead there was an unfamiliar man polishing the wood of the bar to a lustrous sheen with a cloth; he raised his head to nod politely at Sasha, who had only glimpsed him briefly before, lurking in the back of the kitchen while Rosie brought in the orders. Now he paused in his polishing to remove the pencil tucked behind one ear and enquire, 'What can I get you for breakfast, my love?'

For once, the thought of eating held no appeal for Sasha. 'Just a pot of tea, please,' she said quietly, looking around for Rosie.

The man glanced at her over his pad. 'Are you sure about that?' he asked, apparently a little surprised. 'No eggs or sausage; not even a slice of toast?'

Sasha smiled a little. 'Tea will be fine,' she said, her fingers plucking nervously at a napkin. Before the man had a chance to turn for the kitchen, she asked hastily, 'Is Rosie around this morning?'

The man shook his head briskly and replied, 'Nope. She left early today to go into town to do a bit of shopping.' He then headed into the kitchen, returning shortly with a pot of tea and a pretty china plate upon which he had arranged a variety of shortbread biscuits and fruit. When Sasha looked up at him gratefully, he smiled kindly and said, 'No need for you to go out on a day like this with nothing but tea in your belly.'

Sasha glanced out of the window. It was another grey Yorkshire day, the nearly denuded trees sketched against a heavy curtain of mist, the near-whiteness of the fog and the bare skeletons of the trees suggesting a damp, cold day in winter rather than early fall. Sasha glanced at her watch while she sipped her tea and wondered what the weather was like in New York. Biting thoughtfully into a piece of apple, she worried about what Rosie might be thinking, and hoped she wasn't angry that Sasha had spent the night with her lover in Rosie's very own pub. Surely not, Sasha resolutely decided, cutting off another slice of apple: hadn't Rosie assured her that she wanted Sasha to see this thing through? After all, Rosie knew the whole story: she knew that it wasn't so much that Sasha was interested in Johnny, but rather that she was seeking some kind of closure to Amelia Asher's story. It was the story itself, not John Blakeley the

241

man, which Sasha found so enthralling, and which she sought to unravel.

Having said that, John Blakeley the man had offered her so much passion and pleasure last night in her bed that, had circumstances been different, she could easily have been tempted into delaying her journey back home and staying up here for some indefinite period of time. But that wasn't to be. She really needed to go back home and try to figure out a new direction to her life, now that her journey seemed to have reached some kind of conclusion. She wanted to discover a new project to pursue, one which would provide her with the kind of inspiration and excitement she'd experienced since first hearing Amelia Asher's voice in her hotel bedroom.

But there were some loose ends that needed to be tied up first, one of them being the completion of her mirror, which meant a trip to the shop of John Blakeley, Carpenter. With a final mouthful of tea, Sasha set down her cup and returned to her room for a quick reapplication of her lipstick before preparing herself to once again confront the man she had come all this way to find.

As Sasha drove the short distance to Johnny's shop, she tried to fight back the nervous fluttering in her stomach, the thought of seeing him again so soon after last night causing her to feel somewhat tense and a little bit shy. This was so different from the way she had felt just yesterday morning as she and Rosie had sat, companionably sipping coffee, the ease and familiarity of their breakfast together merely a continuation of the intimacy they had enjoyed the night before. But as Sasha pulled into the parking lot of John's shop, knowing that in a very few minutes she would once again be close enough to touch him, the tremors in her belly began to change into a more excited sensation, more a feeling of expectation than anxiety.

She stood in the open doorway and watched him for a moment. He had his back to her, and he was concentrating intently on an intricate carving of wood which was, she saw with delight, the spiralling base of what must be her mirror. She gazed at him in silence, admiring the tight curves of his buttocks beneath the loose embrace of his battered blue jeans, and the way the muscles of his back flexed under his T-shirt as he bent over the piece of wood to impatiently flick away some untidy shavings of sawdust. She could have stood and watched him a while longer, just marvelling at the intimate knowledge she now had of his body beneath his clothes, smiling a little to herself at the memory of how those flexed muscles had felt under her fingers, and remembering the taste of his skin against her tongue, the taut pucker of his nipples, the silky-rough curls on his chest, the tense planes of his stomach, the pulsing swell of his cock. Ah, yes, he could have been the man for her, if only things were different, if only the situation which had brought them together hadn't been complicated by a centuries-old manuscript and the weeping ghost of a long-dead woman. And, of course, there was Rosie.

Stooping to retrieve his drill from the floor, Johnny turned slightly and caught sight of Sasha standing there silently in the doorway. He immediately dropped the drill and straightened up, pausing to regard her almost enquiringly for a moment, before shrugging off any awkwardness or embarrassment that might have dogged a lesser man, and coming forward to usher her further into the shop.

'Come inside, there, woman,' he greeted her almost gruffly, reaching behind her to shut the door. 'It's bloody cold out there this early in the morning, and you're not even wearing a coat.'

It was true. In her haste to get on with her plans and see John before her nerve failed her, Sasha had neglected to dress herself adequately for the chill grey of the day. Now, however, she felt anything but cold in the warmth of his presence, and as she looked into Johnny's blue eyes, she wondered fleetingly if she could somehow coax him back into bed, just one more time.

But he had already moved away from her. 'If you've come to chide me about leaving you in the night, I should tell you that I never stay in a lady's bed till morning on the first date.' He grinned at her then, gently mocking her unsmiling face, before adding more seriously, and with a trace of guilt, 'Besides, I thought it might be a little uncomfortable for us all if I happened to run into Rosie on the way downstairs in the morning.'

Sasha nodded, coming over to run her fingers along the upended base of the pedestal he had been working on. 'It's OK,' she said almost absently, stroking the polished twists of the wood. 'I understand.' She looked up at him, and indicated the mahogany base she was touching. 'Is this part of my mirror?' she asked.

John smiled. 'Aye,' he replied, then pointed to a slab of glass propped up in the corner. 'And that's part of it as well; it arrived first thing this morning, just as I'd been promised.' He indicated the glass again and continued, 'It came early as a special favour from a friend. That's another reason I had to leave you last night: I had to be sure I would be here when it arrived.' His fingers joined hers as they continued to move, now a little nervously, over the wood. He trapped her hand beneath his, his palm sliding seductively over the backs of her knuckles. 'Last night was good, you know,' he said softly, his eyes gazing into hers. 'I really was sorry to leave you.'

Sasha's breath caught and held in her throat as she looked up at him, the weight of his hand over hers causing her heart to pound heavily. 'It was more special than you know,' she breathed, craving the feel of his body all over again. 'I'll remember it for the rest of my life.'

He moved even closer. 'What, Lady, you're not thinking of leaving now, are you, after what we shared last night?' His breath was warm in her hair, his mouth stirring a few chestnut tendrils which covered the tips of her ears. Sasha felt her body begin to melt into his, and she could almost believe that she might really mean something to this man, but she remembered what Rosie had said about the women's hearts Johnny had broken, and the dangerous charm he exhibited which was not really to be trusted. Nevertheless, Sasha's body began to urge her, what harm could it do, to feel him against her just one more time, to know again the thrill of his lips and hands on her skin, secure in the fact that she would be leaving Yorkshire that very day? And so she turned up her head so her mouth could meet his, the pressure of his lips against hers causing her to moan softly in her throat. Then there was the exquisite feel of his hands on her waist, their thighs pressed together, the velvet of his tongue as she rubbed hers against it, and the strong blades of his shoulders as she curved her hands around them, and Sasha was lost for the moment to any thoughts other than the wonder of the man she embraced. As Johnny lifted her up to wrap her legs around his waist, the leather of her skirt creaking out in protest as the fabric strained against the seams, Sasha clung to his strength and his hardness as he

245

deposited her on the upturned column of wood he had been carving for the base of her mirror. He drew back to smile down at her suggestively, then arched an inquisitive brow in the direction of her handbag, and Sasha understood the tacit intention of his question. With a shy little nod, she reached out for her bag; he handed it over and she began to root around inside for her packet of condoms, while Johnny busied himself with unlacing her boots, causing Sasha to squirm with delight as his fingers drew teasingly along her stockinged feet, while he slowly drew off their heavy leather casings. As Rosie had done only a few nights before, Johnny knelt on the floor to run his mouth along Sasha's foot, imprinting little kisses which tickled her tiny polished toes, her graceful arch, and the sensitive underside of her sole. When at last he rose to his feet, it was to slide off Sasha's heavy dark tights: she leant back on her hands and arched up her hips, allowing him to ease down the cumbersome elastic waistband and roll down the clinging cotton lengths, leaving her legs bare and fully exposed, her protesting leather skirt now hiked up around her waist. She reached up to kiss him, sitting on the pedestal of wood, her naked legs reaching out to wrap around Johnny's hips as he bent over to answer her mouth with his, never once closing his eyes as his face drew down to hers. With his mouth still clinging to hers, Johnny reached up under the peach silk of Sasha's shirt to run his hands over the expanse of bare skin between her bra and her skirt, the warmth of his fingers as they gripped her to him causing her knees to tremble as they pressed around his waist. When Johnny's hands moved upward to cup themselves around the full curves of her breasts, Sasha urged herself closer to him, tugging his white T-shirt up over his head, breaking the kiss only to allow her to bare

246

his glorious chest before claiming his mouth again with hers, cupping her hands against his body the way he was doing with hers. Eager to taste more, Sasha slid her mouth downward over the arc of Johnny's throat, pausing to nip playfully along his smooth skin, burying her lips in the hollow at the base of his neck before licking along the broad width of one shoulder. He tasted so sweet and he smelt so good that Sasha began to mew a little with delight, until Johnny nudged her away from him so he could bend to press his mouth against the shadowed valley of her cleavage, his hands simply pushing her shirt up impatiently around her shoulders, not even bothering to strip it off her completely. With his mouth, Johnny released one rosy-tipped breast from the confines of Sasha's bra, and as his lips closed around the puckered scarlet crest, she moaned and gripped his head with her hands, pressing him closer to her body. She had a momentary image of how the pair of them would look to any casual customer entering the shop: sitting on the unfinished base of her mirror, Johnny bared to the waist, her naked legs wrapped around his thighs, her hands buried in his hair, his open mouth pressed against her naked bosom. But as Johnny licked softly at one nipple before sliding downward to suck more fully on Sasha's breast, she let go of all other distractions at the wonder of his kisses on her creamy skin.

'Come here,' she said, nudging Johnny's head from her breast and reaching for the promising bulge that throbbed behind his fly. 'Let me get at you.' She reached down and deftly unbuttoned his jeans, reaching her fingers inside to clasp them around the satisfyingly long and heavy shaft within, delighting in the contrasts between the satiny smooth tip, the silken drop of opalescent dew which slicked her busy fingers, the textured ridges of his cock, and the lush softness of his cowl. She stroked up and down in a strong, steady rhythm with one hand, while the other reached underneath to lightly fondle the downy covering of his balls, then she smiled a little to herself when she felt his hand on top of hers guiding her in the motion he preferred, before stopping her hand entirely and reaching for the condom she'd placed on the wood beside her. With a rapid jerk, he tore open the packet and shook out the disc, hurriedly covering himself in the wafer-thin sheath before positioning himself back between Sasha's open thighs.

'I need to feel you all around me,' he growled softly, then grunted in frustration as the tip of his cock butted impotently against the slippery barrier of Sasha's satin panties. He paused only briefly to look questioningly into Sasha's face as he gripped the sides of her delicate lingerie in both of his strong hands, then, at her excited nod, he took a tighter grasp on the thin fabric and, with one sure, swift tug, he ripped her panties in two, leaving her suddenly, startlingly naked from the waist down. Sasha reached out for him and drew him to her as he glided sweetly inside to fill her up, his cock snugly enclosed, his arms tightly around her, their bodies locked together. And then he began to move, slowly at first: a long, tantalising, near-complete withdrawal, and then the tense pressure inside as he moved back in, his hands moving down to grip Sasha's buttocks, her own hands braced behind her to support herself as she arched her hips forward to meet his increasingly rapid drives inside her. She arched back her neck and closed her eyes, her hair hanging halfway down her spine and her head flung backward, her legs clasped around Johnny's hips and her sex thumping forward, nearly off the edge of the pedestal upon which she sat, as Sasha urged herself eagerly on to Johnny's deep and thrusting cock. Sasha opened her eyes and caught sight of herself in the piece of glass John had said was part of her mirror; it was propped up against the wall a little to her left, and if she turned her head she could clearly see the two of them making love, Johnny's body hovering over hers, bent slightly at the knees as he adjusted himself to the differences in their heights. Sasha stared, fascinated, at the image of herself in the mirror as her orgasm began to approach, and she noted with a kind of odd detachment the flush in her cheeks and the brightness in her eyes as they widened with the intensity of sensation. Johnny's orgasm erupted almost simultaneously with her own, and as his climax joined with hers, he gently turned her face back so she was looking straight at him, their eyes meeting seconds before their mouths did, their mutual kiss sealing the culmination of their pleasure.

'Well,' Sasha said, and laughed a little shakily as Johnny finally withdrew and discarded the condom, 'I certainly didn't expect this to happen when I came by today to say goodbye.'

John looked at her then as he finished buttoning up his jeans. 'Goodbye?' he echoed, flipping a wayward curl out of his eyes. 'You really are leaving, then?'

Sasha finished struggling into her tights before she answered him, aware of how undignified she must look. 'I'm driving back down to London today before I fly back to New York tomorrow,' she said quietly. 'It really is time for me to return home.'

Johnny looked at her intently for a moment, then nodded. 'Aye, that's probably for the best,' he said softly, but when she looked enquiringly at him, wondering what he meant, he merely shrugged and leant back against the wall. 'Rosie and all that,' he said, then paused a bit before adding, 'I'll miss you, though, lass.'

'But I'll have my mirror to remember you by!' Sasha tried to sound breezy, uncomfortable with this sudden sombre mood. She made a motion towards her handbag. 'Why don't I pay you for it now,' she suggested, deciding it was best to leave before things got too maudlin.

Smiling, Johnny shook his head. 'Payment isn't due until completion, remember?' he said lightly, indicating his cluttered desk in the back of the shop. 'I've got all of your New York details, haven't I, so there's no need for you to worry. I should be done with it in a couple of days, so you should be receiving it within a fortnight. Here,' he said suddenly, reaching into the back pocket of his jeans. 'Let me give you a card for the shop: that way, you'll always know how to get in touch with me.'

Sasha accepted the card, laughing a little at the absurd business-like formality of the situation. She glanced at the small white square, which merely bore the name of the shop and a telephone number, before slipping it into her purse. 'I was wondering why there was no Blakeley listed in the white pages in the telephone book,' she said, half to herself. 'I guess you must have been listed in the yellow pages by your shop.'

John Blakeley looked at her curiously for a moment, as though wondering what she was talking about, but said nothing.

'Well,' Sasha said again hesitantly before coming forward to embrace him. 'I guess I really should go now.'

His arms came around her and he held her close to him, as though reluctant to let her go. 'Look after yourself, lass,' he murmured into her ear. 'I hope you'll come back up here again someday.'

Sasha stepped away from him. 'Goodbye, Johnny

Blakeley,' she whispered somewhat sadly. 'I'll never forget you.'

She then turned and made her way out of the shop, not stopping to look back once, so she never knew if he stood to watch her leave or not.

When Sasha returned to the pub, having made a brief stop on the way, it was close to lunchtime, and Rosie was still nowhere to be found. For a panicky moment she feared she might actually have to leave Yorkshire without speaking to Rosie in person, for she wanted to reach London before nightfall, but as she settled herself at the bar, planning to wait around for a while, the red-headed bartender came bustling out of the kitchen and straight over to Sasha as though she'd been expecting her all day.

'Hello there, my love,' she said cheerily, with no trace at all of envy, anger or sorrow. 'I was wondering when you'd be back for lunch.' She peered closely into the other woman's eyes for a moment, then smiled. 'Everything all right with Johnny?'

Sasha blushed, and looked at her friend. 'You knew I was with him just now?'

Rosie smiled again. 'I saw your car as I was driving back in from town,' she said gently, then reached over to pat Sasha's hand. 'Come on, love,' she said. 'I told you I wanted you to do what you felt was right, and there's no need for you to look so guilty.'

'Actually,' Sasha said, still feeling a little bit uncomfortable, 'I stopped by to tell him I was leaving, and to say goodbye.' She looked at Rosie and smiled mournfully. 'He left in the middle of the night last night before I had a chance to tell him.'

Rosie hooted. 'I told you our Johnny could be a bit of a bastard sometimes!' she said cheerily. 'He's a rude one, that one: he's never been known to stay the whole

251

night in a lass's bed, not in all the years that I've known him!'

Sasha still couldn't quite get used to the idea that Rosie was so comfortable knowing that her lover slept with countless other women, but she decided it wasn't her place to say anything about that.

'So come on, love, what'll you have for lunch?' Rosie asked warmly. 'The cabbage soup is especially nice today.'

Sasha wasn't particularly in the mood to eat, but she didn't want to seem rude, and so she made a brave effort at spooning up the rich, slightly salty, slightly sweet soup with the delectable shreds of red cabbage and beetroot floating around on the top. Rosie seated herself across from Sasha and watched her.

'So,' Rosie said conversationally, pushing over a basket of bread to Sasha. 'You're leaving us today then.'

Sasha glanced unhappily at her friend, then looked away. 'You know I can't stay here,' she said, diving for an elusive slice of carrot at the bottom of her bowl.

Rosie placed a comforting arm around Sasha's shoulders and gave her a squeeze. 'You know, Sasha,' she said, as she brushed away a strand of chestnut hair from the other woman's forehead, 'I know you've only been here for a few days, but I feel as if I've known you for ever. I'm really going to miss you when you're gone.'

Sasha leant her head on the younger woman's shoulder. 'I'm going to miss you too, Rosie,' she said sadly, then pushed away her empty soup bowl and looked appealingly at the bartender. 'I've finished my soup like a good girl,' she said smilingly. 'Can I have a shot of whisky for the road, please?'

Rosie sat with her while she finished her drink, and then tried to wave away Sasha's request for her bill.

252

'Come on, Rosie,' Sasha insisted. 'Don't be silly. I have to pay for my room and my meals.'

Rosie hesitated. 'All right,' she finally conceded. 'I'll let you pay for your room, but I just can't let you pay for your food.'

Sasha considered the compromise. 'OK, it's a deal,' she said, grinning. Rosie then came upstairs with Sasha to help her pack, and they loaded her suitcases into her hired car. When they were finished, the two women stood silently for a moment by the driver's-side door, both reluctant to be the first to say goodbye. Finally, Sasha enfolded her friend in her arms and whispered, 'Johnny's all yours again, Rosie.'

Rosie held on to her and gripped her hard. And then, just as Johnny had, she said, 'Promise you'll come and see me again someday.'

The other woman wiped away the tear that was falling from her eye and sniffled. 'I will,' she replied. 'I promise.'

She then climbed into her car, started up the engine, and waved once more to Rosie before pulling out of the carpark at the Swan and Rose and heading back towards the road that would take her back to London and the Asher Hotel.

Sasha finally arrived back at the hotel some six hours later, tired, hungry, and stiff from her long drive. She hadn't bothered to call to reserve a room for herself, simply trusting to fate that there would be something available, and there was, but it wasn't number 323, Lady Amelia's old room. Instead it was a comfortable, pretty room on the first floor, and Sasha was so exhausted by recent events that she simply took a shower, ordered dinner from room service, and tumbled into bed to sleep without dreaming for nearly the next twelve hours.

When she awoke, the sun was streaming brightly into her window; she made a quick telephone call to the airline to reserve her seat on that afternoon's flight to New York, then dressed hurriedly. She had a few more errands to complete before she could leave for the airport, and she didn't want to miss her plane. She ate a quick breakfast in the hotel dining room, then darted out to her hired car in the carpark, returning a few moments later bearing in her arms the Amelia Rose rosebush she had bought at a local nursery in Yorkshire, shortly after leaving Johnny Blakeley's carpentry shop. After a careful appraisal of the empty hallway, Sasha darted into the deserted library, quickly located the empty facade of Walpole's *The Castle of Otranto*, held her breath, and pulled the metal ring. As the door in the wall swung outward, she slipped behind it and found herself back in the cold stone passage with the imposing wooden door. Sasha went over to the bolt that locked the door, still clutching her bundle, uttered a brief prayer of supplication, and prised open the lock. She then stepped outside into the quiet little churchyard and looked around, half-expecting to see a vision or a ghost of either the long-departed John Blakeley or Amelia Asher. She saw no one, however, so she walked over to the dead woman's grave and, kneeling down, carefully planted her rosebush next to her headstone.

'I found him, Amelia,' she whispered. 'You don't have to weep any more. Johnny hasn't forgotten you, and I hope this means that you can now be together ... wherever you are.'

She gave a final pat to the earth in which the roots of the rosebush were embedded, then stood there a moment longer, feeling oddly comforted and calm, and not at all sad. She pressed her fingers to her lips, then pressed them to the cold stone that bore Amelia's name, before turning to head back to the wooden door and cold dark passage. As she slipped back into the library, pulling the door shut behind her, she smiled in satisfaction, quite pleased with the way things had turned out. She now had but one more thing to do.

Sasha approached the desk and enquired politely, 'Excuse me, but could you tell me whether Claire is working today or not?'

The receptionist shook her head, a puzzled lift to her brows. 'No, Claire has today off,' she said. 'Is there something I can help you with?'

Sasha smiled reassuringly, and placed the carefully wrapped parcel on the desk. 'Could you please see that she gets this when she comes in tomorrow?' she asked, and handed over the letter in its sealed envelope. 'And this as well.'

She returned to her room, picturing Claire's excited face as she opened the parcel to discover inside Lady Amelia Asher's manuscript; Sasha knew that she would treasure and protect it just as she, Sasha, had done, until one day perhaps Claire might pass it on to someone else, another woman who would continue to cherish and look after it. Her letter to the girl was brief; in it, she simply thanked Claire for bringing her to Amelia so many months ago, and said she hoped to see her again sometime. Sasha had debated whether she should mention the curious Michaelmas Ball in her letter, in the hope that Claire would be able to clear up that particular enigma, but she then decided that perhaps there were some mysteries that were better left unexplained.

Sasha made it to the airport in plenty of time to browse through the bookshops before boarding the plane that would take her back to New York. She regarded the shiny new novels displayed so enticingly on the shelves, then, shrugging, she walked over to the rows of so-called 'classics' hidden away in the back. With a rueful smile, she chose copies of *The Mysteries of Udolpho*, Mary Wollstonecraft's *The Wrongs of Woman*, and Daphne Du Maurier's *Rebecca*; as she paid for her purchases, the clerk took a dubious look at the bulky length of *Udolpho* and shook her head with a disbelieving look at her customer. Sasha merely laughed and said to the girl, 'You should try reading it sometime: it really is a great book.'

Once she was comfortably seated on the plane, Sasha realised with a little jolt that she had another week's holiday coming to her, which was a great relief, as she couldn't face the thought of going back to her job at ALM and having to face Valerie. Well, she thought with a shrug as she looked out of the little round window, there's no reason why I have to go back. I've got over a week to decide what I would rather do instead. In fact, the more she thought about it, the more she realised that she wanted to get out of the advertising and marketing business altogether; she had long stopped feeling entirely comfortable with the idea of manipulating consumer consciousness, and she'd always faintly disapproved of the underhanded methods some advertisers used to sell products. What she'd loved most about her job had been the constant contact with other people her work had demanded, and the creative talents it required for her to devise and complete projects. Well, there were thousands of jobs she could do that employed similar skills, but for different, more people-friendly ends than simply coercing them to consume yet more useless products. And as Sasha settled herself deeper into her seat, she contemplated the various post-graduate courses and training programs she could enter, shivering with pleasure at the thought of a whole new world opening up to her. She dug out a pad and a pen from her handbag, and started to make a list.

It was ten days later. Sasha had just returned from matriculating at one of the biggest and most well-known universities in New York City, where she was registered to begin the post-graduate degree program in genealogy early in the new year. She sat on the couch, flipping through her textbooks with excitement, fascinated by the idea she had recently conceived of helping people to trace their ancestry, when the door-bell rang. Puzzled, she glanced at the clock: surely she wasn't expecting someone at this time of day? As she opened the door, however, her stomach flipped with excitement: there, standing in front of her, looking a little tired and cross, were two parcel post delivery people, one woman and one man, carrying between them a very large, bulky-looking packing crate. Ushering them in, Sasha rapidly scrawled her name across several forms and handed over her credit card, shifting impatiently from foot to foot as it was being processed, and eagerly directed the deliverers to position the parcel in her bedroom. As soon as they left, she hastily unscrewed the lid of the crate, damaging several nails in her haste, then stepped back to admire the hand-carved magnificence of her double-sided cheval-glass mirror, the wooden frame glossy and handsome, the pedestal completely unrecognisable from the unfinished column upon which Sasha had made such passionate love with Johnny only a few weeks before.

Sasha gazed at herself in her mirror. Her cheeks glowed, her eyes shone, her lips were moist and parted. She reached up to turn the mirror over. As the glass swung over to reveal its doubled side, Sasha gasped with shock and surprise. Reflected in the mirror she saw herself, but she also saw, not reflected *in* the mirror but actually *inside* it, the lovely young woman with brilliant blonde hair and sparkling green eyes. But she wasn't weeping: oh no, not this lady. This lady was laughing with joy. Sasha came closer, and looked again.

Oh yes, she was definitely laughing.

BLACK LACE NEW BOOKS

Published in March

RAW SILK
Lisabet Sarai
£5.99

When software engineer Kate O'Neill leaves her lover David to take a job in Bangkok, she becomes sexually involved with two very different men: a handsome member of the Thai aristocracy, and the charismatic proprietor of a sex bar. When David arrives in Thailand, Kate realises she must choose between them. She invites all three to join her in a sexual adventure that finally makes clear to her what she really wants and needs.

ISBN 0 352 33336 7

THE TOP OF HER GAME
Emma Holly
£5.99

Successful businesswoman and dominatrix Julia Mueller has been searching all her life for a man who won't be mastered too easily. When she locks horns with a no-nonsense Montana rancher, will he be the man that's too tough to tame? Will she find the balance between domination and surrender, or will her dark side win out?

ISBN 0 352 33337 5

Published in April

HAUNTED
Laura Thornton
£5.99

A modern-day Gothic story set in both England and New York. Sasha Hayward is an American woman whose erotic obsession with a long-dead pair of lovers leads her on a steamy and evocative search. Seeking out descendants of the enigmatic pair, Sasha consummates her obsession in a series of sexy encounters related to this haunting mystery.

ISBN 0 352 33341 3

STAND AND DELIVER
Helena Ravenscroft
£5.99

1745, and England is plagued by the lawless. Lydia Hawkesworth feels torn between her love for Drummond, a sea-faring adventurer turned highwayman, and her all-consuming passion for his decadent younger brother Valerian. With the arrival of the icy Madame de Chaillot, Valerian's plans to usurp his brother's position and steal his inheritance turn down a sinister and darkly erotic path – one which Lydia is drawn to follow.

ISBN 0 352 33340 5

To be published in May

INSOMNIA
Zoe le Verdier
£5.99

A wide range of sexual experience is explored in this collection of short stories by one of the best-liked authors in the series. Zoe le Verdier's work is an ideal reflection of the fresh, upbeat stories now being published under the Black Lace imprint. Many popular female fantasies are covered, from sex with a stranger and talking dirty, to secret fetishes, lost virginity and love. There's something for everyone.

ISBN: 0 352 33345 6

VILLAGE OF SECRETS
Mercedes Kelly
£5.99

Every small town has something to hide, and this rural Cornish village is no exception. Its twee exterior hides some shocking scandals and nothing is quite what it seems. Laura, a London journalist, becomes embroiled with the locals – one of whom might be her long-lost brother – when she inherits property in the village. Against a backdrop of curious goings-on, she learns to indulge her taste for kinky sex and rubber fetishism.

IBSN: 0 352 33344 8

Special announcement!
THE BLACK LACE BOOK OF WOMEN'S
SEXUAL FANTASIES
Edited and Compiled by Kerri Sharp
£5.99

At last, Black Lace brings you the definitive Book of Women's Sexual Fantasies. This special collection has taken over one and a half years of in-depth research to put together, and has been compiled through correspondence with women from all over the English-speaking world. The result is an astounding anthology of detailed sexual fantasies, including shocking and at times bizarre revelations.

ISBN 0 352 33346 4

If you would like a complete list of plot summaries of Black Lace titles, or would like to receive information on other publications available, please send a stamped addressed envelope to:

Black Lace, Thames Wharf Studios,
Rainville Road, London W6 9HT

BLACK LACE BOOKLIST

All books are priced £4.99 unless another price is given.

Black Lace books with a contemporary setting

ODALISQUE	Fleur Reynolds ISBN 0 352 32887 8 ☐
WICKED WORK	Pamela Kyle ISBN 0 352 32958 0 ☐
UNFINISHED BUSINESS	Sarah Hope-Walker ISBN 0 352 32983 1 ☐
HEALING PASSION	Sylvie Ouellette ISBN 0 352 32998 X ☐
PALAZZO	Jan Smith ISBN 0 352 33156 9 ☐
THE GALLERY	Fredrica Alleyn ISBN 0 352 33148 8 ☐
AVENGING ANGELS	Roxanne Carr ISBN 0 352 33147 X ☐
COUNTRY MATTERS	Tesni Morgan ISBN 0 352 33174 7 ☐
GINGER ROOT	Robyn Russell ISBN 0 352 33152 6 ☐
DANGEROUS CONSEQUENCES	Pamela Rochford ISBN 0 352 33185 2 ☐
THE NAME OF AN ANGEL £6.99	Laura Thornton ISBN 0 352 33205 0 ☐
SILENT SEDUCTION	Tanya Bishop ISBN 0 352 33193 3 ☐
BONDED	Fleur Reynolds ISBN 0 352 33192 5 ☐
THE STRANGER	Portia Da Costa ISBN 0 352 33211 5 ☐
CONTEST OF WILLS £5.99	Louisa Francis ISBN 0 352 33223 9 ☐
BY ANY MEANS £5.99	Cheryl Mildenhall ISBN 0 352 33221 2 ☐
MÉNAGE £5.99	Emma Holly ISBN 0 352 33231 X ☐

Black Lace anthologies

PAST PASSIONS £6.99	ISBN 0 352 33159 3	☐
PANDORA'S BOX 2 £4.99	ISBN 0 352 33151 8	☐
PANDORA'S BOX 3 £5.99	ISBN 0 352 33274 3	☐
SUGAR AND SPICE £6.99	ISBN 0 352 33227 1	☐
SUGAR AND SPICE 2 £7.99	ISBN 0 352 33309 X	☐

Black Lace non-fiction

WOMEN, SEX AND ASTROLOGY £5.99	Sarah Bartlett ISBN 0 352 33262 X	☐

---------- ✂ --------------------------

Please send me the books I have ticked above.

Name ....

Address ....

....

....

.... Post Code ....

Send to: Cash Sales, Black Lace Books, Thames Wharf Studios, Rainville Road, London W6 9HT.

US customers: for prices and details of how to order books for delivery by mail, call 1-800-805-1083.

Please enclose a cheque or postal order, made payable to **Virgin Publishing Ltd**, to the value of the books you have ordered plus postage and packing costs as follows:
   UK and BFPO – £1.00 for the first book, 50p for each subsequent book.
   Overseas (including Republic of Ireland) – £2.00 for the first book, £1.00 for each subsequent book.

If you would prefer to pay by VISA or ACCESS/MASTERCARD, please write your card number and expiry date here:

....

Please allow up to 28 days for delivery.

Signature ....

---------- ✂ --------------------------